Damascus Street

Cathy Sultan

**CALUMET
EDITIONS**

Minneapolis, Minnesota

**CALUMET
EDITIONS**

Minneapolis, Minnesota

FIRST EDITION MAY 2018

This is a work of fiction. All of the characters, names, incidents, organizations, and dialogue are either the products of the author's imagination or are used fictiously.

Printed in the United States of America.
10 9 8 7 6 5 4 3 2 1

ISBN: 978-1-939548-92-4

Book design by Gary Lindberg

Colleen McElroy, Professor of English, University of Seattle; author of 14 books including *Over the Lip of the World: Among Storytellers of Madagascar* and *Queen of the Ebony Isles*, which received the American Book Award

TRAGEDY IN SOUTH LEBANON: THE ISRAELI-HEZBOLLAH WAR OF 2006

Tragedy in South Lebanon provides vital information about a topic often misreported by the mainstream media. I particularly liked the interviews with both Hezbollah and Israeli soldiers describing the same battle. This is an important book that should be read by anyone interested in Israel and Lebanon.

Reese Erlich, foreign correspondent and author of *The Iran Agenda: The Real Story of US Policy and the Middle East Crisis*

As someone who works with other organizations to ban the use, sale, and transfer of cluster bombs, I applaud Cathy Sultan's discussion on the effects of these lethal weapons on Lebanese civilians, many of them children, who continue to be killed and maimed by these odious, unexploded Israeli cluster munitions.

George Cody, Ph.D., Executive Director, American Task Force for Lebanon

Finally, finally, finally, there is a book that looks at the complex issues in Lebanon for what they are—complex. And even more importantly, Sultan has taken her experience and transported all of us into the region to better understand the complexities from the people themselves. We have had enough of the bumper sticker slogans and five second sound bites. Great.

Jack Rice, journalist and former CIA officer

Sultan gives a fair and accurate account of what went on in South Lebanon. As a UN official who has spent 24 years in South Lebanon, I say she also lends refreshing voice to those who would otherwise never be heard.

Timor Goksel, Senior Advisor and Official Spokesman for the United National Interim Force in Lebanon

PRAISE FOR CATHY SULTAN'S WORK

ISRAELIS AND PALESTINIAN VOICES: A DIALOGUE WITH BOTH SIDES

Standing in the shoes of those who face each other daily across this dangerous divide forces us to see beyond media stereotypes often reduced to terrorist and victim. This fast-paced narrative and compelling interviews brings to life a conflict whose complexities Americans must try to understand."Janice Harayda, Minneapolis StarTribune

Sarah Harder, President, National Peace Foundation

THE SYRIAN

In *The Syrian*, Cathy Sultan has achieved a master trifecta of political thriller, historical fiction and romance. This wickedly smart novel reminds us that politics is all about relationships and dares us to conceive that women are just as capable of sexual power plays as the men who have made careers by them for millennia. Sultan's expertise about the contemporary Middle East brings a breathless authenticity to the surprises that come at every turn.

Antonia Felix
New York Times Bestselling Author

A BEIRUT HEART

There is nothing like an intelligent woman, spouse and mother of small children, to carry one into the midst of war, with its horrors as well as its capacity for soul-building. Sultan's narrative enfleshes our disjointed 'news' of the Middle East.

David Burrell, C.S.C, Hesburgh Professor in Philosophy and Theology, University of Notre Dame; Director, Tantur Ecumenical Institute, Jerusalem

...a view drawn from a camera obscura that moves behind the screen of invading armies, détentes, and broken treaties...a compelling story of survival that settles for no less than the promise that this family will remain together and safe at all costs...

To the people of Syria, that they may be left alone to choose their own leaders and solve their own problems without Western and regional interference

Also by Cathy Sultan

Nonfiction

Israeli and Palestinian Voices: A Dialogue with Both Sides
A Beirut Heart: One Woman's War
Tragedy in South Lebanon: The Israeli-Hezbollah War of 2006

Fiction

The Syrian

Damascus Street

Cathy Sultan

CHAPTER ONE

This was no ordinary abduction.

Nadia Khoury woke in a very dark room. She lay in a large, soft bed between freshly laundered satin sheets. Someone had removed her clothes and put her in a nightgown. Her first instinct was to feel between her legs to see if she had been raped. She hadn't. She was unaware, at first, of where she was until finally she remembered what had happened.

It was shortly after nightfall, and she had been hunched over the back seat of her father's car, searching for Sonia's laptop. A big hand had nimbly reached in and covered her mouth, and with his other arm wrapped around her waist, a man had pulled her from the vehicle. She had flailed about, kicking her assailant in his shins and scratching his face with her nails, and when he tried to get her into the waiting car, with her still thrashing about like a wild cat, he accidently hit her hard in the mouth with his elbow, dazing her. Another man strapped her into a seat belt, stuffed a handkerchief into her mouth, tied her hands with plastic twine and blindfolded her.

She remembered her chest heaving uncontrollably. She could not breathe. She told herself to take deep, slow breaths through her nose, but the sense of utter helplessness had already taken hold, and the fetid smell of fear began to seep from her pores. In her mind's eye, she saw her late husband, Elie, sitting, for thirteen years, in a rat-infested, ten-foot-square cell smelling of urine and feces. She also remembered Leila from Marjeyoun, who had endured torture and multiple rapes during her eight years in Khiam prison. What godforsaken hell-hole would she end up in, or would it simply be an unmarked grave? She had no idea where these men were taking her or what they intended to do to her, and she lost what little sense of decency she still had and wet her pants.

They had driven for what seemed like hours without speaking a single word. It was only when the car came to a halt and she heard the Syrian dialect being spoken that she realized she was probably at the border crossing. The man next to her opened his door and got out. The man in the passenger seat did the same while someone big slipped in beside her. Instinctively, she knew it was Hassan Jaafar. Was it the way he sat or the smell of his cologne as he leaned over her body and gently removed her blindfold? When he pulled the handkerchief from her mouth, she gasped for air and sobbed uncontrollably.

"*Ya Akrout!*" Nadia screamed, her chest heaving as she struggled to catch her breath. "You arranged this! I almost died. How could you do this to me?"

"I'm sorry it had to be this way, Nadia."

"Take me home, now."

"*Rawee*, Nadia." When he touched her arm, she shrank against the door and glared at him. She knew what was going to happen and could find no more words. Just hours earlier, while escaping war-stricken Marjeyoun, she and her fiancé, Andrew Sullivan, had witnessed a bomb from an Israeli jet slice their friend's upper torso from the rest of his body and behead another man. The blood and bone and sinew had splattered over the hood of their car and onto their faces, a horror indelibly etched in her mind.

Nadia watched the three kidnappers walk to a waiting Mercedes while Hassan's chauffeur, probably the same one who had driven him to Chtaura, climbed in behind the wheel. She glanced out the window as the car began to advance and realized, in the commotion, that she had just been transported across the Lebanese-Syrian border at the Dabousie crossing without official papers of any kind, a feat only a man as powerful as Hassan Jaafar could have carried off. How would she ever get back into Lebanon?

When the driver passed Tartus and turned east just before Lattakia, Nadia realized Jaafar was taking her to Slunfeh, his fiefdom high in the mountains some sixty miles east of Lattakia, where, as Syria's former Intelligence chief, he could hold a woman against her will—no questions allowed, none asked.

It was another hour up a winding mountain road before Nadia saw, in the distance, a large, well-lit house dominating an otherwise dark landscape. Minutes before their arrival, she had watched the driver speak into his phone, and as they approached the estate, double wrought iron gates swung open. She looked behind her as they passed and watched her prison gates begin to close. She panicked, and even with her hands bound, managed to get the car door open, intent on jumping out and rushing to the gates before they shut.

Jaafar had grabbed her arm and closed the door. "What were you trying to do, Nadia? You could have gotten seriously injured." She threw her head against the back of the seat and screamed, the roof of the car spinning in her vision.

The car stopped, and the back door opened. She fought off anyone who tried to come near her until finally two men pulled her out by force and dragged her inside the house.

"*Da Kheelik,* Hassan, take me home," she tried to say through her sobs, and as the men wrestled with her, yanking her across the foyer toward a flight of stairs, she tried to brake with her feet. From somewhere Nadia heard a soft, female voice call her by name, and when she looked up and saw a thin, pretty, thirty-something woman coming down the carpeted stairs toward her, she calmed herself.

"*Sitt* Nadia, my name is Ani, and I'm going to take you to your room."

"My room? No, I'm not staying here."

"Yes, it is just at the top of the staircase. Come."

Finally, too exhausted to resist, Nadia gave in and let Ani take her arm and guide her to the second floor. When she reached the landing, she peered over the banister and saw a large crystal chandelier dangling over a polished, white marble-floored foyer and Jaafar, standing in the middle, staring up at her. Her heart, or was it something in her brain, went numb, and instead of spitting at him, or hurling insults, she turned away and let herself be escorted into the bedroom. Ani closed the door behind them and directed Nadia to sit on the side of a bed. Ani undid the plastic twine around her wrists and slipped off Nadia's shoes, then asked her to stand so she could also remove her clothes.

"Let's get you into the shower, *Sitt* Nadia. You'll feel much better once you've been cleaned up."

"I don't want to be here, Ani. I want to go home."

"There's nothing you can do, *Sitt,* so just relax. This is your life now."

Nadia thought better than to discuss her predicament with this woman and, instead, followed her through an open door into the large bathroom where everything, from the walls and the double sink and shower, to the bidet and toilet, was white.

Ani had Nadia sit on the stool in front of the sink so she could tend to her swollen lip and, more urgently, the raw gum line where she had been hit.

"Were you in a fight?" Ani asked.

"I wasn't very nice to the men who abducted me."

"Never mind. I'll take care of fixing you up."

Ani ran the cold water, dampened a washcloth and gently dabbed Nadia's swollen lip and gums until she felt some relief. While Ani worked on her mouth, Nadia looked in the mirror and saw a weary-faced woman she hardly recognized. Her eyes were dark circles, her skin drawn and pale, her hair tangled and dirty. Through swollen eyes she saw Andrew, too, on his knees, lungs bursting, his heart pounding after a desperate attempt to rescue her. Nadia jumped when Ani swabbed her lip with antiseptic. The woman paid no attention and, taking hold of Nadia's hands, tended to her broken nails, filing them down before dabbing them with some curative oil.

"Tomorrow I will give you a proper manicure," Ani said, "but now, to the shower."

She ran the water, got it to the right temperature and helped Nadia in, closing the glass door behind her. Nadia tilted her face upward, raised her arms above her head and, as the water ran down her body, she cried uncontrollably. A shower was what she had wanted when she arrived at her father's house from Marjeyoun, thinking she and Andrew had finally won their life together. A shower with the love of her life, to dry each other with the scented towels her mother would supply, and then make love in a safe bed rather than cowering as they had under Israeli bombardment. Instead, here she was in this shower, separated from Andrew, in a foreign but luxurious prison instead of some hellish cell or crypt, and none of it made any sense.

On a moulding stood a small bottle of shampoo and a bar of lemon scented soap. The warm water ran over her and washed away the sweat and smell, but cleansing herself would be a capitulation, she thought, an insult to the way Elie had been kept for thirteen years. She imagined refusing to bathe for as long as Hassan kept her. How would he like that when the time came... raping an unkempt, filthy, angry woman who stank? But she could not do it, so used was she to being pampered and clean. She folded shampoo into her hair and brought it to a lather, smelled the filth still in it and rinsed and lathered again. She used the lemon soap and washcloth, and feeling like a traitor to Elie, acknowledged the terrible disparity between their circumstances. Perhaps she could refuse to bathe another time, but now she had to wash away the blood and sweat from Marjeyoun and her cruel kidnapping and cleanse herself.

When she had finished showering, Ani was waiting with a warm bath towel to dry her off and slip her into a white silk nightgown, matching robe and slippers.

"Do you usually sleep with wet hair, or shall I dry it?"

"Dry it, please. Otherwise, it will be a tangled mess in the morning."

Again, Ani sat Nadia on the stool and pulled out a hair dryer from one of the side drawers.

"Would you like some cognac and a sedative to help you sleep?"

Nadia felt her emotions welling up and nodded. "Yes, knock me out. I don't want to be here. And maybe I will wake up tomorrow and find out this was all a bad dream."

Ani, always maintaining a slight, polite smile, did not answer. She handed Nadia a pill and a plastic bottle of water. She then poured the cognac into a round glass. Nadia cupped it in her hand and took small sips while Ani dried her hair. Over the low hum of the dryer, they chatted.

"How do you know my boss?" Ani asked.

"We were very close some fifteen years ago. He asked me to marry him, but I didn't agree with what he did for the Syrian government, so I refused and married someone else instead. Hassan got very angry and had my husband disappeared and thrown into a Syrian prison."

"I know nothing about such things," Ani said. "To us, Mr. Jaafar is our savior. He takes very good care of us."

"How many of you are here?"

"We are twelve. We used to work in Mr. Jaafar's Damascus home, but when his wife died he closed that house and brought us here. It's quite a nice place. It's your home now too."

"It's a prison, Ani, and I don't want to live here."

Again, Ani kept that slight smile of hers in place instead of answering.

Nadia had no recollection of the rest of their conversation. The last thing she recalled was falling asleep in a soft bed. She did not remember that Ani had turned down the bed covers or helped her in or taken the empty cognac glass from her hands and wished her a good night before leaving the room, but all those things must have been done.

* * *

Nadia lay in the dark room, listening to faint sounds and distant voices. She could not recollect anything at first. She was woozy, and her head spun a bit, and then she remembered the strong sedative. And when she pulled a strand of hair from her mouth, the taste of cognac was still there. She had no notion of how long she had slept, only that it must be daytime. Ani had removed her watch before she showered but had not returned it. Finally, she heard the rattling of a trolley coming along the corridor. A key turned in the door, and light from the hallway streamed in. Ani swept through the room, pulling open the drapes and letting in a flood of light. Then she rolled in the trolley and set it next to Nadia's bed. A petit woman with a pretty face, her thick, black hair in a ponytail, she wore no makeup, but a gold cross and chain hung from her neck. She fussed about with Nadia's bed, puffing up her pillows, folding down her sheets and inviting her to sit up so she could eat.

Employing such luxuries to gloss over her forced detention deeply offended Nadia. She considered throwing the food in Ani's face or beginning a hunger strike, but she was famished. She had not eaten since she had left Marjeyoun, and the smell of the Arabic coffee was impossible to resist as were the warm, chocolate-filled croissants. Damn Hassan for remembering they were her favorite.

As Ani puttered about the room, Nadia glanced at the bare cream-colored walls, the pure white ceiling and the gold and white settee with a mahogany coffee table—all seductive, soothing colors and shapes Hassan knew she favored. Even the two Queen Anne chairs had cream and gold filigree on the mahogany arm rests, as did the deep-blue carpet on the floor. Through the double glass door, Nadia saw the rolling hills with thick foliage and beyond, the Mediterranean. This isolated fortress was now her prison. Any conceivable way of escape eluded her. But the passing of time often let the answers to problems present themselves. In Elie's case, she had waited thirteen years. Would it take as long this time? What was it her father used to tell her when she was trying to solve a problem? Fix your attention too much on the center and you will not find the answer. Look peripherally where the visual perception is oftentimes clearer. But would such logic get her back to Andrew?

Maybe the first step was to win over Ani. It could be that this completely sweet little Armenian woman had been specially trained to deal with this kind of situation. She could be an expert at calming dragons and be completely loyal to Jaafar. She could be both jailer and spy, but there was something about her soft black eyes and sad sympathetic smile that quieted Nadia's anxiety. She had always felt sorry for Armenians with their tragic history, but they had a reputation for being astute and linguistically adept. To test what she thought she might know, Nadia said, "Ani, that's an Armenian name, yes?"

"It is, *Sitt* Nadia."

"You speak several languages then."

Ani laughed and said, "Yes, I have that gift, like many of us."

"Do you know English?"

"No, *Sitt,* Arabic we speak and Turkish and French, and, of course, my own tongue, but not much English."

The thought of Andrew exploded in Nadia's mind. He wanted to learn Arabic because he found it beautiful. Nadia had to hold back tears and could not speak anymore.

She finished her coffee and pastry, and Ani took the tray and left the room. Nadia got out of bed and walked to the balcony. Thoughts cruised at random through her mind… how Hassan would rape her and whether she should fling herself from the balcony beforehand; how poor Andrew was coping; if her father had called every important person he knew to demand her release; and how Elie ever survived his brutal treatment. How should she handle a man who had gone through such desperate measures to capture her? She was feeling weak and vulnerable and knew that any form of resistance would be ineffective, yet resist she must, at least for now.

She felt someone touch her shoulder. Startled, she turned and saw Hassan, his face clean-shaven with a clipped mustache that matched his salt-and-pepper hair, elegantly dressed in an open dress shirt and jacket.

"Why didn't you announce yourself?" she snapped.

She saw the color drain from his face. For a second, even his coal-black tired eyes looked frightened, rather like a dog about to be kicked, but he quickly recovered and with a bit of one-upmanship replied, "And a good morning to you too, Nadia. I'm relieved to find you a bit calmer. I was very worried about your condition last night."

"I'm touched," she sneered and turned away.

Be careful, Nadia thought. *You need time to think through your strategy going forward. Do not get him angry, or you could end up in the same place as Elie.*

"I've come to tell you I'm leaving."

Relieved, she said, "Have a nice trip."

"I'll be gone about a week. Ani and the other staff will make you comfortable. Feel free to use the library and all the facilities."

He paused, waiting for her to turn around.

"I am an expert at this stuff, Nadia. Don't try to escape. You can't. You will only get yourself hurt, and I don't want any harm coming to you. Please respect the rules here. No one gets in or out of here without my permission."

Finally, he took hold of her shoulders and gently turned her around. "*Manni chaitan,* Nadia, but we are going to do this my way, and I am sorry if you find me a monster. I can be a most exquisite partner if given a chance."

She brutally pulled herself from his grip and stared out the window. She waited until she heard him quietly withdraw, leaving the door unlocked, before she laid her forehead on the glass and cried.

CHAPTER TWO

Andrew's head felt like a fuse about to detonate. There had been no movement that he was aware of and no updates from the Lebanese government as to Nadia's whereabouts. So it was crucial he accept the invitation to appear on CNN International. A live interview might be his only chance to shame local officials into action, and no one was going to stop him from speaking out. If he had not been so deficient in street smarts and firearm use—he could not even shoot the gun he had held in his hand to stop Nadia's abduction—and so politically naive about things regional, he would have already gone searching for Nadia himself. Instead, he and her parents had to rely on the lackadaisical response from authorities when it was blatantly obvious that it was Hassan Jaafar who had abducted her and transported her to Syria. So, the last thing Andrew wanted was Mr. Fouad Nasr, a man he hardly knew, counseling him not to give the interview. He had called late morning suggesting as much.

"Hello, my friend, this is Fouad Nasr. I understand you plan to do an interview with CNN International. Could I have a word with you before you do?"

"If you'd like. The interview is on for six p.m. You're welcome to come anytime beforehand."

"Thanks. I'll be there at two."

* * *

Andrew glanced out the window at the journalists and cameramen from CNN, BBC, RT and Al Jazeera camped out on the driveway where Nadia had been abducted. They had originally set up their media center along the main road opposite the Khoury's home, but Victor had opened the gate and invited them into the family compound. He offered them coffee and sweets and spoke freely to anyone who asked about the heartless beast who had abducted his daughter.

While their major focus was the ongoing war between Israel and Hezbollah in the south, Nadia was also news. She was local. She was a diplomat serving on the UN Commission for Human Rights. Her husband, Elie, had been abducted, some thirteen years earlier, and rescued from his Syrian prison cell by his wife before being decapitated by an Israeli rocket while fleeing Marjeyoun. So, the media was outside, and had been all week, talking into television screens, their sophisticated equipment strewn helter-skelter across the front of the house, unavoidably tramping on Carole's flower beds, monitoring both stories.

At two, Fouad drove through the arched rosemary bushes and overgrown olive trees, steering his Fiat over the lawn to avoid the CNN mobile truck parked smack in the middle of the driveway. He parked his car between the swimming pool and rose garden. He got out, tiptoeing carefully over thick television cables, and made his way toward the front porch. Apparently, the local press corps thought he must be someone important because they surrounded him and, shouting questions, shoved microphones in his face and begged for any update on the Nadia Khoury kidnapping.

Who was this man, and why had he referred to himself as Andrew's friend? They had known each other exactly four and a half hours, the time it had taken to fly from Heathrow to Beirut. Andrew's flight from Washington, DC had a short layover in London and that was when a well-dressed, balding, slightly rotund, fifty-something man named Fouad Nasr had boarded the plane and plopped himself down in first class next to Andrew. Over filet mignon and a bottle of Ksara, he had told Fouad just about everything—how he had met Nadia, their upcoming engagement party and the disappeared husband. Fouad remembered the kidnapping, but mostly he remembered Nadia. She had given interviews, written articles, and met with government officials, even foreign diplomats, pleading for their help, and it did not hurt, Fouad had confessed, that hers was a face not easily forgotten. When their plane landed in Beirut, Fouad had handed Andrew his card, offering assistance should he need it.

That night, while Andrew had dined with his journalist friend, Sonia Rizk, at the Phoenicia Hotel, Fouad had walked into the restaurant. After Andrew made the introductions, Fouad excused himself and went to his own table. Later, when Andrew told Sonia that Fouad had made mention of Building 2-4-8 in Damascus, where Assad was thought to hold his political prisoners, she suspected he was connected to one of Lebanon's Intelligence units. A later inquiry confirmed her suspicion.

And here he was, in sport jacket, jeans and sockless loafers about to knock on the Khoury's front door. Andrew promptly opened it and pulled him in, rescuing him from the over-zealous press corps.

"Greetings, Fouad, it's nice to see you again. Come in and let me introduce you to everyone." And Fouad followed him into the living room.

"Fouad Nasr, I'd like you to meet Carole and Victor Khoury, Nadia's parents."

"Very pleased to meet you," said Fouad, shaking hands first with Carole and then her husband, "although I wish it could have been under more pleasant circumstances."

Carole burst into tears. Victor wrapped his arm around her shoulder and sat her down on the couch.

"Carole is having a hard time dealing with all of this," he said.

"That's quite understandable."

Andrew took Fouad's arm and continued around the room. "This is Leila Chakar. She and her uncle Camille graciously hosted us in Marjeyoun."

"I'm honored to finally meet you, Mademoiselle Chakar. You're a hero to many of us after what you endured in Khiam prison."

Leila smiled at him. "Thank you."

"She came with us in the UN convoy to deliver two little orphans to their grandparents here in Beirut. She's had a calming influence on all of us this week. I dare say, I've needed her as much as anyone, and we're very grateful she agreed to stay when she was so urgently needed back in Marjeyoun."

And then Andrew moved on to the last person in the room.

"And this is Sonia Rizk. You two met briefly at the Phoenicia the night we arrived from London."

"Yes, of course, I remember this lady. How delightful to see you again."

"Please have a seat, Fouad," said Carole, as the maid arrived with a tray of Arabic coffee and sweets. As soon as everyone was served and she had departed, Andrew addressed Fouad.

"You wanted to talk to me about the interview?"

"I've come to urge you not to do it. It's foolhardly and could get you into a lot of trouble."

"I'm afraid you've wasted your time, Fouad. I've given my word, and I'm not backing out. Besides, it's urgent I do the interview, and that's final."

"Please listen to me. You've been involved in some pretty audacious things since you got here and have spent time in a bloody war zone, but you're still that naïve American I met on the plane, and you can't even begin to imagine the danger this interview could put you in."

"What specifically are you referring to?" asked Sonia. "I'd be the first to dissuade Andrew if I thought there was a valid reason not to speak with CNN."

"I'm talking about his life, Sonia. This interview could very likely get him killed. Is that reason enough?"

"Yes, of course," Sonia sputtered, "if that was even remotely possible, but what makes you think he'd be in danger?"

"Hassan Jaafar abhors publicity, and any mention of him could potentially be a death warrant for Andrew. I've no doubt this is a distinct possibility."

"What if he didn't mention him?" Sonia asked.

"I'd already decided I wouldn't mention him for fear of putting Nadia in more danger," said Andrew. "If that's all you're concerned about, you have no worries. I'm only interested in getting the authorities to move their butts and bring her home."

"I understand your frustration, but trust me. There are a lot of people working on Nadia's case, but ever since the Hariri assassination, and with half of Lebanon thinking Assad did it, our normal channels of communication with Syria have gone sour."

"I don't think you fully appreciate our frustration," Victor said. "We want our daughter back, and if broadcasting her abduction to the world so someone other than the Lebanese government might come forward and help, well then, we support Andrew's decision."

"Apparently, I've been overruled, and I'm sorry to hear that," Fouad said, shrugging his shoulders. "I only hope my concerns are for naught."

"And so do we," said Carole. "Why don't you stay and watch the interview with us, and then we'll all have dinner together."

"Thank you, Madame Khoury. I'd like that very much."

Andrew did not miss the pleased look Fouad flashed at Sonia as he responded to Carole's invitation.

* * *

After Fouad left, and Nadia's parents had retired to their room, Andrew sat in front of the television with Leila and Sonia and watched the late evening news.

"It has been another ghastly day across Lebanon," the anchor reported. "After destroying 85 percent of the country's infrastructure and dropping bombs on runways at Rafic Hariri International Airport, the port, and fuel storage tanks, Israel struck Dahiyah again for the ninth consecutive day, reducing most of that vast Shiite suburb to uninhabitable rubble. Some four hundred buildings were destroyed, leaving well over half a million people homeless."

Video footage showed smoke still rising from ten and twelve-story buildings and women weeping as they walked through the debris. Most of the wreckage came from the lives of ordinary Lebanese families— wedding photos, toys, students' textbooks, baby strollers, clothes, pages from the Quran littering the ground—while other targets, Hezbollah's political and information offices, were the more obvious. Everything looked gray, the color of war—the unrecognizable streets choked with blocks of cement, twisted metal, splintered trees, skeletons of severely damaged cars thrown blocks away by the bombs, dead body parts poking through the rubble, Rasoul Hospital with its windows blown out by an air strike.

One of the journalists walking through the rubble said, "This was the most dense residential population in Lebanon. It was a vibrant neighborhood. The people who lived here were not fighters. The fighters are on the front lines, in the south."

"And this just in," said the anchor, his voice cracking. "Israel just fired more than a million cluster bombs over south Lebanon, apparently in the hope that the area would be made as uninhabitable as possible."

"What's a cluster bomb?" Andrew asked.

"It's a canister that opens in midair and disperses small sub-munitions called bomblets," Leila explained. "They're deadly, and when they hit someone they set off pressure waves in the body and cause soft tissue and organ damage."

Suddenly, Leila realized what this meant and jumped to her feet. "Oh my God, I need to check on Uncle Camille in Marjeyoun." Cell phone in hand, she dashed out of the room to find a quiet corner.

When Andrew clicked off the television, Sonia spat out, "Goddamn Israeli cowards. Thousands of innocent people need to die or lose their homes because they want to defeat Hezbollah? Tell me why that makes any sense."

"I've never been anywhere near a war," said Andrew, "but my God, have my eyes been opened. Americans have no clue about what goes on here. According to Camille, Israel has invaded Lebanon five times. Who the hell knows that? I saw the people they killed and the destruction they wrought. It was quite a shock."

"The Israelis do an excellent job of cleaning up their act around the world," Sonia said, "particularly in the States, always managing to appear the victim. It doesn't work here where we know how awful they really are."

CHAPTER THREE

Nadia had been played by Hassan, and if she had not been so bored and so desperate for companionship and intelligent conversation, and so tired of eating meals on her own, she would not have been so happy to see him when he finally came back. His game had been cleverly played. He had stayed away the requisite amount of time to be both missed and appreciated. As a master spy, he knew every trick of his trade—how to get into the heads of others and how to manipulate and make people do things they did not necessarily want to do. And he knew everything about Nadia—her social and intellectual needs, her passions and her weaknesses. She was his obsession, the love of his life.

If Nadia was Hassan's fixation, he was her paradox. She would betray Andrew if she gave in to Hassan, but she would lose any chance of gaining her freedom if she did not participate in his game and try to win his trust. But her dilemma was even more complex. She hated Hassan for taking her from Andrew, yet he stirred a sexual desire she wished was not there. How else to explain that she still remembered, after fifteen years, his Givenchy Pour Hommes cologne or the unmistakable arousal that had wakened when he ran his fingers over hers the day they met in Chtaura. There was no hiding her reaction. He had seen it when their eyes met, and she knew he would exploit those yearnings until she ultimately gave in to him sexually.

She needed to gain time so a solution could present itself. She had begun this game at a disadvantage. He was the warden, she the prisoner. He knew her frailties. She was unaware of his. He was sure of himself. But when it came to Hassan, she was not sure of herself. Given the odds, was freedom even possible? Did it even depend on how skillfully she acted her part?

She was focused on Hassan, but he was not the only one participating. She, too, possessed certain powers. While he could have forcibly taken her at any time, this was not the game he had initiated. Confident he would eventually win, he was offering her an even playing field, and it was hers for the taking. So, to find a way to best her opponent, she concentrated on the outermost limits of her peripheral vision where her sight might be clearer. That was how the wise and witty Scheherazade had won her freedom. Nadia, too, could be cunning, and she certainly had brains and beauty and, if used intelligently, she could successfully exploit his obsession. And Andrew would surely understand if she agreed to do certain things. Regardless, the time for analyzing and planning was over. The road ahead was clearer.

Let the game begin, Nadia Khoury, and may you be the winner.

* * *

On his first morning home, Nadia joined Hassan for breakfast. Wearing a sleeveless summer frock that showed off her tanned arms and trying to appear sure-footed and confident when she really felt like a jittery wimp, she walked across the stone terrace to where he was seated. He smiled when he saw her and stood, pulling out her chair, just as he had done when they had met in Chtaura. With a wave of his hand, he gestured for her to sit next to him. The round table was set with fine floral china, a matching pale-pink tablecloth draped the stone and a centerpiece held cut pink roses.

"Good morning, Nadia, how lovely you look. Thank you for joining me."

She stared at him before she finally spoke. "You're feeling pretty smug about yourself, aren't you, Hassan? You go and steal me away and destroy my life, and now that you've got me here you can do whatever you want. Your government repeatedly raped my country, so I suppose you intend to do the same to me. Is that your plan?"

"*Wallah*, that's quite a bold statement, Nadia. You know I love Lebanon… or did until you and your cronies forced us to leave."

"It wasn't me. It was people like you, the power seekers. Is this the way of the world right now? Is this how we're going to have to live?"

"It isn't how you and I have to live. Look, we've both had some rough spells. All I ask is that you give me time to prove to you that this is the right thing, you being here. I'm not going to rape you or cause you any harm. I love you too much to ever do that. Not everything in life can be as conventional as we want. There isn't only one way the world works. Let me show you another way."

Nadia looked sideways and thought about what he had said. This was her opportunity to say okay, we will see how it goes.

"Do you still play tennis?" he asked.

"I haven't played in years."

"You were an excellent player. You actually beat me as I recall."

"I remember that. You let me win. It was a ploy to try to get me into bed, no doubt."

He laughed. "I tried and tried but…"

"You almost succeeded, but then you went and ordered more killings and kidnappings, and that wasn't any way to woo a woman."

"We'll have to start playing again to see where it gets me now that I've retired and am no longer doing bad things." He laughed, trying to coax her to laugh too, but she held her face neutral.

"Would you like some breakfast, Nadia?" He lifted the lid off of a silver platter. "There's a fresh herb and vegetable omelette here, or if you prefer something else I could have the chef—"

"The omelette is fine."

"I hope the staff treated you well while I was away," he said, as he poured her a cup of tea.

"Yes, and Ani was particularly attentive."

"This is your home now, Nadia. I don't know if Ani showed you all that we have here. There are bicycles and well-groomed trails through the woods, and there isn't a soul for miles to bother you. And I've had an exercise room put in too."

"Just for me?"

"Yes, just for you."

"I did take advantage of your pool."

"Yes, I remember you liked to swim."

"Maids, a chef, bike trails… it's all so… extravagant, Hassan. I never dreamed…"

"I offered you all of this, Nadia, when I asked you to marry me, and instead you chose that pretentious professor of yours."

"Must we dredge up the past again? We quarreled over that in Chtaura, and it got us nowhere."

"I agree… by putting the past to rest, we can begin anew. Splendid."

"I'm surprised you remembered so much about me."

"My dear Nadia, there's not a single thing about you that I've forgotten."

She smiled and he relaxed. They were two people on equal footing enjoying each other's company—that was how Hassan envisioned the game being played. It was nonsense, of course. It was still the prisoner versus the warden, and no amount of wishing could change that equation.

In their previous relationship, she, the young college student, had let herself be seduced by one of the most powerful men in the region. From a wealthy Beiruti family, she was used to being pampered and so quite liked that Hassan treated her like his queen. He was strikingly handsome with olive skin and a Semitic nose. He was well-bred and educated, and if it had not been for her parents' horror at such a marriage, and her opposition to his post in the Syrian government, she just might have said yes. And, she reminded herself, primarily to allay her own misgivings, one does not walk away from such an affair, even if it had not landed her in Hassan's bed, without some latent feelings, however buried she had managed to keep them. On the other hand, Hassan was and still is a monster. He had kidnapped Elie and treated him badly, and now he had Nadia, making their relationship that much more complex and emotionally charged.

After breakfast, Hassan invited her on a tour of his estate. They walked side by side, she listening as he showed her his vast herb and vegetable garden. He boasted, as was his right, that much of what they ate was grown on the premises, and that included his own flock of sheep. She asked questions, all the while keeping her arms folded across her chest, agitated by his presence, feeling herself being irresistibly drawn in, yet needing to find ways to hurt him and keep him at bay.

As though she was already the mistress of his estate, he introduced her to his kitchen crew, as well as to some of the others on his staff—many of whom she had already met—insisting nothing should be denied her, except, of course, her freedom.

Nadia would have found it so much easier if she had disliked everything about Hassan Jaafar, but she was forced to admit that his hospitality and desire to please was genuine. And since she was also her mother's daughter, and appreciative of elegance in both clothing—he had filled her closet with beautiful things—and home décor, she grudgingly commended Jaafar on his home, presumably furnished by an interior decorator with impeccable taste. On the other hand, such enthusiasm did not extend to his art collection.

As he walked her through the house, pointing out certain paintings, he explained without pretense—he was not a boastful man—that he knew various art dealers in Europe who, when they came across an original work, contacted him.

"Well, what do you think of my collection?"

"It's not my taste, I'm afraid, and instead of looking at European artists, I'm surprised you don't have any of our great local painters like Abdallah al Omari or Helen Kahl or Daoud Corm or George Akl. They are all amazing and represent who we are—our culture and heritage. Their work is much more to my liking."

"Why don't you see about acquiring some of their paintings, Nadia? I give you *carte blanche*. You're now officially in charge of our art collection."

"Are you serious?"

"Absolutely. I'm surprised I didn't think of these painters myself."

"Was your late wife a connoisseur of art?"

"No, she was an unpretentious woman who tolerated my excesses, for which I was grateful. She came from a well-connected family, and giving credit where it is due, she played an important role in advancing my career. Her father was an intimate of Hafez al-Assad."

Nadia was not sure how to respond. His apparent callousness both astounded and frightened her. How could she ever hope to outsmart a man who had made a career of outwitting his opposition while taking advantage, without apparent shame, of his wife's wealth and connections for his own personal gain?

"Let me show you my favorite room in the house."

When he tried to take her arm, she flinched.

"Is something wrong, Nadia?"

"I'm feeling a bit woozy, I'm afraid."

He eyed her quizzically.

"Come, have a seat in the library while I order you a camomile tisane."

She had already fallen in love with the room when Ani had shown it to her. And as on her previous visit, the sun's rays poured into the grand room, and as before, it still smelled of cigars and fine leather. A large Persian carpet with its cardinal reds, burgundy and shades of blue, covered most of the parquet floor. Aside from a tall window that encompassed almost an entire wall and overlooked the gardens, thousands of books on shelves that reached to the ceiling filled the other walls. The library even had its own wooden ladder attached at the top by a railing that allowed the reader to reach any desired book. The centerpiece of the room was a massive fireplace with an equally long, dark brown leather couch facing it. A long and wide mahogany desk sat in the far corner, positioned as if to preside over the room.

Nadia marveled once again at the splendor of it all. She had found her center of gravity. She would survive her captivity.

"What a magnificent room," she said, as she twirled around to take it all in, forgetting in her enthusiasm that she had just complained of dizziness.

"I love to read, and now that I've been formally introduced to your library, I will spend every free moment here."

He smiled at her.

"Excellent. I, too, enjoy reading and listening to classical music. Come and sit. Your tisane will be here shortly."

Hassan sat at the opposite end of the couch. "I offended you just now when I spoke of Nadine, didn't I? That's why you didn't want me to touch you."

"Yes," she lied. It was really that he had touched her, and her body felt it. "You sounded calculating and indifferent, as if she meant nothing to you."

More troubling was how perceptive he was and how difficult it was going to be to deceive this master spy.

"Ours was a marriage of convenience. She wanted a family, and I wanted her help promoting my career. We entered our union as equals, Nadia. She was a loving mother to our three children, and I respected her immensely. Considered by the Assads to be part of their clan, she knew what was expected of her. She never questioned me about my role as Intelligence chief, nor my frequent absences. My children and I were profoundly saddened when she was diagnosed with terminal cancer. Now that I've been completely honest with you, I hope we can leave that sadness behind us."

Nadia nodded. "Yes, of course."

"Now, shall we take our tisane here or in the garden?"

"Here, please. I'd like to look around your library and choose a book or two to read."

* * *

The day following Hassan's return, they sat together in Nadia's room to watch the morning news. When it ended, Hassan was about to turn off the television when the anchor announced a special interview from Beirut. Suddenly, in front of her eyes, without the slightest bit of warning, she saw Andrew. He was seated in her father's living room. Her heart ached, and her eyes swelled. Her darling Andrew, the man she loved, the man she might never see again.

With the war in south Lebanon winding down, Nadia's week-old abduction was apparently also headline news.

The anchor began:

> "Earlier today we recorded an exclusive interview
> with Dr. Andrew Sullivan, the fiancé of Nadia Khoury,
> Special Representative to the UN High Commission on
> Human Rights, who was kidnapped a week ago outside

her father's Hazmieh villa. Nadia and Andrew had their lives dashed in the most extraordinary way. When, after thirteen years, her disappeared husband, Professor Elie Khoury, was declared dead, she became engaged to Dr. Sullivan only to discover that her husband was still alive in a Syrian prison. In an incredible feat of courage, Madame Khoury got her husband out of prison and brought him back to Lebanon. In a final amazing turn of events, during the war with Israel, her husband was killed while trying to escape from Marjeyoun in a UN convoy.

"Some in our audience might recall that it was Professor Khoury who, in 1993, famously criticized Syrian troop presence in Lebanon, calling it 'an evil, autocratic power that kept the Lebanese under constant surveillance and then manipulated the odds of survival by selecting some for abrupt removal.' Shortly after making that statement, Professor Khoury was kidnapped from his classroom at the American University of Beirut.

"Nadia Khoury's fiancé, Dr. Andrew Sullivan, a cardiologist who practices at the prestigious Georgetown Hospital in Washington, DC, witnessed her kidnapping.

"Welcome, Dr. Sullivan, and thank you for taking the time to speak with us. I realize this is a very difficult time for you and the Khoury family. Do you have any idea who kidnapped your fiancé?"

"No, it was dark. I heard a muffled scream and saw her being forced into the back seat of a car, but I couldn't see the assailant's face. And even if I had, he probably wasn't the one who ordered the abduction."

"Did you try to intervene?"

"Yes, of course. I ran after the car. I got close enough to see the dashboard lit up and could identify the car as a Mercedes, but then it charged up the driveway."

Nadia felt tears run down her cheeks. She dared not look at Hassan. She had hoped to keep Andrew her secret, out of Hassan's reach.

Andrew's voice cracked. After a brief pause, he continued:

"I ran after the car, but it rounded the corner at the
end of the driveway before I could get there... and she
was gone."

"Have there been any demands from the
kidnappers?"

"No demands and no leads."

"Is it true that the two of you were to be married?"

"Yes, the day after her abduction. The ceremony
was to have taken place in Ghazir where Nadia's parents
have a summer home."

"What are your immediate plans, Dr. Sullivan? Do
you intend to return to your practice in Washington, DC?"

"Absolutely not. I will stay in Lebanon until I find
Nadia." And then turning to the camera, he said, "This
is a message to Nadia's kidnapper. Whoever you are,
wherever you are, I am coming after you."

Hassan turned off the television and looked at her steely eyed.

"How long were you with him?"

"Six months."

She felt a brick sink through her torso. She knew what was coming.

"I presume that as a good Christian woman you would not sleep
with someone until you were married. I hope I'm in time."

"In this day and age, Hassan, isn't that a bit naïve? How many
women have you slept with who you weren't married to?"

"So, did you sleep with him?"

She thought to lie and say no, but she decided to cut him to the
quick.

"Yes, of course. This is the twenty-first century."

Without a word, he walked out on the balcony. He took hold of
the railing and, flexing his arms and shoulders, roared into the wind.
When he returned, he promptly fled the room. She remained seated, too
frightened to do anything else. If this was how the game was going to be
played, she wondered if she had made a very wrong move.

For a while the house was silent, and then from somewhere on the first floor, probably his study, Nadia heard his voice, whether speaking to someone in his presence or over the phone she could not tell. He sounded angry and shouted what sounded like orders. When he returned to her room, he appeared to have calmed down. He sat down beside her.

"I apologize, Nadia. I shouldn't have asked you those questions, but I learn from my mistakes."

She looked into his clouded eyes and knew he was not sincere.

"I'm going away for a while," he said.

He was playing her, and she had to play him right back.

She put her hand over his. "I can see you are very hurt, Hassan, but surely you understand that this is none of your business. I didn't know that you wanted anything, and I had to live my life. I didn't think I would ever get Elie back, and then Andrew came into my life when I least expected. I see now that you've been manipulating me. You knew I had a new love interest, and you tried to spoil it by telling Sonia that Elie was still alive, knowing that I would come to get him out. And then, you patiently waited for the right moment so you could abduct me. If you want any relationship with me, you need to be completely honest."

"And will I receive the same from you?"

She lied and said, "Yes."

CHAPTER FOUR

onia pushed back her hair, placed the side of her face near Andrew
and, crying softly, stroked his hand. If he had died, it would have
been her fault. When she had orchestrated Nadia's kidnapping, she had
unintentionally made him Jaafar's prey.

He had been conscious for about ten minutes but had not recognized
anyone—not Fouad, standing at the end of his bed, checking his cell
phone, or Victor reading his newspaper or her, seated by his side. Still
heavily sedated and fighting hard to keep his eyes open, he slipped in
and out of sleep and then, when she least expected it, he whispered,
"Nadia, is that you?"

"No, this is Sonia," she said, replying to him, as everyone did, in
English. Traitor that she was, she stood and kissed him gently on the
forehead.

She watched in a state of panic as he studied her face. Did her eyes
betray her? Could he remember how she had grabbed hold of his arm,
trying to prevent him from saving Nadia? Or, maybe he recalled her
talking on her cell phone outside the house as soon as they had arrived
from Marjeyoun. Would he connect that to Jaafar's thugs turning up a
short time later, or wonder who told Jaafar he was Nadia's fiancé? Did
he ask himself why it was Leila who had walked him back to the house
after his failed rescue attempt while she had stood on the sidelines and
let it all happen?

"Don't stare like that," she said, laughing in between sobs. "I know
I look horrid... no makeup, my hair's a straggly mess. It's your fault,

you know. I've spent the last three nights sleeping beside you on a cot, praying you'd survive your injuries… and," taking his hand and kissing it, "I'm enormously relieved that you have, even if you've aged me a good twenty years."

"I'm here too," said Victor, squeezing his other hand, "and very grateful you're alive."

"So am I, friend," said Fouad. "You sure as hell gave us a scare. Emergency surgery for a ruptured spleen, a massive infection, not to mention a number of other injuries, which I'm sure you're painfully aware of. No pun intended." He laughed. "Sorry, I didn't mean to imply any of this was funny. According to your doctor, your assailant used either a heavy metal bar on you or a slab of wood. The bastard tore open your side and almost severed your spine."

"Do you remember anything?" Victor asked.

Andrew shook his head and closed his eyes. "Yes," he finally said, "on the Corniche… an errand or…"

Sonia watched him struggle with words, his tongue seemingly refusing to cooperate with what it was he wanted to say. "Andrew, have some water." She lifted his head and guided the straw into his mouth. He nodded when he had enough.

"That's right," said Victor. "I dropped you off on the Corniche while I ran an errand."

"You wanted to buy…" started Andrew, before his words fell off.

"Yes, a Beretta… just too bad I wasn't there in time to help you."

"And then what happened?" asked Fouad.

"More water, please."

"Wouldn't you prefer a 7Up instead?" asked Sonia.

"Yes… long time since I had one." She turned to buzz the nurse, and when she looked back, he had dozed off.

When he woke, she put the straw to his mouth.

"How delicious!"

"What else do you remember?" asked Victor.

Andrew closed his eyes. "Nadia… forced into a car…"

Sonia dampened a washcloth and sponged his forehead. "You were on the Corniche, Andrew," she whispered. "Victor dropped you there."

"Yes, watching the sunset and…"

"Andrew, and then what?" asked Fouad.

He became agitated. "Two men grabbed me… too strong. I couldn't resist… A black car at the curb, dark windows… pushed into the back seat. A man, bulging biceps, tied my wrists, blindfolded me."

Andrew closed his eyes. Tears streamed down his cheeks. "I thought I was going to die."

"Stop it, you two," said Sonia. "Can't you see this is too much for him?"

Andrew shook his head. "No." He continued. "Don't remember how long… the car stopped. I was pulled out, told to walk. We were by the sea… still blindfolded… I fell on the sand. Someone strong grabbed my arms and yanked me up. My blindfold ripped off… a man shouted in my face, 'Mr. Jaafar didn't like your interview on CNN,' and he punched me. I buckled. Someone pulled me upright… more punches. Hit across my back and…"

Fouad came to the side of the bed. "They took you to a public beach near Damour. There's a factory there, and two of their guards were on cigarette break when they saw you being attacked. They came running, firing their guns in the air, and chased away your assailants but not before snapping a few photos of the thugs. They saved your life."

Andrew nodded. "I didn't mention Jaafar in the interview, so why was I attacked?"

"No, but you identified yourself as Nadia's fiancé," said Fouad. "I assume up to that point Jaafar didn't know you existed. Nadia wouldn't have told him. She would have wanted to protect you. This revelation must have pissed him off. At least you refrained from talking about the Israeli whose head he'd severed. Otherwise, you would have definitely been a dead man."

"You're upset…"

"Frustrated is more like it. You insisted on doing the interview." He turned to look at Sonia and Victor. "Your friends here encouraged you, and you almost got yourself killed. You don't listen to sound advice when it comes from an Intelligence officer who knows what the hell he's talking about. So yes, I'm annoyed."

"We don't know if Jaafar wanted you killed, or just roughed up, but we're taking no chances," said Victor. "We've posted two security guards outside your room."

"Tell me about Nadia."

"We've nothing yet," said Fouad.

Andrew closed his eyes and shook his head. "What if…?"

"Let's just concentrate on you making a full recovery for now," said Fouad.

"Yes, and it starts right now. No more questions for today," said Sonia, standing up to face the two men. "You've exhausted him, and he needs to rest. I'm ordering you two out. Go home and come back tomorrow."

Sonia smiled, hands on her hips when she said that, but they knew she was only looking after Andrew, and they stood to leave.

"What about you?" Fouad asked, looking at her. "Isn't it time you took a break? You look exhausted. Why don't you sleep in your own bed tonight now that Andrew is out of danger?"

"Thanks for your concern, but I'll stay. I want to make sure Andrew has a restful night. We'll see you both tomorrow."

* * *

After an agitated sleep on an uncomfortable cot, Sonia was relieved to see Andrew alert and sitting upright when she woke.

"And a good morning to you," she said, standing to stretch stiff body parts. "You, at least, appear to have slept quite well."

"I did, and I'm even hungry."

She laughed and cried and rang the nurse to order breakfast.

After eggs with zaatar and manoushe and tea, Sonia left Andrew to rest and read the local English daily while she showered and dressed, checked her emails and got a bit of work done. And before she realized the hour, it was mid-afternoon and Fouad and Victor had returned.

"How is our patient today?" asked Fouad, standing at the end of Andrew's bed and wiggling his toes.

"As you can see, he's doing very well," Sonia said, without giving Andrew a chance to respond. "He even had a ferocious appetite this morning."

She noticed Andrew's broad smile. A small recompense, she thought, after his brush with death.

"Wonderful news," said Fouad, addressing Andrew. "Listen, my friend, Victor and I have had a chat, and we need to talk to you."

"This sounds serious," Andrew said.

"It is," Fouad said. "We both agree that the best thing you can do, and we say this as friends, is return to the US and forget Nadia Khoury."

"Why would you ever suggest such a thing?"

"Carole and I fear for your safety," said Victor. "And Nadia wouldn't want anything to happen to you either. It's possible Jaafar will come after you again, and he'll kill you if he does. We'll be in constant contact, and if we discover anything about Nadia's whereabouts, you'll be the first to know."

"I thank you for your concern, Victor, but as long as Nadia is held captive, I will never abandon her."

"I urge you to give this a bit more thought," said Fouad.

"I don't need to. My mind is made up, and that's the end of this discussion."

"Well, if that's the case, I'm going to have you transferred to a private clinic in Broumana in the Metn Mountains where you'll be well-protected, just in case Jaafar decides to send his dogs to finish you off."

"That's very generous of you, Fouad, and I'd welcome that."

"And if you're going to insist upon staying, you'll need some training, but that will come only after you've fully recovered. Your doctor thinks that will take at least six months."

"That long?"

"You're a middle-aged man, my friend, who has been beaten almost to death. Your body will need that time to heal. Once your doctor gives us the green light, you'll start working out with a buddy of mine who's a personal trainer. He takes wimps like you and turns them into warriors. He'll work with you, get you strong and teach you some survival skills and street smarts. Lord knows you need them. Oh, and while you're in recovery, I'm going to suggest you start Arabic lessons."

"Sure, I'd like to learn the language, but this is hardly the time to be tackling such a challenge."

"I disagree," said Sonia. "Since you're determined to stay, I think it's absolutely the right time. And the sooner you get back to being a physician, the better you'll feel. I have a friend in the Shatilla Palestinian camp who works with Doctors Without Borders. They need doctors, and this would be the perfect fit for you, but in order to work in the camp, you'll need a decent command of Arabic."

"And I'm confident this is the kind of work Nadia would want you to be doing," said Victor. "Don't you agree?"

Andrew nodded. "Yes, but you're not suggesting this precludes me from trying to find her, are you?"

"Not at all," said Fouad. "Once you're well trained, your Arabic is solid, and I've determined the timing is right, maybe then we can slip into Syria and rescue Nadia. In all likelihood, that's where Jaafar took her."

Fouad continued. "There are some bad winds brewing in Syria right now. Bush wants regime change. The CIA is already in Jordan training mujahedeen crazies to fight the Assad government. Within the next few years the country will go up in flames, and hopefully before that happens we can get Nadia out, and maybe it will be through Doctors Without Borders."

"A year, maybe two?" said Andrew. "That's a hell of a long time to have to wait for something to happen."

"Not really," said Fouad. "Between your full recovery and training, we're looking at a year and a half, and that's a pretty realistic time frame. And then, you'll need at least six to eight months in the camp to acclimate yourself and practice your Arabic."

"Do you have a plan?" asked Andrew.

"Not yet, but I'm working on one."

"Who do you work for, Fouad?"

"Who I work for isn't important. What matters is that I'm very good at my job. And my priority is to get you ready for whatever plan I come up with."

Sonia saw that this was a bit more than Andrew was prepared to handle at the moment.

"Why don't we leave you to rest a bit," she said, "and give you time to mull this over. It's time I got a bit of fresh air, and besides,

you're probably tired of seeing my face. I'll be back in the morning."
She kissed him on the forehead and then grabbed Fouad and Victor's
arms. "And these two are coming with me. We could do with a walk
along the Corniche." She escorted them out of the room.

CHAPTER FIVE

Sonia woke thinking she was in an explosion, the sun shining directly on her face, hot and dazzling. She closed her eyes and nestled into Fouad's underarm. Like a cliff offering protection, he put his arm around her. After leaving the hospital and accompanying Victor to his car, they had walked from the Corniche to Zaitunay Bay, the upscale promenade adjacent to Beirut's yacht club. Over several bottles of Ksara, an abundant mezee and grilled meats at Babel's, they had celebrated Andrew's recovery, and before either of them could make sense of their conduct, they were back in her rooftop apartment in Achrafieh trying to take off each other's clothes. Sonia recalled how sweet it had been, both of them a bit tipsy—she trying to unzip his pants, he fumbling over buttons—until finally undressed they had fallen into bed, their love making crazy and easy and fun. For Sonia, sex had too often been a means to some ulterior motive—a query, a secret divulged in the moment, a better career posting. How wonderful, she thought, that the most natural thing between two people had happened for the sheer joy of it all.

When Sonia tried to slip out of bed, Fouad pulled her back. "Where do you think you're going, my lady?"

"I thought I'd surprise you with breakfast."

"How delightful, but there's really no hurry. Andrew is recovering nicely, and it's my day off."

"Ah, but the sooner I feed you, the hungrier you'll be for me." She smiled as she climbed out of bed.

He sat up and leaned on his elbow. "You know a lot about men and what they like, don't you?"

"Yes, I do, and I'll show you," she said, glancing back at him as she walked into the bathroom.

"I can't wait," she heard him say as she closed the door.

Be careful, Sonia, she told herself while standing under the shower. Do not get cocky and let your guard down. He is a spy, and clearly no one's fool. Not to worry... I will move ahead cautiously until I figure him out.

After toweling off, Sonia decided on a sleeveless, mid-calf-length dress, a distinctly feminine choice given that Fouad had only seen her a disheveled mess in the hospital. While she forewent her usual amount of makeup, she could not resist a dab or two of her favorite Jasmin Noir behind each ear, and instead of brushing her hair into a chignon, which would have been much sexier, she wore it loose and casual. She gave herself one final check. Pleased, she went to the kitchen where she donned an apron and busied herself preparing their meal, something she rarely got a chance to do. Any other time, it would have been her maid's job, but Hasna had the day off. She was glad. She wanted to show off her culinary skills.

She chopped bananas, apples and a few strawberries and tossed them with orange blossom syrup. She divided the fruit between them and topped each bowl with a lebneh-honey mix. When she heard Fouad go into the bathroom, she fried four eggs, sprinkling them with sumac, heated the manoushe and laid out an assortment of cheese and olives. She set everything out on a small table on her balcony, concealed from public view by tall shrubs and flowering plants. A Damascene rose, her favorite, had just opened. She cut it, put it in a small silver vase and placed it in the middle of the table. *Perfect,* she thought, except she knew it was anything but and began to cry.

She was responsible for the assault on Andrew's life, and that had unhinged her. She had also betrayed Nadia to Hassan Jaafar in exchange for information that proved Israel had killed former Lebanese Prime Minister Rafic Hariri and, in the process, had almost gotten her killed. Ah yes, at the time Sonia thought nothing could be easier. Deceive Nadia in exchange for a good story and plenty of accolades. Why not? Hassan only wanted to have sex with her. What did she care? She disliked Nadia, and some sexual escapades with a seasoned man like Jaafar would do the perfect Nadia Khoury some good. No, that was not the whole truth. She was jealous of Nadia. She had expected a marriage proposal from Elie. They had been having an affair for years. Neither of them were particularly nice people. They recognized that about themselves so, in her mind, the logical next step was marriage to a fellow scoundrel. Only that was not what happened. Elie surprised her and chose, instead, the beautiful Nadia to be his wife. In revenge, she had no qualms about arranging Nadia's kidnapping, but things had not gone as planned.

She jumped when Fouad came up behind her and kissed her wet cheek.

"I hate to see a beautiful woman cry," he whispered in her ear.

She wiped her cheeks and turned around. "But I'm fine now that you're here. Take a seat. Would you like tea or cappuccino?"

"A double cappuccino, if you don't mind."

He looked pleased as he took in the profusion of colors around him, and, as Sonia suspected, even more content to rest his eyes on her. "Gorgeous lady, you've set an inviting table in an intoxicating garden. Is there some special occasion?"

"Very special." She smiled as she joined him at the table. "Bon appétit."

Fouad finished his eggs, wiping up every remaining bit of yolk with a piece of pita bread before speaking again.

"Victor told me you'd wrapped up your Hariri investigation."

"A bit of an exaggeration, I'm afraid. I have what I consider solid evidence, but it doesn't necessarily mean much when accusing the Israel government of a major crime."

"You're a well-respected journalist, Sonia. You wouldn't have boasted such a feat if you hadn't verified all the facts."

"You seem to know a lot about me, Fouad."

"I've made it my business to know what you do, just as you've made it yours to know who I am and what I do. After we met at the Phoenicia. It seems like ages ago… do you remember? The night Andrew flew in from London—you had me checked out. I've been intrigued by you ever since. You're a force unto yourself, *ya Sitt* Sonia."

"You knew all along about my call to Internal Security?"

He smiled. "Your friend is also mine. Our Intelligence unit is a tightly knit bunch. When I knew it was you asking, I gave him permission to confirm what you thought you already knew... that I had former connections to Intelligence when, in fact, I still do. Then, when you realized I could be useful, you had Andrew call me the following day to help get him a visa to gain entry into Syria.

"And before you accuse me of grossly exaggerating my skills as an Intelligence operative, I'll admit something else. Your crooked little friend Nehme works for me too."

"Nehme, the drug dealer in the Bekaa Valley?" she said, with as confident a voice as she could muster. "You knew all along that I was using him?"

He nodded.

"But he spent years in prison for selling—"

"That's right, for selling drugs to minors. I put him there and made sure he paid dearly for crossing that red line. He's grateful I arranged his early release, and now he does anything I ask of him."

"Okay, we've established that we both know Nehme. So what?"

"As it happened, I also had a known Israeli spy followed when he left Beirut. Little did I know that he'd end up in your bedroom at The Park Hotel in Chtaura. Imagine my surprise when Nehme informed me that you'd asked him to keep twenty-four-seven surveillance on the man. You were playing a dangerous game, Sonia."

"I understood the risk," she replied, by now unnerved by the breadth of irrefutable evidence he had on her.

"*Ya Allah,* not the half of it," he replied. "And what you did in south Lebanon was even more foolhardy. Meeting that same Israeli spy so publicly in Hezbollah territory? You were lucky one of their thugs only beat you to within an inch of your life. I'm surprised he didn't finish you off. And then, when the Israelis found out what you were up to, they issued an order to have you killed, but they got your journalist buddy, Ali, instead, with a bullet to his head. Their way of telling you, in case you hadn't understood, to forget about accusing them of murdering Hariri. So yes, that's pushing all limits of reasonable risk."

Eyes flooding, she looked across the table at Fouad. "All my adult life I've dealt with fear by burying it. This has allowed me to walk into war zones and cover massacres and report the horrendous survivor stories, all the atrocities a good journalist is supposed to write about. But the fear I have now is different. I can't make it go away. It visits me every night. In my dreams, I'm tortured and killed in terrible ways."

She stopped and wiped her tears. "I'm frightened, Fouad. I don't want to die."

"Frightened enough to listen to some sound advice?"

"Yes," she said, accepting his handkerchief to blow her nose.

"I have as much interest in proving Israel's guilt as you do, maybe even more. In my case, it's a matter of national security. Some might call me completely unrealistic, but I have this vision of a successful nation-state and what it should be, and it can't be one with thirty thousand Syrian troops undermining our authority, or Israeli aggression, or the US fostering sectarian violence, or lawless, uninhabitable refugee camps like Shatilla. So yes, I promise you'll get to write your story and reap the rewards you so rightly deserve for speaking truth to power, but it will be done my way so I can provide you the necessary security you're going to need."

"Israel will try to kill me once my story gets out."

"I know it."

"So, it would appear that I am entirely at your mercy."

"You needn't be. We're not at odds, you and me. In fact, we're on the same team."

"How is that?"

"I know what you did to get your story."

Sonia stared at him. "You don't know the half of it."

"Oh, but I do. And since you and I are now lovers, I'm going to be honest and open with you."

Sonia shook her head. "I'm not sure I can handle any more surprises."

"Hassan Jaafar and I are old acquaintances. At one time, we were actually close friends. While we stay in regular contact, we haven't seen each other in years… different politics basically. He had an agenda handed him by the Syrian government, and I had mine, all of which was normal given the occasional animosity between our two countries. We trained together at the CIA, two Middle Easterners shunned by the trainees from the elite colleges, another reason we bonded. He returned to Syria to become Assad's Intelligence chief, while I stayed on at the CIA until I tired of its culture and finally came home."

Unsettled, Sonia listened. Defeat was not something she abided easily, but it appeared she had been out-witted on all fronts by a master spy.

"All of this to say your secret is safe with me."

"What I did was wrong, Fouad. I've got to find a way to make things right."

"You will, and I'll help."

Through tears she stared at him. She had never had a truly honest relationship with anyone; she had never felt the need. She had always gotten what she wanted through sex or lies, and gross deceptions. Fouad knew all of this about her and yet, here he sat, offering unconditional support and loyalty and, above all, forgiveness for all she had done. For years she had been out there experimenting with other men, mostly the wrong kind, and now here was someone from her own Christian Lebanese clan, a man who, for a spy, had a mellow and easy manner about him, who actually wanted to take care of her. She desperately wanted that to happen. She stretched her hand across the table and took his.

"Thank you, Fouad," she said, wiping away more tears. "I'd appreciate your help."

"My dear lady, look at you. I never intended this conversation to turn so dreary. I think you could do with a bit of cheering up. Am I right?"

"Yes." She laughed, blowing her nose again.

"*Eh bien.* I propose a relaxing drive up the mountains to the Broumana retreat. You can meet Andrew's trainer, and if you're so inclined, we can have a quiet, candle-lit dinner there and stay the night. What do you say?"

"I think that's a perfectly splendid idea."

* * *

The drive from Beirut to Broumana in the Metn Mountains took them through small, long-established Christian villages, each with their own unique character, some with vistas that stretched to great expanses, a wondrous illusion in a country only about three times the size of Rhode Island. The landscape spanned pine forests, deep valleys and rocky cliffs where, on some of the highest pinnacles, one invariably found either a monastery or church, and oftentimes an elite private school. Every village laid claim to both fine restaurants and take-out food joints, to women and men's apparel boutiques, coiffeurs and barber shops, pharmacies and even small grocery stores. The much larger Broumana, once the most desirable summer destination of Lebanese Christians had, with the advent of better roads and urban sprawl, grown into a year-round Beirut suburb. The "retreat," as Fouad called it, was the most luxurious estate in the Metn and was located at the entrance to Broumana.

"I'm surprised you don't know it, Sonia."

"I know where it is, but it's always been under private ownership and off limits to the uninvited. I remember when a Saudi prince purchased it. The locals were outraged, claiming Muslim encroachment on their exclusive turf."

Fouad laughed. "That kind of nonsense obviously didn't faze the prince. He went about completely remodeling it and spent, I'm told, some twenty million on the place, and then for whatever reason he turned around and put it on the market a few years later. At the time, Langley was looking for a safe house–private guest facility and snatched it up."

A scandalous use of American taxpayer dollars, thought Sonia.

"You never mentioned that Andrew was being transferred to a CIA-owned facility, Fouad."

"I didn't think it mattered. My primary concern was getting him the best care and keeping him safe, and this place does both. Regardless of what you may think, I intend to take good care of Andrew, even if I can't be completely honest with him."

"Why not?"

"Because I know where Jaafar's keeping Nadia. I also know that she's being well-treated."

Sonia stared at him. "What are you saying?"

"I have a reason for keeping Jaafar safely tucked away with Nadia. As long as he's happy, he has no reason to return to Damascus or be in the public eye."

"Hold on… you're spy-speaking and making no sense."

"In certain elite Washington circles, Jaafar has an enemy or two. He did something years ago, which I personally thought was justified, that angered certain people, one of whom is currently serving in the US embassy in Iraq. Now that he's stationed in the region, he's made it known he wants revenge on Jaafar, and I'm not about to let that happen. As for Andrew, Jaafar wanted him dead. The retreat, the trainer, Arabic lessons, and finally his work in Shatilla—all of this fits into my plan to ensure he's carefully looked after. Now, that's all I'll say about the matter, so no questions, please."

"I don't know if I can resist, Fouad. You've gone and stoked a journalist's curiosity…"

"No, I haven't, Sonia. I've simply entrusted you with a secret, just as you've entrusted me with yours. Now you and I are bound by secrecy, are we not?"

She had just been ensnared into his spy world, but that didn't trouble her. She had already decided to trust this man with her life, and now their bond had been made even stronger. Whatever he asked of her, she would do.

"Yes, we are, Fouad, completely."

"By the way, the man you're about to meet, Joe… he's ex-CIA too."

"Well, what a surprise." She laughed. "Would he have been anything else?"

"Okay, Miss Smarty Pants, I'll take care of you later."

She laughed and slipped her hand between his legs. "I'll be waiting."

"As I was about to say, he lived in the States for some twenty years. After he retired from Langley, he moved back here where he runs a training facility for people like Andrew who want to learn survival skills."

"Why come to Lebanon?"

"He grew up here. His mother's Lebanese. He speaks Arabic, French and Russian."

"Russian?"

"His father was a diplomat, apparently with close Kremlin connections."

"You're not worried about possible dual loyalties?"

"No, he's 100 percent loyal. Besides, his possible connections could be helpful if Russia openly allies itself with Bashar down the road. Don't forget Russia and Syria have had long-standing ties. They've had a naval base in Tarsus since 1971."

"And didn't they also sign a treaty on military cooperation?"

"That happened in 1980. So, don't worry about Joe, even if he has a foul mouth and sometimes talks like a gutter rat. And when he starts cursing in Arabic, holy shit… it's outright embarrassing."

Sonia laughed. "And many of our curses are sexually explicit like *ahu charmootah,* you're the brother of a prostitute. My favorite is *kiss eikhtai,* the vagina of your sister."

"Yes, Joe's quite the enigma. One minute he's uncouth, the next he's quoting Confucius… and then…" Fouad looked at Sonia. "He's also my counter-terrorism expert."

"What are you getting Andrew into, Fouad?"

"Joe's been working undercover in Shatilla. One of the camp leaders, a woman named Aziza, works closely with him. They're monitoring al-Qaeda-linked jihadist groups that have begun infiltrating Shatilla and other camps over the past year. Having Andrew in Shatilla will give them an additional set of eyes and ears."

"Jesus Christ, you promised you were going to protect Andrew, and now you're going and putting his life in danger."

"I don't agree. He'll not only be under the auspices of Doctors Without Borders but the watchful eye of Joe and his team."

"Why bother about what goes on in the camps? It's not as if anyone gives a shit about the Palestinians. I wish I had more sympathy for them, but I'm one of those Lebanese who can't forgive what Arafat and his men did during the civil war. Of course, the Phalangists and Israelis committed monstrous crimes during the Sabra-Shatilla massacre, but Arafat set up a state within a state and did his part to destroy Lebanon too."

"Arafat was an arrogant, self-serving bastard who didn't care a damn about his people, but that doesn't excuse the horrific conditions in the camps. No one should be made to live like that, and the jihadists are there taking advantage, preying on the unemployed youth, recruiting them to carry out sectarian strife. My boss and his Sunni powerhouse are funding these jihadist bastards, so I have a moral obligation to try to stop them."

"Even if it gets you killed, Fouad?" She stared at him and finally said, "Your plan sucks and has zero chance of succeeding."

"I've been doing this work a long time. I know what I'm doing."

"This is different. You've never come up against these kinds of people before."

Sonia sat silently staring out the window for a long time. When she finally turned, she said, "Do you think Joe and Andrew will get along?"

Fouad heard the resignation in her voice.

"Confucius says a superior man understands what is expected of him."

"You and your Confucius. You're an enigma yourself—one minute a spy master with this crazy idea he can save his country and defeat jihadists, the next a philosopher. I'm impressed."

"Damn right. You better be impressed." He laughed. "As for Andrew, he knows he needs help. He'll make it work with Joe."

Finally, Fouad brought his car to a halt before the retreat's iron gate.

"I need to warn you," she said. "I may not be allowed in this place."

"What are you talking about?"

"Years ago, the CIA approached me to be one of their Middle East correspondents. I've not many redeeming qualities, as you know, but posting their disinformation would have surpassed even my limits of unscrupulous behavior."

Fouad laughed. "You've nothing to worry about, dear lady. They're all locals working here, albeit with the proper security clearance, and vetted by Internal Security. They wouldn't know anything about an attempt to recruit you."

"Let me get this straight. The men who work here were handpicked by you?"

"More or less an accurate statement." He smiled. "Any other questions?"

"No," she said, laughing. "And if I did, you'd just have another smart-ass answer."

"And just so you know, Langley's need for total control of information requires media complicity which means either recruiting journalists who have no qualms about peddling disinformation or, as in in your case, handpicking a well-known journalist who might agree to be their mouthpiece, so consider it an honor, of sorts, that you were asked. Being the savvy journalist you are, you were able to see through their deceptive practices and refuse."

"Thank you, dear spy master." She laughed out loud.

He looked at her and smiled. "That's how I like to see you, Sonia, happy and relaxed."

"It hasn't happened much lately, but I agree it's long overdue."

Fouad buzzed and gave his name. Seconds later, Sonia marveled as they drove along a narrow cobblestone driveway lined on either side by ivy-covered stone walls, emerging finally onto a plateau of manicured lawns, sculptured shrubs, a circular pond and vine-entangled trellises shading red-cushioned teak chairs and matching tables.

Fouad stopped the car in front of the arched entrance of a two-story, red-tile-roofed stone building. An attendant, a local who addressed Fouad by name, appeared, opened Sonia's door and helped her out while Fouad grabbed their overnight bags. He gave the man the keys to the car and, hand in hand, he and Sonia walked up a wide marble stairway and through sliding glass doors.

While Fouad went to speak to another local at the reception desk, Sonia perused the lobby.

She found it unsettling to be inside such an opulent CIA-owned facility. What bothered her most was the privileged way it took care of its own while caring little for the countries, particularly those in the Middle East, it had so willfully destroyed, whether for their own agenda or that of their regional ally, Israel. It was not as if the agency could lay claim to a successful track record either, except maybe in Afghanistan where they had thrown out the Russians, but that had come at the expense of leaving al-Qaeda and its minions, not to mention American troops, behind to wreak further havoc on a desolate, poverty-stricken country. And if the rumors were true, Langley had already called up the next generation of these same jihadists to help them overthrow Assad and destroy Syria.

Despite her misgivings about the place, Sonia could not help but marvel at the flawless sarcophagus sitting atop a sturdy wooden frame in the center of an otherwise sparsely furnished lobby. In her cynicism, she wondered if Langley had asked permission to display such a valuable object d'art in their facility or had simply lifted it from one of Lebanon's many archeological sites, claiming it as their own.

"Is this Roman or Phoenician?" Sonia asked as she walked around the artifact, examining the intricate, well-defined figures chiseled around its marble base.

"It's Phoenician," Fouad said, returning to her side with a room key in his hand. "When we leave here tomorrow, we'll stop in Beit Meri. I'll show you the treasure trove of ancient ruins there."

"Yes, I'd like to see them again," she said, vaguely remembering a profusion of relics she had seen there in her youth.

"Come on then," he said, "let's put our bags in the room."

On the second floor of the guest house, Fouad ushered her into a well-appointed suite with a balcony that overlooked a vast pine forest extending deep into the valley and up the other side of a steep mountain range.

"This is all so…" *Extravagant*, she thought, and wondered what Americans would say if they knew their tax dollars were being spent on a privileged few. Sonia had lived for extended periods of time in the US and had even kept a small townhouse in Georgetown. She held the much-sought-after green card and had a great fondness for Americans—a kind and generous people—even if they were uninformed and too often complacent about what their government did in their name. She understood this human frailty. She had been guilty of the same kind of behavior during the civil war when, on those days when other parts of the city were being bombed, she had felt selfishly relieved her neighborhood of Achrafieh had been spared. So yes, she understood complacency and selfishness, but when a powerful country like the US went about initiating wars and supporting criminal behavior because it suited their agenda, she considered it the responsibility of its citizenry to sit up and pay attention.

Fouad pulled her out of her reverie, saying something about his plans for the evening.

"How nice," she responded, not quite sure what he had just said.

"Well then, let's go find Joe," he said, taking her hand and whisking her out of their suite.

From the guest house, they descended the stairs, walked across the driveway and followed a stone walkway alongside a swimming pool until they reached the gym—a large, brightly lit room furnished with every imaginable piece of workout equipment. Fouad scanned the room, and when he spotted Joe, he pointed toward the boxing ring.

"There he is."

Joe was boxing rather rigorously with a husky, middle-aged man, possibly Russian by the sound of the accent they heard when he shouted he had had enough. Aside from the requisite padded gloves and head gear, each was dressed in a sleeveless T-shirt, shorts and high-top, thin-soled boxing shoes. In her mind's eye, Sonia had imagined Joe a macho iron-man, ex-GI type, with short-cropped hair. Instead, she stared at a statuesque, olive-skinned, Greek-nosed figure with wavy, dark hair. When Joe saw them, he excused himself from his sparring partner, climbed out of the ring and hopped to the floor. He approached Sonia and took her hand.

"Who is this ravishing beauty?" he asked, staring into her eyes.

"This is Sonia Rizk," said Fouad, "and she's already spoken for, so don't get any ideas."

"*Quel dommage*," Joe said, lifting her hand to his mouth and kissing it.

Quite the charmer, she thought, loving his attention.

"I've heard a lot about you, Joe. I'm pleased to finally meet you. We'll be seeing more of each other once Andrew gets here."

"It will be my pleasure," he said.

"Fouad, when do you expect Andrew to be transferred here?" he asked.

"I suspect it will be at least another four weeks. He's only just come out of an induced coma. I'll let you know as soon as I've gotten the okay from his doctor to have him transferred. And even when he finally gets here, he'll only be able to handle the most basic stuff for a good long while."

"I agree," Joe said. "Rest assured I won't do anything without his doctor's permission."

"We're very grateful that Andrew will be in such capable hands, Joe," Sonia said, extending her hand. "We'd best let you get back to your sparring partner. *A tres bientot.*"

"If you're free tonight, why don't you two join me for dinner," said Joe.

"Sorry, but we already have plans."

Surprised, Sonia looked at Fouad, but refrained from asking what they were.

Once outside, Sonia asked, "Why did you refuse his invitation?"

He shrugged. "I have my reasons."

"Are you by chance jealous? No doubt, he'd be quite the catch."

Fouad laughed.

"Why hasn't he already been snatched up by some lucky woman?"

"Maybe he hasn't found the right one yet. I hadn't either until you came along."

Sonia smiled and slipped her arm in his. "I think we're both lucky people, and I love that you're jealous. It makes me feel special."

She kissed him on his cheek. "I hope your plans for this evening include food because I'm famished."

"They do, dear lady." They chatted as they walked back to the guest house.

With a simple command on the room's phone, a waiter arrived a short time later with a food-laden trolley. He went about setting the table on the balcony with a linen tablecloth, fine china and silverware. When he finished, he lit the candles and left, leaving it up to Fouad, as he had requested, to serve dinner at his leisure.

"Shall we?" he asked, inviting Sonia to take her place at the table.

He lifted the dome on the first silver platter and announced, "Some foi gras and chilled sauterne to begin our meal."

Sonia clapped her hands. "Fouad, you're spoiling me."

"The pleasure is all mine."

"And later, to go with our filet mignon, they found us a vintage Musar in their wine cellar. I know you prefer Ksara, but this is my favorite red. I hope you'll like it. And for dessert…"

"Darling, I'd like to have you for dessert."

"I can arrange that," he said, laughing.

From the foi gras to the filet and Musar, Sonia found it easy to be in Fouad's company. He was comfortably predictable, which she realized was a silly thing to say. With any other man, she would have found such behavior boring. Yet, here she was… content and feeling very safe and relaxed with a new lover she hardly knew. She reached out and took his hand.

"I think we're ready for dessert, my darling."

"I agree." He pulled her to her feet and took her to the bedroom. Unlike their drunken foray the night before, he took his time undressing her, and she him. When he led her toward the bed, she suggested they try it on a chair instead. She had him sit, and legs spread wide, she straddled him. Both in full arousal, she slipped him into her. She rode him, slowly at first, trying not to climax too soon. Aware of him coming, they soared to the stars together. When she caught her breath, she burst out laughing.

"What's so funny?"

"It was amazing," she said, and she was not kidding. She had been in a war zone in south Lebanon. Sex with Fouad these past two days had been her first since the decapitated Israeli. Poor useful fool, that trauma had been such that she had not realized how much she missed sex until she had climaxed.

"You're pretty amazing yourself, Sonia. I've never made love to a woman quite like you. You completely lose yourself. It's almost as if you weren't even present."

"You're right. I wasn't. You took me to a purely joyful place and gave me an incredible high."

CHAPTER SIX

Fouad was fifty-three years old. A number of women had shared his bed, and until now, that arrangement had suited him quite nicely. No commitments, no messy entanglements, no hysteria—everything clear from the first—but that was before he had met Sonia Rizk, a curious riddle of a woman not easily defined. She was gutsy and sly, yet sophisticated and well-seasoned. She was righteous in her devotion to journalism and truth-telling, a quality that did not necessarily translate to other parts of her life, but he did not hold that against her. She had, after all, expressed remorse over Andrew's near demise. He was willing to overlook her betrayal of Nadia too. She had done it to prove the enemy's guilt, a forgivable malefaction in the eyes of most Lebanese. Beyond her faults and qualities, Sonia was a woman so intoxicating and so passionate he found himself drawn to her like a bee drone to his queen. At the same time, she frightened him. The sexual attraction was so strong he risked losing the one thing he had always cherished—his freedom.

* * *

Before Fouad climbed out of bed the next morning, he turned to Sonia and, with a kiss, wished her a good morning.

"Tell me this hasn't all been a dream, dear lady. I've just spent an incredible forty-eight hours in your company, and I don't want it to end."

Sonia smiled up at him and stroked his arm. "Oftentimes the best and most enduring affairs are accidental. I sense this is one of them, and I don't intend to let you go."

"I'll hold you to that promise." At least he hoped he would, miserable wimp that he was, afraid to make a commitment.

"What do you say we spend the day in Beit Meri. I promised you Roman and Phoenician ruins, and I wouldn't want to disappoint you."

"A day with the ancients it is."

"I'll order breakfast while we shower and dress."

"I suggest you call for breakfast after we've showered. No telling how long we'll take." She smiled, climbed out of bed and followed him into the bathroom.

* * *

Fouad stopped his car on the outskirts of Beit Meri.

"Come, let me show you my favorite view of Beirut," he said as they climbed out of the car. "During the war, I used to drive up here just to remind myself that we were still a civilized people living in a cosmopolitan country and that we were not the savages we'd become. One night in particular, the Syrians were bombing the hell out of Beirut. It was complete mayhem, but, for whatever crazy reason, I agreed to meet friends for dinner at Mounir's. I stopped here to watch the fireworks. I wondered what the hell I was doing when I should have been back home, hiding in my building's shelter."

"But that was how we survived the war, wasn't it," Sonia said. "We defied it. We refused to cower in fear and, instead, lived each day to the fullest as if it was our last."

"It's still hard to believe that *pour un oui ou pour un non,* we turned into barbarians, killing each other over religion and societal inequities."

"And for what?" she asked. "All we did was play into the hands of outside forces who orchestrated and manipulated every turn of tragic events to their benefit."

Sonia stood with arms folded across her chest, looking down at the city.

"I'm glad we stopped here. I haven't been up here in years, and you're right, it's one of the most scenic spots in Lebanon."

Sonia shivered and pulled her sweater around her shoulders. "And I'd forgotten how deliciously cool it can get."

"It wasn't so obvious last night in Broumana because we spent the evening indoors, but we are at about eight hundred meters here."

"When I was a small child, we used to spend our summers in Broumana," Sonia said. "The hotel we stayed in had a pool. We spent every day there, never once feeling the need to go down to the sea."

"Which hotel was that?"

"The Broumana Hotel."

Fouad whistled. "Pretty ritzy place, at least it was in its heyday."

Sonia smiled. "I guess it was."

"I spent my youth camping here with the Boy Scouts... during Easter break if the weather cooperated, and then during the summer for two weeks. Finally, after incessant begging, my parents agreed to rent an apartment not far from here so I could spend every free day during summer recess exploring the ruins."

"I'm surprised you didn't become an archeologist."

"I'm an amateur one… that's good enough. Besides, I doubt I'd have been able to make much of a living as an archeologist."

"Well, do you earn much more being a spy?"

"No, not really." He laughed. "But enough of what might have been. Let me introduce you to my Beit Meri."

At first glance, as they drove through, it appeared to be little more than a dense pine forest with the occasional red-roofed luxury villa dotting the landscape, each with a view of the city and sea below. A more careful look revealed a treasure trove of Roman antiquities, some of which, in their day, had matched the grandeur of Baalbek's temples.

Fouad pulled up in front of a church and parked his car.

"I know this place," Sonia said. "It's the old Maronite Monastery of St. John the Baptist."

"Do you know its history?"

"No, I'm afraid I don't."

"Well then, permit me to enlighten you."

"Please do, Mr. Amateur Archeologist."

As they walked toward the monastery, he began.

"The present complex was built on the ruins of an ancient Phoenician temple dedicated to Baal Markadi, one of their great gods. You can still see some of the original work that adorns the area in front of the church. Come, I'll show you."

They walked along an elevated stone wall etched with warriors and their chariots and gods on their thrones, all clearly indicative of antiquity.

"Are these Phoenician?" Sonia asked, as she studied the ancient carvings still amazingly identifiable.

"Most of what you see here now is Roman. When they arrived in 64 BC, and as was common practice, the Romans destroyed the Phoenician temple that was here and rebuilt their own over it. Curiously, they kept the same name."

"Why would they have done that?"

"Probably because Baal means Lord and Markadi means quake—the god who shows his force by making the earth tremble.

"When Emperor Constantine converted to Christianity in 312 AD, he ordered the demolition of all the pagan temples across the country, replacing them with places of worship dedicated to the one true God.

"As though Baal Markadi was upset at Constantine, there was a devastating earthquake in 550 AD, and this monastery, along with most other edifices along the coast, including Rome's law school in Beirut, was destroyed."

"Pretty powerful god to have pulled off such a trick, given the size of the temples."

"According to available records, this particular Roman temple was some forty-two meters long, eighteen meters wide and fourteen high. Across the façade, there were six columns some seven meters high, five meters round, weighing fifty-one metric tons."

Sonia whistled.

"There were several other temples of equal size built nearby, one dedicated to Juno, the wife of Jupiter, the other to the daughter of Saturn."

"How were the Romans, and the Phoenicians and Greeks before them, able to construct such massive temples? We're talking about weights measuring eighty tons or more."

"For the lower blocks of stone, they apparently used iron forceps or tongs. As for the columns, they weren't solid single pieces but individual drums stacked one on top of the other, with a beam placed across the top to hold the roof structure in place."

"Okay, you're building a column and pretty soon it's reaching great heights. Then what? How do you get the last drums in place?"

"According to the experts, they used a system of ropes and pulleys to lift the higher drums in place and move any of the other massive pieces around."

"What amazing engineering skills."

"Look over here," Fouad said, pointing just outside the wall. "You can still see the thermal baths that provided central heating to the temple. They accomplished this by using conductors made from terra cotta pipes manufactured near Saida. They even preserved the heat in jars for individual use."

"And we think we're so sophisticated. But where did they get their water?"

"They built reservoirs above the village."

"How ingenious."

"Come," he said, taking her hand, "there's one more thing I want you to see."

They left the church and walked across the road, climbed over a stone wall and landed in an area so crowded with fallen columns, crumbling walls and broken earthenware it was difficult to navigate a way forward. Sonia followed Fouad as best she could toward the remains of what was probably a house, some walls of which still stood. In what she imagined had been the kitchen, with some of its blue and green floor mosaics still visible, Fouad pointed to an opening in the ground.

"Guess what this was."

"A well, of course."

"No, the remains of a wine press."

"You're not serious."

"The Romans venerated Bacchus, the god of wine. They built dozens of wine presses throughout the village."

"Didn't the Romans cultivate the first Cabernet Sauvignon?"

"Indeed! By the first century AD, they had not only cultivated the variety, they had planted vineyards and produced the first Bordeaux wines."

"And thanks to them, we're still enjoying our fine red Lebanese wines. *Magnifique!*"

Fouad and Sonia climbed back over the wall to the main road.

"Had enough, or do you want to see more?"

"I've seen enough. We'll come back another time."

As they walked toward the car, Sonia asked, "I haven't seen any sarcophagi here. Where did the one in the retreat's lobby come from?"

"It's from Tyre where there are hundreds of them. The most important ones, of course, are in the National Museum."

"Did Langley ask permission to use the sarcophagi, or did they just take it?"

Fouad laughed. "We actually have strict rules governing our archeological sites that even the American government can't ignore."

"Glad to hear it."

"You really dislike the CIA, don't you?"

"I do, and with reason. They have a sordid record of coups, regime change and assassinations just about everywhere. Don't you remember what they did here in 2004 when the US embassy coached a group of unwitting Lebanese youth in CIA 'Triple U' techniques? That stands for uncontrollable urban unrest, doesn't it?"

Fouad nodded. "Yes, smart woman."

"God only knows what bullshit they fed those boys to make them such willing participants. And what happened?" asked Sonia, unable to disguise her anger. "Some three thousand Christian student activists show up for a rally downtown demanding 'Syrians out,' and carrying signs that read 'Bush Help Us Save Lebanon,' all in English, by the way, even though this was Lebanon. They even had one student dress up as Osama bin Laden with the words 'Syrian terror' written across his chest. On orders from the American embassy, no one was arrested for this unlawful demonstration."

"I remember it well," Fouad said. "We were powerless to stop it."

"Apparently that was a practice run for the so-called Cedar Revolution that took place within days of the Hariri assassination. That rally was engineered by London-based Saatchi & Saatchi with the CIA picking up the tab, which included a Freedom From Syria tent city that distributed food, flags and posters with pictures of George W. Bush standing next to a Lebanese flag. There were even bouncers in black bomber jackets wearing Oakley sunglasses and earpieces who encouraged the crowd to shout, 'Out Syria!'"

"Yes, it was outrageous and embarrassing," Fouad said.

"So why the hell didn't the Lebanese government put a halt to such an outrage?"

"Because the power players in Parliament wanted this to happen, Sonia, and worked with Langley to organize it. Getting the public worked up about Syrian presence after thirty-five years wasn't that difficult to pull off since everyone was tired of having them here. The whole show went off as planned. The public thought it was a spontaneous response to Syria's supposed involvement in the Hariri assassination."

"The CIA had no business meddling in our affairs."

"Of course they didn't, but the US and Israel had an agenda. Get the Syrians out of Lebanon, then carry out regime change in Syria to weaken Iran so Israel would then have a free hand to attack Hezbollah.

"Why do you think I finally came home, Sonia? After years of seeing this kind of shit carried out around the world, I'd had my fill of the CIA and its skullduggery."

"Promise me you'll protect Andrew and not let those monsters get their hands on him."

"You have my word," he said, hoping he and Joe could keep that promise.

CHAPTER SEVEN

Good morning, Sonia," Andrew said, kissing her on her cheek when she arrived at his hospital room. "You're late. I've been waiting for hours."

"How can I be late?" she asked, checking her watch. "It's only nine thirty in the morning."

"I hardly slept. I was showered and dressed by five a.m. It's been six long weeks. I can't wait to be out of here."

"That's understandable, but how do you feel?"

"Better, stronger, and as long as I take my meds, the pain is tolerable. It's my back that gives me the most trouble. I'll just be glad when this is all a distant memory."

"We all will, but considering the injuries you sustained, you're a very lucky man, Andrew."

"I know, and I'm grateful. I only wish Nadia were…"

Sonia heard the crack in his voice. "You'll be in a better frame of mind once you're out of here. Hospitals are depressing places."

As he watched Sonia pack his few remaining things, he grabbed hold of her hand. "We both know you're a little shit, Sonia. I've told you that often enough."

She laughed. "Yes, you have, more times than I can count."

"But you're also a good friend. Thank you for pulling me through this ordeal."

"I'll always be there for you, Andrew, whenever you need me."

He kissed her cheek again. "I know that. Nadia's parents were amazing too. They treated me as though I was their own son. Nadia's brother and sister have also been wonderful. Both have their own lives now, dividing their time between London and Paris, yet they managed to come visit me. This has all been a very humbling experience."

"Nothing beats old fashioned Lebanese hospitality," Sonia said, "definitely one of our better qualities. And if you'd been a native, your entire village would have moved in. Seriously," she insisted, seeing his wrinkled forehead mocking her, "and they'd have arrived with baskets of food and decks of cards and had extra beds brought in so one or two of them could keep vigil over you at night."

"Guess there's a reason we only allow two visitors at a time in our hospitals back home," Andrew said with a laugh. "On a more serious note, the person who's amazed me the most is Fouad. How can I ever repay him for everything he's done? My God, he's the brother I never had. I'd only met him on the plane and seen him once after that, and yet he stepped right in after Nadia was kidnapped and practically took charge of everything. What a remarkable man."

"Yes, I agree. You couldn't find a nicer person."

Andrew noticed the starry-eyed look she had on her face as she said those words.

"Are you and he…?"

Sonia nodded, smiling.

"Well, well, you've finally made an exceptional choice of a mate, Sonia."

She laughed. "I agree. And it did take me a long time, didn't it, but yes, he's a keeper. I haven't told him as much, but I will, in due time… wouldn't want his head to swell too much."

"And speaking of nice people, guess who came to visit me yesterday."

"Who?"

"Camille and Leila. They popped in late afternoon, and what a delightful surprise it was to see both of them. I hardly recognized Leila. I'd only seen her in jeans and T-shirts, and there she was dressed like a lady. She wears her hair down now, and it becomes her. And when she heard I was going to learn Arabic, she offered to help."

"How was Camille?" Sonia asked, ignoring, he noticed, his comments about Leila.

"He's still mourning Tony. He teared up talking about his life-long friend and how much he missed him."

"I hope he didn't have to see Tony without his head," she said.

"Poor dear man, it will take some time—"

"Enough sad things," she said, cutting him off. "I have some good news to share. I've finished writing my series of articles on the Hariri assassination."

Damn it, Sonia, does everything have to always be about you? he thought. *You could at least have let me finish my sentence.*

Andrew half-listened to her ramble on.

"The *London Review of Books* has agreed to publish them. I'm pleased and relieved, and frightened too… no telling what retaliatory measures Israel will take against me."

Why would she not expect the worst, he thought. She had slept with an Israeli spy to get her story, and then when Kamal lost his head, poor sap, Andrew had been obliged to dispose of it, an ordeal he would likely never forget. And that horror had come on the heels of the episode at the morgue, Sonia insisting Nadia accompany her when Jaafar almost succeeded in kidnapping Nadia. So, no, he was not in a mood to listen to her accomplishments when all he could remember were her crimes and misdemeanors.

"No one in the States would touch the story, of course," she continued, "too terrified of repercussions from the Israel lobby."

"Oh?" he replied, half listening.

"Just this past March, the *London Review* published an essay by Stephen Walt and John Mearsheimer entitled *The Israel Lobby,* and the usual suspects raked the authors over a bed of hot coals. Fouad said they'd just written a book—*The Israel Lobby and US Foreign Policy*— due to come out next August. Israel will go ballistic when it does. In the meantime, I'll bask in the…"

He had just remembered another one of Sonia's crimes. She had accused Jaafar of raping her while a prisoner in the Hezbollah jail, a claim Camille, who had been in the cell next to hers, denied ever happened. Why was he remembering all of this now? Was it because his intuitive Nadia, toward the end of their stay in Marjeyoun, had begun to question Sonia's motives, or was he just finding it unbearable to listen to Sonia boasting when Jaafar, in the end, had finally gotten his hands on his Nadia?

"Oh, there you are," said Sonia, greeting the two nurses who had just walked into the room. "He's all packed and ready to go."

"Not before I say a proper good-bye," insisted Andrew, taking the hands of the two nurses and kissing them. "I'll never forget the extraordinary care I received. My recovery is due in large part to you and your staff. Please extend my gratitude to everyone on this floor."

"It was our pleasure, Dr. Sullivan. We wish you well." And they helped him into the wheelchair and pushed him into the hallway.

"Thank you," said Sonia to the nurses. "The security guards will accompany us down the back elevator." She then leaned close to Andrew's ear and said, "Fouad is waiting for us outside the emergency room."

"Goodbye and good luck," said the nurses when the elevator door opened. "We'll miss you." And Andrew waved until the doors closed.

"Fouad thought it best no one see you leave the hospital," said Sonia as they rode to the ground floor. "He's not sure if Jaafar's thugs are still around, so he's pulled his car into the ambulance entrance. From there, we'll slip away through one of the back streets."

"How long will it take to get to this safe house?" asked Andrew, feeling fatigue already setting in.

Sonia consulted her watch. "It's not quite noon which means we'll miss the mid-day traffic. I estimate about three quarters of an hour."

When the elevator door opened, Fouad was standing there with a huge smile. "*Enfin,*" he said, pulling Andrew to his feet. He hugged him and patted him on the back before helping him into the back seat of his car. "I've put a blanket and pillow there in case you want to take a nap."

When the car doors were closed and Sonia was settled in next to Fouad, Andrew watched her lean over and kiss him on the cheek. "You've thought of everything, darling. Well done."

I hope I'm not going to have to put up with this kissy-stuff the rest of the day. They're just happy, Andrew. I know, and I'm jealous. I miss Nadia.

* * *

This was Andrew's first time to the Metn mountains. How different from a city devoid of greenery. Trees, and lots of them, luxurious villas, and clear skies and air that didn't smell like car exhaust. But, as carefully as Fouad drove, Andrew could feel every bump in the rutted road, every turn, every abrupt foot on the brakes.

"A bit slower, Fouad, please. Any jerky motion throws my back into spasms. I don't mean to complain but…"

"Sorry, my friend."

He finally felt relief when Fouad brought the car to a halt in front of a closed gate.

"Well, what do you think?" asked Sonia, indicating with a tilt of her head that they had arrived at their destination.

"This is where I'm going to be living? Bless me, I must have died and gone to heaven."

Sonia chuckled. "You almost did, darling."

"Seriously… it looks like someone's private mansion."

"It is private, and it is a mansion," replied Fouad, "and since it was purchased with your tax dollars, we thought it only proper that you stay here."

"What are you saying? That the US government owns this place?"

"Yep, more specifically the CIA," said Fouad, pushing a button beside the gate. "It's a luxurious multi-use facility. We use it as a safe house and get to enjoy the amenities that come with it. It also has a four-story wing of royal suites for VIP visitors, the kind who arrive on private planes for top-secret meetings and expect discretion. We also host regional conferences, not for the general public of course, that are tailored toward the needs and pleasures of influential regional businessmen and elites."

Fouad parked the car in front of the entrance, and the same attendant appeared, this time with a wheelchair. While Andrew was being pushed up the handicap entrance, Sonia and Fouad walked up the stairs and joined him at the main door.

"Someone please pinch me. This can't be real," said Andrew as he perused the lobby. "How did you manage such a feat, Fouad?"

He shrugged and said, "I told you I was good at what I did. We'll take a quick look at your room to drop off your things, and then we'll have lunch."

Andrew reflected on Fouad's friendship. Why was it so immediate and powerful? He hardly knew the man. Okay, he had felt sorry for the naïve American, and as a courtesy had helped him obtain his Syrian visa, but then to go to the trouble of placing guards at his hospital door and arranging this safe house... it simply went beyond any reasonable norm and made no sense. Was there an ulterior motive? Did Fouad want something from him? At some point, was he going to ask him to carry out some secret mission on behalf of his spy agency?

And then there was this luxurious suite. Andrew was taken aback by the expensive video and audio entertainment system, the wine and beer-stocked fridge, not to mention a private balcony with a postcard view of the distant coastline. And what of Sonia, seemingly working in tandem with Fouad, unpacking his suitcase, setting up his toiletries in the bathroom, his clothes in the closet and his pajamas and slippers near his bed? What was she up to? And how could her affair with Fouad have happened so quickly? Aside from a brief glance at the Phoenicia Hotel, they had actually only begun conversing in his hospital room six weeks ago. Your affair with Nadia began like that, did it not, Andrew? Yes, but we were normal people. Here you have a spy and a woman who could not be trusted to tell the truth or perform a service without an ulterior motive. And since he and Sonia were friends, and had been for years, Andrew could confirm this assertion with a high degree of certainty. They had also had a short-lived wild, sex-filled affair some twenty years earlier when he was doing a medical residency in London and she was studying at the London School of Economics. After their breakup, he had watched her go through career advancement moves and men, lots of them, discarding them like used pieces of Kleenex, to get what she wanted. So, what were they up to? For the time being, he was in recovery mode and in need of their help. His only option, short of returning State-side, was to bide his time, stay alert and hope he was wrong about both of them.

"Come on," said Fouad, breaking his reverie. "You'll be spending enough time in your room. Let's get you some food before you pass out." Once he had secured Andrew back in his wheelchair, he and Sonia pushed him back down the corridor to the elevator, through the lobby and out to a shaded outdoor dining area alongside the pool.

"There will be menu choices delivered to your room every morning," Fouad said, as he brought Andrew's wheelchair to a halt, "and aside from breakfast delivered to your room, this is where you'll usually take your meals. It's near the gym, where you'll work out, and the library where you'll have your Arabic lessons. We also have an indoor shooting range here. Once you're in better physical shape—"

"And that will be Joe's job, I presume," said Andrew. "Tell me more about him."

"He's Russian by his father, Lebanese by his mother. He plays up being Lebanese more than most, probably because he likes the idea of claiming Phoenician heritage."

"Phoenician?" asked Andrew. "How does he figure that?"

"Some Lebanese Christians, particularly the Maronites, that's what Joe's mother was, claim the Phoenicians as their ancestors rather than admit to being Arabs," Sonia said.

"What we call Lebanon today first appeared in recorded history around 4000 BC as a group of coastal cities," said Fouad. "It was inhabited by the Canaanites, a Semitic people, whom the Greeks called Phoenicians. These same Christian Lebanese claim that since Lebanon has been inhabited uninterrupted since Phoenician times, the current population, therefore, descends from them."

"Sounds like a solid argument to me," said Andrew.

"It's yet to be proven scientifically, but try telling that to snobs like Joe."

Andrew's attention was drawn to the inviting table set for three. There were two salads—tabbouleh and fattoush—and kebabs, both lamb and chicken, along with French fries, a platter of hummus, baba ghanoush and falafel.

"Look at this table full of food," he said. "You brought me here to eat, so let's begin. I'm famished."

"You're absolutely right," Sonia said, as Fouad pulled out her chair. "Who wants to join me for a glass of wine?"

"Not I. I'm on too many meds to drink alcohol."

"I'll join you," Fouad said.

In between bites, Andrew asked, "What do you know about Joe's Russian father?"

"He was a diplomat with Kremlin ties," Fouad said, "apparently killed in some bizarre accident. For whatever reason, Joe suspects foul play. Did the father fall out of favor? Did he have enemies? Maybe you'll glean those details from Joe when you get to know him a bit better. I suspect he joined the CIA because of his father's work. He severed his ties with Langley, but does he still curry favor with the Kremlin because of his father? I don't know."

"Here, darling," said Sonia, putting a piece of lamb in Fouad's mouth. "Succulent… just taste how delicious it is."

She wasn't even listening to the conversation, thought Andrew.

"I'll see what I can find out," he said, not sure anyone was listening to *him* either. "In the meantime, I think I'll retire to my room. This is all a bit overwhelming for someone who's just been discharged from the hospital."

He did not feel like hanging around those two love-birds. They were having fun, and he was not. He had eaten enough to satisfy his hunger but wrapped a few falafel in a napkin in case he wanted an afternoon snack.

"How thoughtless of us," Sonia said. "Of course, you're exhausted."

Sonia called the waiter over to their table and ordered Andrew a tisane.

"It'll relax you and help you sleep."

"Andrew, before you retire, I'd like Sonia to tell you about her idea…"

Fouad stopped in mid-sentence. His eyes followed a Mercedes as it drove by their table. It stopped in front of the main entrance. A man he recognized as the US ambassador to Lebanon descended the stairs to greet the man climbing out of the car.

"I'll be damned. You see that man?" he asked, inclining his head toward the new arrival. "I know that son of a bitch… Robert Jenkins, number two man at the US embassy in Iraq."

Sonia remembered what Fouad had said. Jenkins was the man looking for Jaafar.

"Why is that a big deal?" Andrew asked, as he studied the two men still talking beside the car, both dressed in suit and tie, apparently the ubiquitous uniform of diplomats, regardless of country or climate. Robert Jenkins, aside from his steel-rimmed eyeglasses, his pale skin and fading sandy-blonde hair, did not appear to have any other remarkable features.

"Normally it wouldn't be," said Fouad, "but this guy has a history of showing up in countries that are about to burn. Ever heard of the Salvador Option?"

"The Central America debacle?" asked Andrew.

"Close," said Fouad. "During the '80s, US Special Forces trained and funded the Salvadoran military and turned them into death squads. El Salvador became a virtual killing field. Oscar Romero, Archbishop of San Salvador, the slain Jesuit priest, remember him? All classic counter-insurgency tactics to quell the opposition. The cost was a staggering seventy-five thousand dead."

He stopped and stared at Jenkins again before he spoke.

"In Iraq, the US is doing the same thing—targeting the Iraqi insurgency—but apparently that isn't enough mayhem. According to my sources, this guy's now going around Syria inciting groups to overthrow the Assad government and offering military aid to some al-Qaeda-affiliated rebels if they agree to play."

"But what's he doing here?" Andrew asked.

"It would appear he's also a guest. Why don't you chat him up and find out?"

CHAPTER EIGHT

Andrew stretched out on his bed, closed his eyes and listened to a chorus of male crickets, the only perceptible sound in an otherwise still twilight announcing the end of another day. Aside from post-trauma fatigue and back pain, his body was healing, his mind was sharper and his memories of Nadia were acute and constant. It had been almost two months since her disappearance. The images manifested themselves at night when he thought he was asleep but was not. His failure to protect her, his ineptness with guns—everything he sought to forget rushed back full-fury. He dared not speculate on what Jaafar had forced Nadia to do, or he would have gone mad with rage. By nature, he was neither violent nor vindictive, but he was prepared to do whatever was necessary, with no regrets or apologies, to rescue her even if it meant committing some unspeakable act.

He was scheduled to meet his trainer in the morning, the man charged with restoring him to his former fit self. Fouad had described Joe, a former Intelligence officer, as a bit gruff around the edges. None of that mattered to Andrew. He was there to be pushed and prodded, and he was ready.

* * *

At first glance, Andrew estimated Joseph Lavrov to be in his late forties. Aside from some streaks of salt and pepper, his thick, wavy hair was still pretty solidly black. When he saw Andrew approaching, he got up from his chair and walked toward him with a confident, relaxed stride. His white polo shirt and shorts accentuated his warm olive skin.

"You don't look like a man who was near death a few months ago," Joe said, clasping Andrew's hand in his.

"I had an excellent team of doctors."

"That's not surprising. You were in the region's best medical facility."

Andrew liked the way Joe's lively eyes smiled into his when he spoke, a sign, he thought, of a man sure of himself, not in a cocky, macho way but amiable and respectful.

"I didn't fully understand the extent of your injuries until I read your doctor's report. I called him this morning. I wanted him to approve my rehab program, and he did. So, I'd like to begin with an overall assessment of how well you can move your limbs, and then we'll take it from there. Today we'll just walk around the premises and see how you do. We'll eventually work up to brisk walks then on to slow jogging.

"We'll also work in some light weights… no more than ten pounds for now, given your abdominal incision. Once that's healed, we'll begin some core Pilates work. How does that sound?"

"Cautious, yet well thought out," said Andrew. "In a former life, before I came here and got caught up in wars and disappearances, I exercised and swam every day." He stopped and shook his head. "It feels like a hundred years ago."

"That's the nature of a major setback, Andrew. You're a physician, so I don't need to remind you that as a forty-five-year-old man your body will need some extra time to heal. Given your overall physical condition— you're not overweight, you've no blood pressure, heart or cholesterol issues—I'm confident that with daily workouts, lots of rest and proper nutrition, you'll respond quicker than you ever thought possible."

"I hope so."

"Well then, let's get started."

* * *

You did well today, Andrew. I purposely hastened our pace, and you kept up."

"It felt good. I'm pleased and encouraged."

"Good, that's the right attitude. Before you shower, why don't you join me in the sauna so we can chat, get to know one another better."

Andrew grabbed a towel and wiped the sweat from his body. He quite liked challenges, and while the discipline of getting himself into shape would be arduous, as would his upcoming Arabic lessons, everything was interconnected, and the sooner it all came together, the sooner he and Fouad could cross into Syria and rescue Nadia.

He laid his towel across the hot cedar bench and sat down.

"How are you doing?" Joe asked.

"I'm here, aren't I, so I guess—"

"It's your mental state I'm asking about. Fouad told me what you've been through... the war, friends dying under horrific circumstances, Nadia's disappearance. That's a lot of shit to be dealing with."

Andrew stared at him and rolled his eyes. "Tell me about it."

"I'm worried, okay? I've taken care of men like you who've returned from combat with severe PTSD, so I know what I'm talking about."

"Maybe you should have been a shrink, Joe, since you like to give advice."

"Shut the fuck up... I'm just concerned, that's all. Have you considered seeing a shrink? We could arrange to have one come visit you here."

"No, because I know he'd tell me to give up trying to find Nadia. Look, Joe, no offense. You're a nice guy, but I'm here for one reason and one reason only."

"You really love her, don't you?"

"Have you ever been in love?"

"You're reaffirming my assessment of women. They're a pain in the ass, and your situation proves it."

"Joe, you're a handsome man and likeable, but," Andrew laughed, "you're a cynical old fart."

"Yes, I know... been told that many times."

"Do you want to know why I'm so driven? I'm nothing without Nadia. She's with me always. I hear her voice. I hear her passion and her gentle sighs when we make love. I hear her scream, her plea for me to save her. It's an echo in my head that replays itself over and over again. So, I'll work hard and make you proud, and in return, you'll prepare me for whatever I need to do."

"So, I'm training you to take revenge, and being well paid to do it, and I should be proud of that? You've no idea who you'll be dealing with once you get out there. I'm the nice guy, Andrew. Others will take advantage of you, even do you harm or worse, use you as fodder to get what they want. Look what they've already done to you. I know what I'm talking about. I worked for them for twenty-five years. So, remember what Confucius said... 'Before you leave to seek revenge, dig two graves.'"

CHAPTER NINE

Any self-respecting woman would have been as offended and as frustrated as Nadia by Hassan's frequent and prolonged absences over the last four months. During those rare moments when he was in residence, he remained aloof, took his meals alone and addressed her curtly whenever they encountered one another around the estate. If asked her opinion as to why he acted so irrationally, she would have argued that Hassan suffered from an exaggerated case of wounded manliness that he had harbored far too long. He was a proud man, loathe to lose face, and if this intolerable situation was to be rectified, she knew she would have to be the one to make the first move.

While she also suffered from boredom, she, at least, had at her disposal Hassan's exhaustive library, and during this last longer-than-usual absence she had concentrated on learning more about the region's history. Her latest read centered on the great Kurdish warrior Saladin, born in 1138. He led the Muslim military campaign against the Crusaders and reconquered Jerusalem in 1187, and because of his prowess he was awarded the title of first Sultan of both Egypt and Syria. As impressive as was his military career, it was, in fact, his wife, Ismat al-Din, who most intrigued Nadia, particularly because of the similarities in their lives.

Ismat was the daughter of the regent of Damascus and wife of the two greatest Muslim generals of the twelfth century, Nur al-Din and Saladin. During the time of her father's reign, Damascus's rival cities, Aleppo and Mosul, were united under the Zengid dynasty. In 1147, Ismat's father negotiated an alliance with its emir, Nur al-Din. As part of the agreement, Nur al-Din was given Ismat's hand in marriage. When he died in battle in 1174, Saladin, his general, became his successor and took Ismat as his wife.

Like Saladin's claim to Ismat as his prize, Hassan, too, considered Nadia his. Ismat's first husband had died in battle. Nadia's husband, Elie, had also died in battle, blown to bits in an Israeli air strike.

Although she lived in luxury, Nadia, in her mind, could have been held, as was Ismat, in Saladin's castle. Like Hassan's estate, it, too, sat in high mountainous terrain mere miles from Ismat's prison on a ridge between two deep ravines. Surrounded by a dense forest, Saladin's castle was unassailable. While Hassan's estate was accessible by car, it may as well have been impenetrable, for Nadia had not been allowed to leave since she arrived.

Ismat had been described as having courage and intelligence beyond that of most women. Nadia was a lawyer, her expertise being international law, with a PhD in law from the London School of Economics and a prestigious appointment to the UN Commission on Human Rights.

As Ismat must have frequently felt when Saladin went off to battle, Nadia, too, was lonely, not necessarily for Hassan's company, but for someone to converse with other than staff about an interesting book or music or a meal they had both enjoyed.

Just this morning, Ani had informed Nadia that Hassan had traveled again. As with each of his absences, he left no note and no indication as to when he planned to return. Saladin, when absent, wrote to Ismat every day. Hassan did no such thing, nor would he. He was still pouting because she was not the unsullied woman he thought he was getting when he had kidnapped her.

* * *

As had become her routine after a long, lonely day, Nadia tuned in to the evening news. This particular night the top story felt like a bomb exploding in her head for the revelations portended widespread destruction and death.

The anchor, barely able to contain himself, began the broadcast with some startling news from Washington, DC.

"Good evening and welcome to the *Nightly News Hour.*

"According to the whistleblower website WikiLeaks, the US State Department has apparently been funneling millions of dollars to the Movement for Justice and Development, a London-based dissident organization which broadcasts anti-government news into Syria.

"This afternoon, David Denny, a state department spokesperson, was asked to comment on these accusations."

The anchor played the video from Mr. Denny's press conference while providing a simultaneous translation in Arabic across the bottom of the screen.

We're working with a variety of civil society actors in Syria with the goal of strengthening freedom of expression, Denny said.

According to the news anchor, recently released diplomatic cables from the US mission in Damascus admitted the risky optics of the funding.

Some programs may be perceived, were they to be made public, as an attempt to undermine the Assad regime, the embassy spokesperson said. The Syrian Arab Republic government would undoubtedly view any US funds going to illegal political groups as tantamount to supporting regime change.

The feed returned to the Syrian news anchor.

"WikiLeaks provided the diplomatic cables to the *Washington Post* which first reported them. The files are part of some 271,000 secret US diplomatic documents the website says it has in its possession.

"Additional state department diplomatic cables released by WikiLeaks reveal that as early as 1996, under Benjamin Netanyahu's first term as prime minister, Israel hatched a plan to overthrow Assad by engineering sectarian strife in the country and isolating Syria from its strongest regional ally, Iran.

"Leaked emails belonging to Secretary of State Hillary Clinton seem to confirm Israel's current role in covertly creating the conflict and securing the involvement of the US.

"The fall of the House of Assad could well ignite a sectarian war between Shiites and the majority Sunnis of the region drawing in Iran, which, in the opinion of Israeli commanders, would not be a bad thing for Israel and its Western allies.

"A second Clinton email reiterated Netanyahu's remarks: 'Bringing down Assad would not only be a massive boom to Israel's security, it would also ease Israel's understandable fear of losing its nuclear deterrence to Iran.'

"For a response to these startling revelations, we turn to Madame Khattib, a Syrian government spokesperson."

"This is a deliberate plan by the US-NATO alliance to trigger social chaos, to discredit the Syrian government of Bashar al Assad, and ultimately destabilize Syria as a nation-state. As to Israel's involvement, it is well known that its strongest motivations are Syria's vast oil reserves along with its territorial expansion in the Golan Heights, which Israel annexed in 1981, and where, since then, it has transplanted some one hundred thousand settlers."

Dating as far back as ancient times, Nadia knew that this tiny area of the Middle East had seen empires come and go. Egyptians, Assyrians, Babylonians, Macedonians, Romans, Israelites, Philistines, Crusaders, Arabs, Ottoman Turks, and finally the British, had all claimed strong historical connections to this land either through bloody warfare or benign conquest. Was it now, she wondered, the turn of the US and its regional ally to leave their murderous mark on Syria and possibly Lebanon?

As she listened to remarks made by the Israeli prime minister, she was reminded of a passage she had read years earlier in *Demonic Male* which claimed that males had, without precedent, the capacity for both creation and destruction. *And here we are*, she thought, *thousands of years later, and they are still initiating wars and destroying nation-states because they have the wherewithal to do so. Curious how history repeated itself, never bothering to learn from its mistakes!*

Nadia wondered where she stood in this potential horror show. She was a captured maiden, being kept for Hassan's pleasure on his estate that was not only in the heavily dominated Alawite part of the country but was the fiefdom of the Assad clan. When the battles did finally begin, and the Sunni jihadists began attacking the Alawites outside her prison walls, who was going to save her?

CHAPTER TEN

Sonia expected to be gloating over the reception and overall favorable reviews her stories on the Hariri assassination had generated in the *London Review of Books*. The British journal of literary essays, whose contributors included such luminaries as Tariq Ali, Patrick Cockburn, Susan Sontag and Edward Said, had a penchant for political controversy. Her articles, which stirred up a plethora of raucous discord, were no exception. Ever since the last of the three-part series had appeared in print, accusing the Israeli government of assassinating former Lebanese Prime Minister Rafic Hariri, and with the absence of other serious news, there had been an on-line debate that had raged on as relentlessly as a wildfire in a drought. No one had ever accused Israel of such high crime and walked away unscathed. Sonia understood this. Ali, her former lover and colleague had paid the highest possible price. He should have been sitting next to her during a recent interview with Al-Jazeera since he had collaborated on this project. Instead, he lay buried in a mass grave in south Lebanon, shot in the head by a Mossad agent.

Neither the success of the biggest story of her life, nor the accolades that had elevated her to celebrity status mitigated her torment. She felt full of lead and could not seem to muster the energy to even get out of bed. She was leaving for London in the morning. She had been invited to participate in a high-level panel about the Middle East. What if she broke down in front of her audience? The thought terrified her. What if the same people who sent her hate emails and accused her of antisemitism, and wished her a grisly death, filled the conference hall and started booing her. She kept breaking into high emotion. If only she could rip the past from her memory.

She was fantasizing a dozen ways to end the painful remorse that sat in the back of her mind like a tumor when Camille called to say he and Leila were in Beirut and on their way to pay her a visit. A call to prayer echoed somewhere in the distance. For whatever reason, it became the fulcrum that forced her out of bed and into the frock she had worn the previous night. She brushed her hair but did not bother with makeup. When they arrived, they would know she had been crying, but so what.

The buzzer from the downstairs lobby announced their arrival. She opened her door and stepped into the hallway when she heard them reach her floor. Leila pushed a wheelchair out of the elevator and turned it in her direction. She made her way with Camille, a blanket covering the lower part of his body. When they got closer, Sonia realized Camille was missing his legs. She burst into tears, covered her mouth to hide her sobs, and ran toward him. She flung her arms around his neck and kissed his cheek.

"I'm so sorry. I had no idea. Why didn't...?" She looked up at Leila.

"You know my uncle," she replied, lifting her shoulders and rolling her eyes. "He's still the stoic elder who never wants to bother anyone, even when he can no longer take care of himself. Thankfully, that's about to change. We've just come from America University Hospital, where we met with specialists who will make uncle a pair of artificial legs. He'll soon be up and walking on his own. We're very excited."

"And I'm delighted I get to share in this good news... but we mustn't stand in the hallway. Please come in." She took over the handles and wheeled Camille into her apartment and directly to the terrace. "I'll bring some wine, and we'll talk until lunch is ready. I apparently have a lot of catching up to do."

Overcome with emotions, Sonia dabbed her eyes before returning to her guests with a tray of hors d'oeuvres and white wine.

"When we arrived, you looked like you had been crying," Leila said. "Are you ill? Did we come at a bad time?"

"No, not at all. You two are just the medicine I needed," said Sonia, now sorry she had acted like a little shit when Andrew had mentioned that Leila and her uncle had visited him at the hospital. Leila had, indeed, transformed herself into a very attractive woman.

"You got me out of bed and made me put on some clothes. I've been a bit down since my articles on Hariri's assassination appeared in The *London Review of Books*. I thought I'd be excited, but I'm not, and everything is awful. And I shouldn't even be mentioning it to you, of all people. You spent eight years in Khiam prison, and you have your own demons. I can't imagine how you've kept your sanity. You're whole and well and vibrant, and I'm not handling all this war and death shit like I thought I would, and it's tearing me apart."

"Don't think I'm not immune to depression, Sonia. There are times when my demons come roaring back, and I have a hell of a time trying to fend them off."

Wiping away more tears, Sonia pointed to Camille's missing legs. "Tell me how this happened."

"When Leila brought back news of Tony's death, I was grief-stricken," said Camille. "We'd known each other for close to sixty years. We went to the American University of Beirut together and had been best friends ever since. You may recall that Tony went on to teach history there. We were a threesome… me, Tony and Yousef."

"Yes, I remember your buddies with great fondness," Sonia said. "They had a crush on me. I enjoyed their flirtations… made me feel like a young girl again."

"For quite a while, I couldn't bring myself to visit Tony's house," said Camille. "I knew he had cancer, knew it would eventually kill him, and so did he. But to die the way he did, it broke my heart. His wife passed away years ago. I don't think you knew that, and his son lives in Beirut, so there were no other family members in Marjeyoun to take care of his affairs. And since Israel had bombed all the bridges and secondary roads, his son, poor man, couldn't even get home for his father's funeral."

"What's the connection between Tony and your legs?"

"In the last seventy-two hours of the war, Israel saturated the south with cluster bombs, one hundred thousand according to UN estimates. You must have read or heard about that. This would have been about a week after you left with the UN convoy."

Sonia nodded. "Of course I knew about it."

"When the bombing stopped, Yousef and I finally went to Tony's house. We inspected the inside for possible damage, found none, and then I went out to check the garden. That's where it happened. I didn't pay attention to where I was walking, and I stepped on an unexploded cluster bomb. The next thing I knew I was waking up in the hospital and being told I'd lost both my legs."

"And if Yousef hadn't been with him, uncle would have bled to death," Leila said. "Speaking of tragedies, is there any news of Nadia? I didn't want to ask Andrew when we saw him in the hospital."

"Not a word, but we assume Jaafar took her to Syria."

"We searched all over Marjeyoun for that bastard after he broke into my house and beat up Elie, leaving him bleeding on the floor," said Camille. "I gave the order to have him shot on sight. Too bad he managed to elude capture."

"Yes, I remember that incident, and how unfortunate he slipped away," Sonia replied. *But how fortuitous for me that he did,* she thought. *Otherwise, I would not have had my story.*

"At least Andrew's recovering nicely," said Sonia. "I saw him a few days ago. His back still bothers him, but according to Joe, his trainer, he's slowly regaining his strength. He has yet to start his Arabic lessons but—"

"I'm relieved to hear that," Leila said. "I promised I'd help him, but with uncle's accident, I couldn't have managed. Once he gets fitted with his prostheses, I should have more time."

"Which means you will be coming to Beirut more often. I insist you stay here to avoid traveling back and forth and tiring Camille out. I've plenty of room, and from here, Leila, you can be in Broumana in no time."

"That's very generous of you, Sonia, and very much appreciated. And once uncle gets his new legs, he'll be able to go back to Marjeyoun, and I'll have time to help Andrew."

"Then it's settled. I leave for London tomorrow. I've been invited to sit on a high-level panel on the developing crisis in the Middle East. I'll also be meeting with a publisher who wants to turn the Hariri story into a book, but I'll only be gone a few days. This will give you the time to return to Marjeyoun, pack up a few things, and be back here when I return."

"That sounds like a perfect plan," said Leila.

"I think congratulations are in order," Camille said. "What an accomplishment, Sonia. It took a lot of guts to write those damning articles… and at great risk to your life. I'm very proud of you. To your success," he said, lifting up his glass of wine to toast her.

"And to your new legs," replied Sonia. "Now, let's have lunch."

"It's so peaceful and beautiful here on your terrace," said Camille, "glancing out at a city, seemingly quiet and beginning to rebuild again. It seems like only yesterday we were all together in Marjeyoun hiding from Israeli bombs."

"If it's any consolation, neither Tony, nor Elie, nor his nurse Anna ever knew what hit them. The Israeli attack was so swift, their deaths were instantaneous."

Camille nodded. "It's a small comfort to know that."

"The baggage I carry around from Khiam," said Leila, "is nothing compared to what happened to the people across the south. Maybe they'll be able to pick up the pieces and get on with their lives, but it'll be difficult and costly. It's been a tragic nightmare."

"For all of us," murmured Sonia, recalling a long and damning list of her many transgressions. Both she and Ali had been targeted for assassination, but she had let him go alone on the mission that had gotten him killed. Camille had been charged with colluding with the enemy and imprisoned because of her scandalous affair with an Israeli. She had caused Kamal's decapitation. She had helped arrange Jaafar's first attempt to kidnap Nadia. She had claimed that Jaafar had raped her when it had never happened and finally, the most recent of her crimes—her betrayal of Nadia. As much as Sonia tried to put a membrane over her eyes, those deeds stuck in her mind like a death knell.

Sonia took a set of keys from a drawer in her desk.

"Here are the house keys. The thicker one," she said, separating the first from the second on the chain, "opens the lobby door, and this one," she pointed to the key with a red dot, "opens the door to the apartment. We're family. My house is your house."

"Thank you," said Leila. She stood and gave Sonia a hug. "I'm afraid we'll have to be going. I can tell Uncle's energy is fading, but we'll be back soon."

"I almost forgot," said Sonia, walking them to the door. "Andrew will be working with Doctors Without Borders at the Shatilla medical clinic as soon as he's proficient enough in Arabic."

"There's my extra incentive to help him get there," Leila said.

"Good," said Sonia, kissing each of them goodbye.

"*A tres bientot.*"

Her phone rang just as she was closing her front door. "Hello?"

"Hi, beautiful lady," said Fouad. "I'm just confirming tomorrow's schedule. You want me there by eight?"

"Yes, darling. We'll have breakfast together, and then we'll leave for the airport by nine."

"What are your plans for the rest of the day?" he asked. *Such a considerate man*, she thought, *always looking out for her.*

"I have an interview with France 2 at six thirty. I need to be there by six for makeup and hair. After that, I'll drive straight home… promise."

"If I hadn't agreed to cover for a colleague, I'd have spent the night in your arms."

"I know, darling, but I'll only be in London a few days."

"Love you, a *domain.*"

"Love you too."

* * *

Sonia was running late. She kept on the same dress and did not bother with any makeup, but she felt a bit better having visited with Camille and Leila. She had given them the key to her apartment and done something good, but would that be enough to lift her spirits? Camille told her that they all needed to forgive themselves. He was right, but he was unaware of most of her sins. She put on her sunglasses, threw her handbag over her shoulder and locked the door behind her. During her interview, she hoped she would not say anything that sounded egocentric or self-serving. She would have to monitor herself.

It was already 5:40. She needed a good half an hour to reach the television station, and it was peak rush hour with bumper to bumper traffic. She had left her car on a side street adjacent to her building earlier in the day because someone had parked in her slot. She clicked the remote as she crossed the street, threw her purse on the passenger seat, climbed in, closed the door and started the motor.

An explosion rocked the car, ripping the left door off. The front end of the car, now a ring of curled metal, twisted inward, pinning Sonia's chest against the steering wheel. She felt a burning, searing pain coming from the left side of her body. She could not see out of her left eye but managed to turn her head just enough to discover her left arm dangling from shredded sinew, looking like a slab of raw meat. She was sheathed in glass—chest, legs, right arm. Probably her face too, because the slightest grimace hurt. As smoke began to fill the car, she coughed, hardly able to breathe for the pain in her chest. And then she saw the flames creeping toward her, first to her dress, then her abdomen and chest. With her right hand, she tried to undo her seatbelt, but it would not budge. She screamed. Could anyone hear her? A shroud of grey haze blinded her, and for a few seconds she was not sure if she had lost consciousness, but then she felt hands grab her underarms and lift her out of the car. Faces reassured her as she pleaded with them to save her arm. As soon as she was placed on a stretcher, the medics administered morphine for her pain, then tended to her wounds. And, as she drifted off, she felt herself being lifted into an ambulance.

CHAPTER ELEVEN

Dressed in a pair of white shorts and polo shirt, Andrew sat under an umbrella pool-side studying his Arabic. After months of nothing but daily workouts with Joe, Andrew relished the intellectual stimulation his Arabic lessons provided. Apparently, he had a natural aptitude for learning languages, even one as difficult as Arabic.

"Can I join you?" asked a voice coming from a man standing in front of him.

Andrew looked up and saw Robert Jenkins. "Sure." He shrugged. "Have a seat."

"I go by Bob," said the stranger, hand extended.

Andrew shook it. "I was just ordering lunch. Are you hungry?"

Andrew turned to the waiter standing beside his table. "I'll have shish taouk with French fries and some Pellegrino. Thank you."

"And you, sir?" asked the waiter, addressing Bob.

"I'll have the same, but instead of water, I'd like an Almaza beer."

"Weren't you here about three months ago?" Andrew asked.

"Yes, I work in the region and often come here for meetings. How long have you been here?"

"Forever… or so it seems," said Andrew, laughing.

"Then you must be agency," said Bob, sitting back in his chair and stretching out his long legs.

He was at least six foot two, thought Andrew, a bit taller than he had originally thought when he had seen him standing next to the US ambassador.

"Agency? No, I'm not, but you are."

"How do you know that?" Bob asked.

"It's pretty obvious. Requisite Oakley sunglasses, navy jacket, grey slacks and government-issued black, lace-up shoes in need of a polish." Andrew laughed. "You guys stand out a mile away. And no one else wears clothes like that in such a hot climate."

Bob sat up in his chair and gave Andrew a closer look.

Andrew shrugged his shoulders. "No offense, I'm just stating the obvious."

"If you're not agency, what are you doing here?"

"I needed a safe house. Someone tried to kill me, so a friend put me up here," replied Andrew, remembering Fouad's advice to give out only bits of his story with the aim of hooking the man into talking about why he was in Lebanon.

"You must have important friends if you're here," Bob said.

"I guess I do. I just hadn't realized how important until now. I assume from your remark that this place is generally not for riffraff like me. You obviously rank, though, if you're here. What do you do?" Andrew asked, surprised by his boldness.

"What did you say your name was?"

"I go by Andrew. Do I get to know what you do, or is that top secret?"

"I work at the US embassy in Iraq under Ambassador Negroponte."

"I know that name from some—"

"Probably because he served as US Ambassador to the UN until he was posted to Iraq."

"I must be thinking of a different Negroponte. The one I'm remembering was involved in the Iran-Contra affair in Central America."

"You have the right man, but he wasn't involved in anything President Reagan didn't ask him to be involved in."

"That could have been any number of things—Contra rebels in Nicaragua, death squads, Oliver North, arms sale to Iran, congressional hearings."

"What's your point?"

"I wonder if what we're doing in Iraq is any different than what we did in Central America."

"That's why we're in Iraq now, trying to fix past mistakes."

"I'm glad to hear that, Bob. I'm sure you'd agree the Iraqi people deserve better than what they've been dealt."

"What do you mean? We did them a favor by getting rid of Saddam."

"A favor? We destroyed their country."

The waiter arrived with lunch, and until they were served and he had left, the two men stayed silent.

"You said someone attacked you?" asked Bob. "What happened?"

"Syria's former Intelligence chief tried to kill me."

"What?" Joe said, choking on his sip of beer.

"You know Hassan Jaafar?"

"Yes, it comes with the job, but I'm surprised you do. No offense, but you and Jaafar are hardly in the same league of players. How the hell do you know him?"

"I don't, never met him."

"Then why did he want you killed?"

"It's a long story."

"I like long stories… and I'm very interested in Syria."

"My fiancé, Nadia Khoury, was kidnapped by Jaafar four months ago. We think he took her to Syria. Unless we can work through the Syrian government, and at the moment they're not cooperating, there's nothing we can do."

"What's Nadia's connection to Jaafar?"

"They knew each other years ago. He wanted to marry her. She refused. Apparently, he's still obsessed with her. When he discovered she was in Beirut planning our wedding, he kidnapped her."

"But why try to kill you?"

Andrew shrugged his shoulders. "I'm her fiancé. Jealousy, I guess. He wanted to eliminate his competition. Okay, my turn for questions. Syria interests you… your words. Why?"

"That's a long story too."

"I've nothing but time," said Andrew.

"We think it's in our national and strategic interests to have a US-friendly Middle East. Assad, like Saddam, is no longer someone we want on our team."

"Post nine-eleven, I seem to remember reading in the *Washington Post* that Assad handed over the al-Qaeda thugs hiding in his country and offered full cooperation with Washington. Sounded, at the time, like a team player to me. Did Assad renege, or do something to offend the Bush administration?"

"Let's just say it was time for a change, and we're working with our local friends to make it as easy as possible."

While chewing his food, Andrew stared up at the sky. What Jenkins was saying did not ring true. According to Camille, the issue was not Syria. It was about dealing a crippling blow to Iran and Hezbollah, and Syria, as their linchpin, needed to be taken out.

"Aren't you advocating regime change in Syria? Isn't that what you're really saying?"

"Damn, you're one smart ass. Where are you getting your information?"

"I have a smart friend who's figured all this out."

"Everyone here has a take on local politics. If I were you, I wouldn't trust much of anything you hear."

"That may be sound advice," Andrew said, flashing on the time when Camille said that anytime a diplomat talked about changes beware of what he was really saying.

"So, hypothetically, let's say you're talking about regime change in Syria. How do you justify doing something like that? You're basically going to destroy a country, kill tens of thousands of people and install a puppet regime. How does this sort of thing make the world right? Isn't this just more of the same madness that keeps repeating itself?"

"It's in our national security interest to keep the region stable."

Arrogant bastard, thought Andrew. *He is the diplomat with all the power, and here I am, a helpless nobody, caring about a people whose country is about to be destroyed.*

"And you do that by choosing the leaders you want in power?" asked Andrew.

"I like you, Andrew. You're heads above the average run-of-the-mill American. Why are you studying Arabic?"

"I'll be making this place home for a while, so it makes sense to learn the local language and, in turn, get to know the people and culture better."

"I'm beginning to suspect that you're not just a man looking for your lady friend. I'll bet you traded in your desk job so you could live an adventure. Are you looking for work?"

Andrew laughed. "If I were, what makes you think I'd be interested in anything you have to offer?"

"I can find your lady friend."

Andrew looked at Bob. He remembered Joe's warning about unscrupulous people offering their help, but then he also remembered Fouad's empty promises. What if Jenkins, the diplomat, a person with obvious influence and power, could find Nadia?

"I can see I struck a nerve there," Bob said. "We'll talk about that next time we meet. As to our political differences, let's agree to disagree."

"A reasonable idea, and if I'm still here, I'd enjoy meeting again."

"You're leaving the retreat?"

"I'm a physician. As soon as I'm more proficient in Arabic, I'll be joining a team from Doctors Without Borders in the Shatilla Palestinian camp."

"A waste of your talents, if you ask me."

"On the contrary, I can't think of a better way to use my training."

"I admire your idealism, Andrew, but if I may, some advice from someone who's spent a lot of time in the Middle East. Nothing appears as it really is, and everyone lies, so don't trust anyone."

Andrew had already begun to suspect as much—Sonia and Fouad came to mind. He was about to respond when his mobile rang. When he saw it was Fouad on the line, he said, "Sorry, Bob, I need to take this call."

Andrew glanced across the table at Jenkins as he answered. "Hello, friend, about time you checked in on me. Where have you been all these months? You—"

He heard what he thought was a sob and turned away from Jenkins. "What's wrong?" he asked, sitting up in his chair.

"It's Sonia... a bomb in her car. She's... I'm not sure she'll..."

"I'll come—"

"No, stay where you are. I don't need someone else to worry about. I'll call you as soon as I know more."

When Andrew closed the line, Jenkins asked, "Is something wrong?"

"A friend had an accident," Andrew said, pulling his chair out to stand. "By the way, I'm in the gym every morning at half past seven. Care to join me tomorrow? We could do some sparring… if that sort of thing interests you."

"I haven't gotten into a ring since college. I'll give it a try. Lord knows I need the exercise. Seven thirty you said?"

Andrew nodded. "Okay then, I'll let my trainer know to expect you." Andrew shook Bob's hand. "See you in the morning."

* * *

J oe, this is Bob, the visiting diplomat from Iraq I told you about."

"Pleased to meet you, Bob. Ever done any sparring?"

"Many years ago."

"We'll warm up first before getting into the ring. Andrew, get on the speed bag and Bob, why don't you jump rope. We'll do two, one-minute rounds with a one-minute rest."

After the warmup, the two men were already sweating profusely. Andrew, his head drooping to his chest, tried to get his breath under control while Bob, breathing heavily, walked around the gym.

"Okay, grab your head gear and gum shields from the table along the side wall, then come back to me for your gloves."

Equipment on, Andrew and Bob climbed between the ropes and into the ring.

"Keep your chins tucked in," Joe yelled, "your eyes forward and your hands up."

They touched gloves acknowledging they were ready to begin. "One-minute rounds, gentlemen."

Bob began throwing jabs at Andrew, but he knew enough to hold his gloves in front of his face. When he threw another jab, Andrew blocked it with his right arm before moving out of range. Bob, for whatever reason, then let his guard down. Seeing an opening, Andrew came back with two jabs, one hitting Bob's cheek. Bob then attempted a left hook but Andrew saw it coming and circled left. A frustrated Bob tried again, but Andrew, seeing another opening, got in another jab. The jumping, twisting and contorting continued for another round until Joe declared the session over. Exhausted, Andrew and Bob removed their head gear and gum shields and climbed out of the ring.

"That was one hell of a workout," Bob said, as Joe pulled off his gloves. "Thanks for suggesting it, Andrew. Another round or two next time I'm in town?"

"You're on," Andrew said, patting him on the shoulder.

CHAPTER TWELVE

Nadia woke when Ani opened the curtains and then came and sat beside her on the bed with a cup of coffee.

"Are you ready to wake up?" Ani asked.

Nadia sat up, stretched and listened to the birds chirping outside.

"Is it a beautiful morning?"

"As usual, *Sitt.* I'll give you a few moments, and then we'll go to the pool."

Ani left Nadia's swimsuit on the end of the bed. Nadia, still in her nightgown, swung her legs over the side of the bed and leisurely drank her coffee. Fully awake, she put on her swim suit and grabbed a loose shirt from the closet. Barefoot, she descended the stairs and walked through the slumbering house and across the stone terrace to the pool. Handing her shirt to Ani, she dove into the cool water and began her laps.

For Nadia, every day was a struggle to stay motivated. She had been held captive in her gilded prison far too long. Swimming followed by a rigorous weight training session exhausted her enough that she was content to spend the afternoon, after lunch on the veranda and a brief nap, reading, feet propped up on the leather couch in the library. All of this was an attempt to keep herself occupied in Hassan's absence. She understood his game, and it was working. She was lonely and missed having him around.

She had been accustomed to a rigorous sex life with Andrew. Until now, she had held Hassan off, but she was at the height of her sexuality, and she missed it. She knew she looked fabulous. She had only to examine herself in the mirror, thinking as she did that someone should take advantage of her beautiful body. That someone should have been Andrew, but she was putting together an escape plan, and she had to push him aside in order to play her Scheherazade sex game. She assumed Andrew would understand what she had to do to survive, but would he? Or was she just fooling herself into believing that because, in the end, a part of her did want sex with Hassan. And then there were Sonia's words that kept repeating themselves in her head—just do it and enjoy it. What's the big deal? It's only sex—and now deprived of it for so long, it was not sounding like such a bad idea.

Nadia knew such reasoning would not have been lost on Hassan. He understood her too well, and she him. His frequent and extended absences were something he had set up so she would finally give in to him.

While she swam, her devoted Ani sat quietly alongside the pool, ready with a towel when she climbed out. Initially, Ani's attentiveness had annoyed Nadia, but she had grown to like this quiet, unassuming woman. Like Nadia, she, too, was a prisoner.

Since her captivity, Nadia had played the compliant prisoner, but that was not going to win her release. She needed to plot a more ambitious plan, one that sorted out potential allies from potential enemies. Ani, she hoped, would be her most important ally.

One morning, Nadia invited Ani to sit alongside her on the adjoining lounge chair.

"But, *Sitt*, I'm not—"

"Of course you are. It's about time you and I got to know each other better. You're usually so formal in my presence. I'd like us to be friends, especially since we have something in common."

"We do?"

"Yes, I'm a prisoner, and so are you, because you're forced to stay here and take care of me."

Ani appeared apprehensive by such talk. She looked around to see if anyone was looking their way before she answered.

"I don't think we should be talking like—"

"Why not?" asked Nadia. "Friends, especially women, talk in confidence."

"I've never had real friends," Ani said. "One of Mr. Jaafar's drivers is fond of me, but he's the first person who's ever paid me much attention. I think he's as lonely as I am."

"Is he Armenian?" Nadia asked, knowing that Armenians, like Jews, were a tight-knit community closely linked by social, religious and cultural ties, and encouraged to marry within their own circles.

"No, he's Alawite, like Mr. Hassan."

"Do you want me to give you back some of the contraceptives you got for me?"

"No, *Sitt,* I would never be intimate with a man before I married him."

"And if I started sleeping with Mr. Hassan, what would you say?"

"Nothing, *Sitt.* It would be none of my business."

Just as Nadia was about to say something, she noticed a man marching toward them. When she asked who he was, Ani explained he was Khalid, Mr. Jaafar's butler and sometime chauffeur.

"How odd, I haven't seen him before."

"He's rather a recluse except with Mr.—"

"Is everything all right, *Madame?*" he asked, standing opposite her chair.

"I'm quite lonely, as you might have guessed, Khalid, so I asked Ani to sit and chat with me. I hope you don't mind."

"I'm not sure Mr. Jaafar would approve, *Madame.*"

"Mr. Jaafar isn't here, is he. In fact, he's rarely here." Nadia smiled up at him and said, "And if he were, I don't think he'd mind. Why don't you take a break from your chores and join us? I'd appreciate getting to know you a bit better too."

"Thank you, *Sitt,* but I have–"

"I understand," Nadia said, cutting him off. "Perhaps another time."

He nodded and walked back into the house.

"Tell me more about Khalid."

"Well, he's a decent man and respectful to staff, particularly to us women… and deeply loyal to Mr. Jaafar. So far, I've managed to stay on his good side, so he treats me fairly."

"If Mr. Hassan is away, why isn't Khalid with him?"

"It depends on where Mr. Hassan goes as to whether or not Khalid accompanies him. I overheard one of the staff say that Mr. Hassan had traveled to Istanbul. If that's true, he wouldn't have needed his driver."

"Still, I find it strange he hasn't shown his face in my presence."

The sneering Khalid was clearly not a potential ally, but Ani was, and even though she didn't wear a cross, she was Christian, as were all Armenians, and clearly more apt to help a fellow Christian.

"Never mind about Khalid. Tell me more about you, Ani."

"I'm thirty-nine."

Early signs of crow's feet around her eyes did not detract from her soft oval face. She wore her coal black hair in a ponytail and dressed in a black short-sleeve dress, white apron and black tennis shoes.

"My grandparents fled Turkey in 1915."

"That would have been during the genocide."

"I don't know much about that, except that the Ottoman Turks wanted them dead. I do remember my mother talking about soldiers capturing some women and children and using them as sex slaves. Those they didn't have any use for, they sent into the desert to one of the resettlement camps. My mother called it a calculated death march. Weak and malnourished, she said many died along the way."

"Such things have happened across the Middle East for millennia."

"Yes, perhaps they have," Ani said. "My grandparents longed to return to their village, but it never happened. Maybe their village isn't even there anymore. When they fled Turkey, they settled in Lattakia. That's where I was born. My father worked as a carpenter. My mother was a maid. I attended public school until the age of fifteen, but when my father lost his right arm in an accident and could no longer work, I had to quit school and get a job to help support the family."

"Do you know how to read and write?" Nadia asked.

"Yes," she answered proudly, "but I hardly do either anymore. It's hard to find the time."

"But you live in a house full of books. There's no excuse."

"I'm not allowed…"

Nadia knew this was her chance to gain Ani's confidence and so pressed on. "Nonsense, Ani. Take any book you want. I'll clear it with Mr. Jaafar when he returns, if he ever does."

"Two days…" she whispered.

"What did you say?" asked Nadia, staring at her.

"He called this morning. He'll be here in two days. Khalid announced it this morning."

Nadia thought to ask why she had not been told, but she already knew the answer.

"How long have you worked for Mr. Jaafar?"

"Twenty years."

"Then you knew *Madame*."

"Yes, poor woman, she died after a long illness."

"Tell me about her."

"She was strict, but if you obeyed the house rules, she treated you well."

"What kind of rules?"

"We were never allowed to repeat anything we heard to anyone. One maid broke that rule. She was found out and promptly removed."

"What happened to her?"

"I don't know. She was never seen again by any of us."

"Do you think that's why you were brought here to this isolated place when *Madame* died… so you wouldn't reveal house secrets?"

"Possibly, but I think Mr. Jaafar just didn't want to live in that big house with the memory of his wife dying there. He was very dedicated to her, especially in the end."

Nadia was relieved to hear that about Hassan.

"*Sitt,* I live and work in this beautiful place. I am fed and clothed and decently paid, and able to send money to my family. When you work for a man like Mr. Jaafar, you learn not to ask questions, and you respect his code of conduct."

"Could you walk out of here if you wanted to?" Nadia asked.

"No. Well, I… I'm not sure."

Nadia had already suggested she was just as much of a prisoner as she was and so was surprised by Ani's answer.

"Maybe we'll leave here together some day."

CHAPTER THIRTEEN

The attempted assassination had unsettled Andrew not just because it had nearly killed Sonia but because the perpetrator, as he had already discovered, routinely carried out brazen, cowardly acts of terrorism with total impunity. As was its habit, the Israeli government had issued the usual denial, and their magnanimous benefactor in the West had turned a blind eye. Case closed.

Andrew's mobile rang. He picked it up on the first ring.

"Sonia's in surgery now," Fouad said.

"Her injuries, describe them."

"They're not sure they can save her left forearm and hand. They're badly mangled." Fouad choked. "She lost her left eye. The bomb was apparently placed under her seat."

Andrew whistled. "It's a miracle she survived. Did she sustain any internal injuries?"

"A ruptured spleen, and her right lung was punctured. The doctor called it a pulmonary trauma... apparently caused by the blast."

"She'll recover from those."

"She has minor burns on her abdomen and chest and facial lacerations from shattered glass. They're doing a CT scan to determine a possible concussion or other brain injuries."

"Anything else?"

"I don't know."

"Sonia's tough. She'll recover."

"Life is so cruel," Fouad said, his voice choking up again.

"Yes, it is."

"I'm forty-three years old, Andrew. I've finally found my equal—flaws, wrinkles, misdeeds, intellect—all of these things Sonia and I have in common. I don't want to lose her."

"She'll get put back together. In the meantime, do something useful."

"Anything," said Fouad.

"Just be there for her, tell her every day that you love her. And another thing, be thankful. At least you still have the woman you love. Not a day goes by that I don't think of Nadia."

"I'll help you find her, Andrew."

Oh, shut up, Andrew thought. *You offer nothing but empty platitudes.*

"I almost forgot... I had an interesting conversation with the American from Iraq... said he could find Nadia."

"Don't get too cozy with him. He's poison. I'll call you as soon as I know more."

"Hey, another bit of news... Joe thinks I'm ready to start working in Shatilla."

"So soon? It hasn't been—"

"It's been almost seven months, and yes, I'm ready. I need to be doing something useful."

"How's your Arabic? You can't already be that advanced."

"My teacher thinks I am. According to him, I have a natural aptitude for foreign languages. And I've been practicing with Joe. My accent makes him laugh, but he concedes I'm pretty damned good. And get this, he thinks I need a bodyguard so he wants us to rent an apartment together."

"Good idea, especially if the bastard from Iraq has you in his crosshairs."

Right now, Andrew thought bitterly, *I'm more inclined to take my chances with him.*

CHAPTER FOURTEEN

With assurances from the doctor that he would call as soon as he came out of surgery, Fouad left the hospital and walked the two blocks to the Internal Security headquarters on Damascus Street. There was a time, Fouad recalled, when no one could safely walk along this major thoroughfare for fear of being killed by a sniper. During the civil war, Beirutis referred to it as the infamous Green Line, a deadly territorial divide separating Muslim West from Christian East Beirut that determined who lived and who died.

Instead of taking the elevator to his office on the top floor, which overlooked the infamous street, he descended a flight of stairs to the forensic lab where the country's most skilled and seasoned specialists collected and analyzed physical evidence taken from crime scenes. The men Fouad worked with were the best in their field. They had years of highly specialized work to their credit, living as they did in the most volatile country in the region, in what many referred to as the battleground of the Middle East. They'd seen it all—civil war, assassinations, hostage taking, drug wars and foreign invasions.

Roger Saliba headed the department. He and Fouad had been best friends since childhood. When they graduated from the American University of Beirut, they were recruited by the CIA and traveled to its headquarters in Langley together. After five years in the States, the Agency recognized Roger's keen scientific skills and recommended he return to Beirut to head the Internal Security's Forensics Department.

Roger settled into his work, married his college sweetheart and fathered four children.

As was his habit when he was on a special case, and in a hurry for answers, Fouad walked into forensics and shouted to one and all, "Hi guys, do you have anything for me yet?" Today was no exception.

"How are you holding up, Fouad?" asked one of the detectives, poking his head out of his office.

"Just heard about Sonia… really tough," said another, patting Fouad on the shoulder as he walked past. "We're praying for her."

"Thanks, I appreciate it. Keep those prayers coming. She isn't out of trouble yet."

Fouad stopped in the middle of the garage and looked around. "Where's her car?" he asked, turning in circles. "Isn't it here yet?"

"I had it moved into the back room," Roger said, coming up behind him. "I didn't want you to see it."

Fouad turned and hugged his friend.

"You know I need to see it."

"Your choice."

He followed Roger as he crossed the garage to a secured area using a key to open the door.

"Here it is," Roger said, watching Fouad examine the burned-out shell of twisted metal.

"How did she survive this?"

"Probably because the bomb didn't go off the right way."

"What do you mean?" Fouad asked, staring at Roger.

"The explosion should have blown Sonia's legs off and bled her to death. It's possible this was just a warning and not meant to kill her."

"Are you suggesting they may try again?" asked Fouad.

"It's one theory, but it's just as possible that Sonia slammed the car door hard enough that she jarred the bomb loose, and that's why she's still alive. I can say with certainty that the bomber used two pounds of C-4."

"What the hell's C-4?"

"It's a plastic bonded explosive, a combination of chemicals and a plastic binder. Powerful stuff! When mixed properly, the consistency is similar to modeling clay. It adheres to just about any surface. A detonator cord is inserted into the plastic and attached, as in this case, to the ignition. That's why I suggested it might have come loose when Sonia slammed the door shut."

"Why use this particular kind of explosive?" asked Fouad.

"It's safe to handle, and it's malleable. Once the ingredients are combined, even an amateur can handle it. All he'd have to know is how to open a locked car door. Once inside, it wouldn't take him long to connect the wire to the ignition, hide the wire under the dashboard or under the floor mat, and then stick the explosive under her seat. As soon as a key was put in the ignition, the bomb would detonate."

"Who makes these explosives?" asked Fouad.

"Every army in the world. As explosives go, it's pretty garden-variety."

"That's no help. Does Israel make them?"

"Sure, why wouldn't they? They're a major arms producer."

"Is there any way to determine if this particular bomb was made there?"

"Not a chance. It wouldn't have to be made there. If they have agents in Lebanon, and we know they do, it could have been assembled somewhere close by."

Roger looked at Fouad. "You look worn out, my friend. Go home. Get some sleep."

"I'm headed back to the hospital. I want to be there when Sonia comes out of surgery. Call me if you discover anything new."

* * *

Aside from her forearm and eye," said the surgeon, "she'll make a full recovery, but she won't have an easy time of it when she learns the extent of her injuries."

"She's a tough lady, doctor."

"I hope so, Fouad. She's looking at months of rehab."

"Can I see her?" asked Fouad.

"She's in intensive care and heavily medicated."

"Please…"

"For just a minute, but you'll have to put on a gown and mask. My main concern at this point is infection."

"I understand."

Fouad was escorted into the unit. He approached Sonia's bed, bent over and kissed her on the forehead.

"I love you, Sonia. Together we'll get through this. I promise."

A promise is a commitment, he thought. *Are you ready to commit to a life with Sonia? Yes, I am.*

CHAPTER FIFTEEN

Andrew was not sure he would reach Beirut in one piece. It was the first time he had gotten into a car with his trainer, and he swore it would be his last. When Joe finally brought the car to a screeching halt in front of Hotel Dieu Hospital, Andrew climbed unsteadily out of the car.

"I'm going to check out a few rental apartments while you visit Sonia," said Joe. "Call me when you're ready to leave."

"I'm not sure I want to put my life in your hands again. You're a fucking maniac behind the wheel."

Joe laughed and waved as he sped off.

The seven-story hospital, squeezed into a crowded space between a public grade school and a police station, was located in one of Achrafieh's poorer Christian neighborhoods, yet close enough to the former Green Line, the wartime divide between east and west Beirut, that it also serviced the abutting Muslim neighborhoods.

The double glass door to the main entrance opened automatically when Andrew approached. At the far end of a rambling, well-lit lobby, its floor a highly-polished white marble, its furniture black leather, he spotted Fouad sleeping, his head slouched onto his chest. His wrinkled shirt and trousers and bristly stubble suggested he had spent more time here than home in the last few days.

Rather than disturb him, Andrew poured himself a cup of coffee from the dispenser at the reception desk and sat quietly beside him, observing the others seated around him—men in suits and open collars, women, some in chador, others in short dresses and heels, bouquets and boxes of chocolates in their arms, chatting among themselves while waiting for visiting hours to begin. Still others juggled bulky patient files and large manila envelopes marked "X-rays" and sat quietly awaiting their turn to see a doctor.

Fouad awoke with a start.

"Sorry, I must have dozed off." He stood and gave Andrew a hug. "You look great, my friend. Joe must be taking good care of you."

"Yes, he is, except he almost killed me on the drive down from Broumana. Have you ever been in a car with that crazy bastard?"

Fouad smiled and shook his head.

"You don't want to," laughed Andrew. "How's Sonia doing?"

"She's struggling. Hell, you know her better than I do. She's vain and accustomed to men fawning over her, so to her a damaged arm and loss of an eye is huge."

"I agree. This won't be easy for her, or for you."

"I know," Fouad said, raising his eyebrows and shaking his head.

"And she has already had a letdown. She was due to travel to London the day after this happened to participate in a prestigious panel of experts on the Middle East."

"I didn't know that. You've kept me too secluded in the mountains, Fouad."

"Purposely, my friend. You've had your own shit to deal with."

"Aside from what you've already told me, did she sustain any head injuries?"

"She's being monitored for possible concussion, although that and PTSD exhibit similar symptoms, or so I'm told, so it's hard to definitively determine any brain damage yet. But listen to me babbling on as if I were her physician. He'll be here soon, so you can ask him all these questions."

"Can I see her now?"

"Follow me, dear man."

When they exited the elevator on the third floor, Andrew was pleasantly surprised to see a welcoming, brightly lit floor, a well-kept and tidy staffing station with wallpapered walls, and he was struck by the old-fashioned uniforms. He had always found the starched and well-creased hats charming and professional. The nurses were duly impressed when they, in turn, discovered that Andrew was a cardiologist from the prestigious Georgetown University Hospital in Washington, DC.

As they walked toward Sonia's room at the end of the corridor, Andrew could not help but notice the respectful silence. There were no clusters of people chatting in the hallway, no boisterous voices streaming out of patients' rooms—both sources of irritation during his stay at American University Hospital.

"You go on in," said Fouad. "I'll look for her doctor."

Andrew knocked gently on Sonia's door before entering. He did not recognize her at first, and for a split second wondered if he had entered the wrong room, especially with a man seated so close to her bed.

Sonia's left eye and part of her head were covered in white gauze, her left arm and hand heavily bandaged, her face red and swollen from multiple glass and shrapnel wounds.

"Andrew," she said, her voice raspy and not sounding at all like the Sonia he knew. He was surprised, with her lungs so damaged, that she could even speak. He made his way to the end of her bed and wiggled her toes.

"How are you doing?"

"You can come around and give me a kiss," she said. "I'm not dead yet. I've only been blown to bits."

Her body smelled of sweat and saline, her lips tasted like burnt metal, and her shallow breathing gave off a wheezing sound.

"Sonia, your lungs need rest. You shouldn't be talking."

"Nonsense, I'd like you to meet my cousin, Paul. He's also a Greek Orthodox priest, so be careful what you say."

He did not look like any priest Andrew had ever seen. He did not wear a white collar or a black suit. His eyes were dark and lively, his nose aquiline with a smile that dimpled his cheeks, and he had straight coarse hair that showed traces of grey.

"Don't take her seriously," Paul said. "She loves to pick on me. Even though we're cousins, she had a mad crush on me and has never forgiven me for choosing priesthood over her."

"That's our girl, never wanting to play second fiddle to anyone, even God. But I have to say, Paul, you don't dress like a priest, and an orthodox priest at that."

"I'm off duty, and I'm not wearing my false beard, so how would you know?" He laughed.

Sonia tried to join in the laughter, but when she started coughing her cousin gently lifted her head and gave her a sip of water.

"Paul," she said, when she had cleared her throat, "this is Andrew Sullivan, the dear friend I told you about. And please don't mind his smart mouth. He's really a special person."

Andrew shook his head and smiled. "Look who's talking. Just out of ICU, and you're already back to being a little shit."

"I'm very pleased to meet you," said Paul. "I know from Sonia that you've had your own recent challenges, but you look fully recovered."

"And as handsome as ever, damn you, Andrew. I'm jealous. I've never looked so bad."

"Stop talking nonsense. You'll be launching a new fashion craze with your eye patch soon enough. The ladies will go wild, wanting to imitate the famous Sonia Rizk."

"Paul, didn't I tell you that he had a smart mouth? And to top that off, he's become a real bullshitter."

"I learned from the best, Sonia."

Paul laughed. "I can see you two have great fun together."

"We actually hate one…" But before she could finish, her eyes closed and she fell asleep.

"It's the morphine. She's been dozing off quite a bit since I got here," said Paul. "Best if we let her sleep." And he took Andrew by the arm and led him into the corridor.

"I saw a waiting room near the nursing station," said Andrew. "We can talk there."

The room had a coffee dispenser, and Andrew poured two cups.

"Thanks," said Paul, taking a sip before he spoke again. "You must be wondering why Sonia was talking to a priest."

"Confused would be more accurate. Sonia's the diametrical opposite of religious."

"She's grappling with a lot of issues—why she survived and what she needs to do to justify such a gift. Throw in remorse for past misdeeds—the usual questions and regrets, I guess, after a close brush with death. You know more about this litany of sorrows than I do—Ali's death, then Elie, Anna and Tony, and Kamal, the Israeli—good thing I never met that son of a bitch."

Andrew took a sip of his coffee as Paul spoke, musing to himself about Sonia's long list of crimes and misdemeanors. From the only window in the room, he could see the school playground next door. It was recess, and the children were playing tag, the boys chasing the girls around the courtyard. *Such innocence. I hope when they grow up, they'll find a more peaceful world filled with better people.*

"That's why I'm here," said Paul. "She said she wanted to talk to someone with God connections. Supposedly that's me."

"It still doesn't make sense."

"Oftentimes people reexamine their relationship with God after a near-death experience. I dare say that's where Sonia is right now."

"Forgive me for being cynical," said Andrew. "I grew up Catholic and haven't practiced in a very long time, but I find it hard to understand how anyone can even talk about God in such a Godless, dark, unfathomable place like Lebanon where people kill one another with impunity and then turn around and invoke religion to justify their actions."

"That's pretty heavy-duty stuff, Andrew," said Paul.

"Why? I'm just affirming what I see around me. If Sonia's going through truth and reconciliation with God, why can't I do it too, but on my own terms and in my own words?"

"I hear a lot of anger and pain in your voice," Paul said.

"Yes, you do. I have a hard time concealing it these days. I apologize. Fouad once called me politically naïve. I used to be, but I'm not that innocent American anymore. And how ironic that I've come to pay a visit to Sonia and ended up confessing my innermost demons to a priest. You must have some pretty special powers, Paul."

"I'm just a mere mortal, like you."

"Not really. You still have your faith. I've lost mine. Hell, I don't even know who I am anymore. Since Nadia's kidnapping and the assault on my life, I feel like I've become one of Beirut's shameless characters who could commit an unspeakable act if it meant I could rescue Nadia. If this is truly who I've become, then I've lost my soul and am beyond redemption."

"If you killed someone to get Nadia back, could you live with yourself?"

On hearing Paul's words, he was reminded of Joe's Confucius quote: "Before you seek revenge, dig two graves."

After a long pause, Andrew sighed. "No, I'd have to find another way."

"Sonia and I talked about a lot of things this morning, but you were her main concern."

"Me?"

"She insisted I help you all I can."

"Maybe you already have, Paul… but what an odd thing for Sonia to say."

"She said she'd done badly by you and wanted to make things right."

"What did she mean by that?"

Before Paul could respond, Fouad appeared in the doorway. "There you are, Andrew. I thought maybe you'd left."

"Sonia fell asleep so we came in here to chat."

"Yes, perfectly understandable," said Fouad. "I was just afraid you'd gone before you had a chance to meet Sonia's doctor whom I've just found. Dr. Richard Salame, I'd like you to meet Dr. Andrew Sullivan."

Andrew stood and shook his hand. He was younger than Andrew had imagined, with olive skin, arched black eyebrows, keen, dark eyes and salt and pepper hair that he wore brushed off his high forehead. He stood a few inches taller than Andrew in his pale-blue dress shirt and grey trousers.

"And this is Paul, Sonia's cousin," said Fouad.

"Paul and I are old friends," said Richard, giving him a hug, a common practice here that Andrew rather liked.

"It's a pleasure to meet you, Andrew. Fouad's told me about your adventures here, or rather your misadventures, but you seem to have made a full recovery."

"I have, and I'm extremely grateful. What's the latest on our patient?"

"I've just been in to see her. She did sustain a concussion, after all, but we're monitoring it closely. Spleen and bowel are recovering nicely. Her lung capacity has improved. Given that she shouldn't even be alive, she's doing remarkably well."

"I hope you told her that," said Andrew.

"Oh, I did. I reassured her she'd be as good as new in no time, and possibly even sexier, although I'm not sure that's possible."

"Hey, let's not get too personal here. Sonia's *my* girl," said Fouad. "I'm the lucky man here."

They all laughed.

CHAPTER SIXTEEN

Nadia had just been through a firestorm of information, and she really wanted to kill someone, and if Sonia had not already been blown up, Nadia would have killed her herself. What a bitching whore she was.

Hassan had told Nadia about Sonia's betrayal, finally, but only after she had badgered him and only after she had compromised herself, something she knew she would eventually have to do. She had assumed she would have to think of herself as Collette putting together one of her novellas—especially the sensuous stuff, the parts that get really raunchy—and pretend she was one of the characters acting naughty. In the end, it had just happened, every lecherous part of it.

It began the night Sonia should have died but survived. Nadia tossed about all night and finally around six a.m. gave up and climbed out of bed. She knew her morning swim would calm her down especially if she did a few extra laps. The household staff was still asleep, and she had the place to herself—no peering eyes to follow her around, no Khalid lurking behind a door to spy on her or listening in on a conversation she might be having with Ani. Nadia no longer thought of herself as the princess locked up in the castle tower. She was a fish in a large glass tank, and she hated it.

After her laps, Nadia swam to the side to exit the pool. As she grabbed hold of the railing, she saw a man standing at the top of the stairs, holding her towel. It was Hassan, home a day early. This was her moment to play the modern-day Scheherazade and make things happen, but she had to be careful not to over-play her part.

As she stepped out of the pool, he wrapped the towel around her. When he kissed her shoulder and told her how beautiful she was, she leaned into his chest and said, "How much longer can I go on resisting you?"

Before she left to shower, she asked him if he had heard what had happened to her friend Sonia.

"She's not your friend," he replied.

"What do you mean?" she asked.

"She's never been your friend, or anyone else's for that matter." He walked into the house before she could ask him what he meant, but then it hit her like a hard kick in the head.

Hassan was right. Sonia had carried on an affair with Elie, Nadia's husband, even after they were married. She had lied when she said she had not heard her scream at the mosque when Jaafar had tried to force her into his car, then covered up her lie by taking her to see Kamal, the Israeli. But there was something else, something Hassan did not want to tell her, and that was what she set out to discover.

When she got to her room, Ani was not there. She now had a new maid. She was sure it was that bastard Khalid who had ordered this. He had not liked her talking to Ani. Did he think two Christian women were some sort of threat? Or had someone overheard Ani when she said that perhaps they would both walk out of there together some day?

After her shower, Nadia dressed herself in a silk dress and panties, nothing else. If her plan was going to work, she had to play the seductress but in a way Hassan least expected. Her lead-in conversation was carefully planned. She joined him for breakfast. He stood, as usual, when she arrived and pulled her chair out. When he had taken his seat and poured her a cup of tea, she told him she had seen the report about the US State Department funding opponents of Bashar Assad to overthrow his regime.

"Using a proxy to undermine a government is nothing new," Hassan said. "In 1979, President Carter signed a directive to give secret aid to the Mujahedeen to defeat the pro-Soviet regime in Kabul. There's an identical script this time, except it's the West and its regional ally dictating who should be removed from power and calling up the newest generation of Islamic jihadists to do the job."

"Can Bashar do anything to stop this?" Nadia asked.

"No, and that's what worries me. He's a physician, not a politician. He has surrounded himself with young technocrats who know nothing about fending off Islamic radicals. To make matters worse, he's put his hothead brother, Mahar, as head of both the army's Fourth Armored Division and the Republican Guard. Mahar is now essentially in charge of keeping the regime in power and doing all its dirty work. If there's trouble, you can be sure he'll be in the forefront of the most brutal fighting, and it will reflect badly on Bashar."

"Tell me more," Nadia said, as she reached over and covered his hand with hers.

"I was away longer than I intended this time because I was making arrangements to send my children and their families to Istanbul."

"Hassan, I'm so sorry. That must have been a painful decision."

"But a necessary one, my dear… nothing you need to worry yourself with."

"If I'm going to be part of your life going forward, I want to worry myself with things that concern you."

"I love you, Nadia. At least a hundred times I've apologized for kidnapping you, but maybe that's not enough. Maybe a thousand times won't be enough for the distress I've caused you. For fifteen years I've thought of you every day, and if I was to go on living, I had to do what I did. I know you have feelings for me too. I've felt it. But you've been afraid to even let me touch you for fear you'd weaken your resolve to resist."

How well he knows me, she thought.

"Yes, you've been very patient with me."

It was here that she took her cue and stood. She had already given herself permission to do this and go all the way to play to her Sultan's passion. As he had already surmised, it was not going to be that difficult. The physical attraction was already there.

She went over to his chair, which he had moved away from the table, pulled up her silk dress and straddled her legs over his lap. She sat close enough that her breasts, which were already hanging out of her dress, pressed against his chest.

"If I let go, let me go completely."

"I've dreamt every day that this moment might happen," he said, as she put her arms around his neck and pulled him even closer.

"Tell me about Sonia. I want you to tell me why she's not my friend."

"It will hurt you to know, Nadia."

"Hurt me," she said, looking him in the eye.

"She set up your kidnapping at your parents' home. She arranged it all."

And, like a scene from a horror movie, she saw in her mind's eye Sonia, standing in her parents' dining room, asking her to retrieve her computer from the car. Sonia had sent her outside because she knew Hassan's goons would be there, waiting to snatch her.

"Damn her, I want you to send her a message—*I hope you die. Nadia.* I want that bitch to know that I know."

Hassan pulled her to him and kissed her. "I love it when you get angry." And he started kissing her more fully.

"Not here," she said, taking his hand and leading him into the house and up the stairs.

Nadia knew she was not in a position to hold anything back. She had to be in full love-making mode, so she pretended it was Andrew making love to her, and her orgasm came naturally and fully, and she was able to fool her new lover. She had succeeded in opening that portal with Hassan, and when they made love again that afternoon, Andrew was no longer needed.

All the way back to Elie's disappearance, and his thirteen years in prison, she had never lost her natural and recognizable innocence. She had only ever slept with two men in her life, Elie and Andrew, and now Hassan Jaafar, who was every bit the lover that bitch Sonia had said he was.

CHAPTER SEVENTEEN

While visiting Sonia, Andrew had mentioned to Paul that he was going to visit Shatilla, and Paul had asked to come along. "I've never visited the camp. It's time I did."

"Sure, come along. Joe, my trainer, will be joining us. He's been there many times and knows his way around."

* * *

The impoverished neighborhood around the camp reminded Andrew of the southeast section of Washington, DC, circa 1968 to 1980, notorious at the time for race riots, crime, drugs, boarded-up buildings, empty store fronts and high unemployment. And while, after years of neglect, that part of DC had finally seen a renaissance, Andrew knew that in a city that showed a blatant disregard for the have-nots, with, ironically, Beirut's only golf course and its private beach clubs just a few hundred meters away, such a revitalization would not happen.

Joe's friend, Aziza, one of the camp's leaders, had agreed to meet them in front of the Shell gas station, opposite the camp's main entrance. When their taxi arrived, Joe nudged Andrew and pointed. "There she is."

Even at a distance, Andrew was struck by her loose, long, coal black hair and large dark eyes. They lit up when she saw Joe exit the cab. After he had hugged her, Joe introduced the two others. When Andrew shook Aziza's hand and had taken in her smoky black eyes and her high cheek bones, long sculpted nose and dimpled chin, he was instantly attracted to her and realized he was back in the game. She may have thought her long sleeve white blouse and jeans sufficiently concealed her figure, but Andrew could see her full breasts and tight thighs and flat rear, and they gave his libido a buzz. He had not thought of another woman since Nadia had been kidnapped, so he was relieved his sexual desire was still intact.

The area just outside the camp bustled with hordes of people, with taxis honking and stopping any which way to discharge passengers, then waiting, motors idling, black fumes spewing into the air, for new customers to climb in. Planes roared overhead as they made their final approach into the Rafic Hariri International Airport. Cars double and triple parked along either side of the road, their drivers deaf to a policeman's shrill whistle meant to hurry them on their way. Food vendors brought out their carts, piled high with any day-old vegetables and fruits they thought they could unload in this poor part of town. Andrew knew he was getting used to this place when he paid no attention to the minaret's call for prayer. Aziza did not either, even while others fell to the ground on their prayer mats and began their recitations to Allah.

As they approached the camp, Andrew paused. Underfoot the ground was damp and reeked of sewage. Decrepit buildings and piles of garbage thrown on piles of rubble lined either side of what looked to be a straight and rather narrow lane ahead.

Aziza stopped at a shaded open space off to the right and, waving her arm, motioned for Andrew and the others to join her.

"I'm afraid this is the only place in the camp where there are still a few trees."

Speaking in Arabic, Joe said, "I'll get us some drinks. It's going to be bloody hot while we walk around. Is everyone okay with Fanta?" Andrew said he was, and then he laughed. That was the first time he had used his Arabic in public.

Sidestepping vendors and squeezing in between motorcycles parked helter-skelter along the pavement and small children huddled in groups playing what looked like jacks and marbles, Andrew and Paul came to a halt at the edge of a vacant lot, empty except for the piles of rotten garbage and a small corrugated metal shack. This, Aziza explained, was the site of a mass grave where victims of the 1982 massacre were buried.

"There are no markers or memorials here, only the memory of unspeakable evil," she said.

"Twenty-seven years later and still no markers? Why?" asked Andrew. "And so much rubbish in such a sacred place? I don't understand."

"People here are too busy cleaning up their own lives and worrying about surviving from day to day."

"It often happens like that," Paul said. "You get caught up in the present. You promise yourself, when there's time, that you'll go back and repair the past with a memorial, or a plaque, only you never do. Look at the seventeen hundred people who were disappeared during our civil war. They don't have a memorial yet either."

"My people know there's more killing to come, more bodies to put in this grave," said Aziz. "Nothing's been settled here. Beirut's still a war zone, and many of the Christians would like nothing better than to get rid of all of us."

"What's this about Christians?" asked Joe, returning with four bottles of Fanta.

"I'll explain while we're walking," Aziza said, taking a bottle from Joe and nodding her thanks.

From the gravesite, they turned back toward the open market.

Everywhere he looked Andrew was surrounded by great hordes of people, literally clogging the road, buying and selling vegetables and cheap household goods. They shouted in Arabic, haggling over a price and countering with a lesser amount.

He saw a corrugated, makeshift hut that sold refurbished television sets, vintage '70s' models. Aziza pointed out a seamstress seated on a small stool, her back pressed against a concrete wall in front of her sewing machine, her clients waiting in line to have their tattered clothes mended. A horn honked, and they jumped out of the way of a motorcycle, a wide wagon full of water bottles configured on its backside. A group of young boys huddled outside a bakery. Aziza explained that the baker paid them a miserly salary to deliver bread, once it was baked and packaged, to the various neighborhoods inside the camp. An auto workshop trained young men in the basics of car mechanics in case they were lucky enough to find employment outside the camp.

"Joe," Aziza said, taking hold of his arm and stopping, "I was referring to the Maronite Christians, the ones who massacred us, not all Christians."

"Not all Maronites are the same. Sure, most don't want you here, but they didn't all agree about the massacre. I certainly didn't."

"You're a Maronite?" Aziza frowned. "All those times we were together, and you never told me?"

Andrew watched their body language and wondered if they had continued their relationship. It was obvious they fancied one another and had dropped their religious differences.

"Because it wasn't an issue that ever came between us. I didn't practice my religion, and as a Sunni, neither did you."

Andrew had been in Lebanon long enough to know that its seventeen different religious sects could all get along just fine. It was only in conflict, when outside forces used the sectarian card, that the Lebanese decided they hated each other, as had happened during the civil war, and the killing had begun.

Rather than respond, Aziza began walking again.

They left the main entrance, turned right and entered a world of darkened, fetid, narrow alleyways. Occasional beams of sunlight streamed in through an open space, with thousands of dangling wires hanging haphazardly, like slithering black snakes, from makeshift lines crisscrossing the walkways. According to Aziza, two children had been electrocuted a week earlier. The walls, many covered with graffiti, still had bullet holes from the 1982 massacre. There were words from Mahmoud Darwish, the Palestinian national poet, splashed on walls alongside photos of young martyrs, Aziza explained, who had been resisting the occupation in Palestine when they were killed.

Parts of the pavement they walked along were cement, other parts dirt-covered, and when it rained Andrew imagined the alleyways flooded with sewage and rainwater.

When they got into the open again, Andrew was shocked to discover dirty looking four, five and six-story buildings rising from the middle of the camp. What had begun in 1948 to '49, when the UN had set up a massive tent city to accommodate the tens of thousands of fleeing Palestinian refugees, had, over the last forty or so years, become a permanent city within a city. It was a stark reminder of the implausibility of any of these people ever being able to return to their homeland.

Some of the buildings looked as though they had been recently bombed and rendered structurally unstable. Andrew saw no sign of windows, only tattered curtains covering what should have been glass and wondered, when the temperature dropped in the winter, how they stayed warm. The rickety narrow stairs were built of cement, but most of them were chipped at the edges. He now knew from Aziza that the camp had electricity only six hours a day, so how did they manage in little or no light without falling? There were elements of life—a table, chairs or bedding, even a television—visible signs that people, sometimes as many as ten to fifteen in each apartment, were actually living in these filthy buildings scarcely penetrated by sunlight.

Aziza stopped abruptly and turned to Joe. "I need to know. Were you a Phalangist?"

"Yes, I was part of that militia. It's not something I'm proud of, but you know me well enough to know I'm not a monster and not a murderer."

Andrew put his arm on Joe's shoulders. He was familiar with Joe's past and knew it could not have been easy for him to admit this, especially to Aziza, or, for that matter, to a priest. Joe had confessed to him that the camp massacre and the emotional toll it had taken on him was the reason he had left Lebanon. What was unclear to Andrew was why Joe had joined the CIA. Was he recruited because of his father's former Moscow connections or because he had been a Phalangist? It was Paul who was amazing in handling this delicate situation. He took Joe and Aziza's hands and said, "It was a terrible time for all of us. We all did things we weren't proud of, but we need to move on and concentrate on the future."

"Aziza, it seems we have a peacemaker in our midst," Andrew said, "and he's a Greek Orthodox priest, so I guess that makes as much sense as anything around here."

"Well, I'll be damned! I've got a priest and a former Phalangist on my hands. Andrew, what do you have to say for yourself?"

"I'm just a doctor who wants to work in your camp."

"And how grateful we are."

"And how wonderful that you have a sense of humor, Aziza," Paul said.

"To survive in this camp, you need one."

"You also need more trash cans," said Andrew. "I've been carrying my empty bottle of Fanta around long enough."

She laughed. "They're well hidden, I'm afraid. We do what we can without any regular garbage collection. Here, let me have all of them." She put them alongside the alleyway. "I'll have one of the boys collect them."

She was about to say something else when Joe started talking almost as though he were in a trance. Andrew realized he was remembering a dark past.

"It was a group called The Youth Special Forces who committed the massacre here in '82. They numbered around four hundred. They were mostly petty criminals marginalized by the rest of us. We wanted nothing to do with them. They had been recruited by Elie Hobeika, who was the Phalangists' liaison officer with the Mossad, and Israel's Defense Minister, Ariel Sharon. Like Hobeika, whose family and fiancé had been massacred by Palestinians in Damour in 1976, these men had suffered similar losses and sought revenge. They were also heavy drug users."

"Did you use drugs?" Andrew asked.

"Hash… if you got yourself high enough, you could pretty much do whatever was asked of you without much thought. But these guys were different. They were heavy cocaine users."

"Why cocaine?" asked Paul.

"It alters how a person thinks and feels emotionally," said Andrew. "Taken in high doses, it can produce anger and can also make you hyperactive. It can even trick your brain into thinking you can do anything and suffer no consequences."

"A massacre still happened, drugs or no drugs," said Aziza.

"Yes, it did," Joe said, "and I'm truly sorry. I was just trying to explain that it wasn't all Maronites who committed the massacre."

"Or all Christians," said Paul. "Unfortunately, the Phalangists are still around, some of them now members of parliament. Sadly, many of them wouldn't hesitate to do the same thing all over again if they thought they could get away with it."

"That's a powerful accusation," said Andrew. "Are you sure?"

Before Paul could respond, Joe said, "I am."

"Me too," said Aziza. "They're the same people who blame us for the civil war and who refuse to allow us our most basic rights or grant us citizenship."

"Citizenship has to do with demographics," said Joe. "The Christians are desperate to keep their hold on power, what little they still have. Tens of thousands of Christians fled the country during the war. A census, were it to take place, would show Christians no longer hold a majority. The Shiites and Sunnis do, and allowing Palestinians who are Sunnis citizenship would tip the balance. This all dates back to the idea of Lebanon as a refuge for Christians fleeing persecution from other Middle East countries and as a guarantee of protection from their enemies."

"Refugees and protection?" asked Aziza. "When will it be the Palestinians' turn?"

"This is history repeating itself, however unfairly," said Paul. "Palestine 1948, Israelis forcibly expelling over seven hundred thousand Palestinians. The Lebanese Christians had the backing of the French government during its mandate here. Sadly, the Palestinians were left to whither in the wilderness."

Aziza closed her eyes and shook her head. Then she did something wonderful. She slipped her arm through Paul and Joe's arms and continued walking. There was an ease to that kind of forgiveness and friendship, and it was something truly beautiful, thought Andrew, and it warmed his heart. This was why he loved these people.

"Were you here during the massacre?" Andrew asked, addressing her from behind.

She stopped and turned around. "Yes, I was a child, but I still remember the day the militias entered the camp. A man, I don't remember his name, came through the camp shouting for everyone to leave because the Israelis were outside the gates with their tanks. My father wasn't there that day, so my mother gathered up all six of us children and rushed us out of the camp by a side entrance. Many of our neighbors ignored the warning and were slaughtered."

"Are your parents still alive?" asked Andrew.

"No, we eventually found my father… in the camp near the entrance. His throat had been slit. My mother died some ten years ago. They're both buried here in the camp."

Andrew could not find the words to describe this place of horror. He realized in that moment that if he were to work in this camp, where the living and the dead co-existed, where squalor and poverty were intertwined with abandonment and restrictions imposed by governments, he would have to leave behind the world he knew and embrace the world of these Palestinians who knew only displacement and slaughter at the hands of an enemy that had confiscated their land and forcibly exiled them. And what of the children here, he wondered, did they not dream the dreams of children, even if the adult world had done its best to extinguish them? Did their parents pray that the refugee camp would not be a sentence of life without parole for them for the sole crime, like them, of having been born Palestinian?

Andrew leaned in close to Joe and whispered, "What a reality check. Here we are, about to move into a luxury apartment, and these people have to live like this."

"There are haves and have-nots in this world for a reason," said Paul. "Secure yourself financially so you can help others. We should all live by that rule. As long as you do this, Andrew, you should never apologize for living well."

"We couldn't possibly run this camp without the charity of others," said Aziza.

"How many Palestinians live here?" Andrew asked.

"We are a total of twenty-five thousand, but Palestinians are the smallest portion at the moment. Some 40 percent are Syrians, and the rest are poor Shia who moved in during the civil war. The UN is doing its best to help everyone. They run several schools inside the camp, and they deny rations to any family whose children do not attend classes."

"You attended a UN school here?" Andrew asked.

"Yes, my lessons began here. I then went on to study at the American University of Beirut. When I graduated with a teaching degree, I came back here to work. It was my way of giving back so that others could have the same opportunities I had.

"Unemployment is a huge problem and makes education that much more urgent," she continued. "In the sectors of low-skilled and low-paid jobs, where Palestinians are permitted to work, the problem has been made even worse by Syrian refugees who have taken over their jobs. They're single men mostly, so they can accept three dollars for a day's work. Palestinian men with families to feed must ask for a minimum of twelve. These are just a few of the complications we have to deal with now."

The end of the tour brought them in front of the Doctors Without Borders clinic. They entered, and Aziza introduced Andrew to the four physicians who worked there. When they, in turn, introduced themselves, and began conversing in Arabic, Andrew joined their conversation. It took him a brief second to realize that he was actually speaking Arabic as if it was the most natural thing to do.

No more inhibitions, thought Andrew, with a deep sense of relief. Most of these physicians were foreigners like him, and they spoke with equally deplorable accents. If they could converse with their patients and be understood, so could he.

Joe gave him a wink and patted his shoulder. "I couldn't be prouder of you. You set your mind to doing this, and you did it."

Andrew gave a bow. "Yes, I did, didn't I? And if Nadia were here, she'd lovingly mock my Arabic, but she'd be proud too."

Aziza warned, "You realize you'll see everything from minor illnesses caused by poor living conditions and malnutrition, to gunshot wounds and heart attacks and drug addiction, especially among our young. Are you sure you want to take all that on?"

"I am," Andrew replied, never more certain of anything in his life.

CHAPTER EIGHTEEN

It had been only three weeks since medics had pulled Sonia from the burning car, and already she could reach out and grab a glass of juice from her bedside table. She was constantly trying to use her left arm, out of habit, and swore it still functioned. In her dreams, it did. She had figured out how to shift her body around and, using her good arm, pivot herself into sitting position, then onto her feet. Though a bit dizzy, with wobbly legs, she was able to walk to the nearby armchair and sit for short periods of time. The swelling in her face had diminished enough that she tolerated the weight of her reading glasses across the bridge of her nose and over her ears. The challenge was adjusting them into the correct position with only one hand. She read the newspaper but rarely got past the first few pages before her eyes grew heavy and closed against her will.

Fouad had saved the articles published in the *London Times*, the *Guardian* and the Lebanese, Syrian, French and Arab newspapers about the attempt on her life and read them to her once she was more alert. In the mode of journalistic sensationalism, the articles had recapped every little detail—the kind of explosive used, with photos of the charred remains of the car, the probable perpetrators, how she had been pulled from the burning vehicle with her clothes on fire yet, with her senses intact, had valiantly asked the medics to save her hand. The attention and notoriety did a great deal to boost her morale.

It was the reconnection to God thing she was still struggling with. As she reflected back on those first few days, she realized it had been Paul, the priest, who had done his best to bring his cousin's soul back into the

Christian fold by taking up the subject of God. She had wondered how and why her life had been spared when an explosion of that magnitude should have killed her. Paul thought the answer was spiritual while she, knowing she was probably one of God's least favorite people, assumed she had been kept alive to suffer punishment for her sins. Her greatest regret was that she had confided in Paul, in a moment of morphine-induced fog, that she had arranged Nadia's kidnapping. As long as she was tucked away in Jaafar's prison, Sonia had no worries about being discovered, unless, of course, Jaafar told her and she somehow got word to Andrew. So, her concern was fear of being found out, not remorse for destroying two peoples' lives, and since God shed mercy on the repentant sinner, Sonia was pretty certain she stood no chance of any possible reconnection with God.

Now if God looked anything like Dr. George Salame, and if he ran a church, Sonia would sign up immediately. He was not only a good healer, he was a keen psychologist who knew how to feed his patient the flattery she needed even when her face was blotchy and swollen and full of stitches, and her eyes were black and blue and her hair filthy and her roots sprouting grey. He was also bold enough to challenge hospital protocol and sit on his patient's bed and hold her hand to deliver a bit of distressing news.

"You're recovering very well, Sonia, but—"

"But what, doctor? I may be a flirt, but I'm intelligent and can be told the truth, whatever it is."

"Okay then, here goes. Against any reasonable expectation, we saved your arm, and that's the good news. There will be some permanent nerve damage but not enough to keep you from doing most things, provided you follow through with a rigorous program of rehabilitation."

"How long will that take?"

"I don't know, maybe as many as six or eight months. The good news is that eventually you'll have a functioning arm with only some limitations. And since you're right handed…"

Sonia looked at him inquisitively.

"Fouad told me." He smiled. "You'll be able to continue writing and, at least in the short term, become the best one-handed typist around. No one, except maybe the Israelis, wants to see you abandon your journalism career. Your work is too important. By the way, that was brilliant writing on the Hariri assassination. I never did buy the story that it was the Syrians who killed him."

Sonia smiled. "You flatter my ego, and I love it. What about my eye, any hope there?"

"Once the tissue around the socket has repaired itself, we'll take the eye out and replace it with an artificial one. Aesthetically, you'll look like you have a normal eye, unless one looks very carefully, but you won't be able to see with it. I'm sure you've noticed that your other eye has already adjusted."

"Yes, I have, but it fatigues easily."

"Yes, and it will for a while. It's a bit like losing a kidney, and the surviving one takes up the workload, slowly at first until it gains full speed."

"Strange analogy, but I guess it works. What actually happened to my eye?"

"Without getting too technical, you suffered a blunt contusion eye injury with shrapnel penetration that destroyed the optic nerve and cornea. So, until the area completely heals, you'll continue to wear your eye patch. There's research being done now on bionic eyes. It's very exciting and has enormous potential."

"What's the difference between a bionic and an artificial eye?"

"You can't see out of an artificial eye, of course, but a group of engineers in California is working on what they call an open-source prosthetic eye with a built-in still and video camera that will substitute for the field of vision in your missing eye."

"I'd actually be able to see with that eye?"

He nodded, smiling. "And blink."

"How amazing, to be living at a time when this is possible and, at the same time, be so blessed because I happen to have the financial wherewithal to have access to these breakthroughs."

"Yes, and how admirable that you recognize your good fortune when so many people take such things for granted. The advances in medical science are astronomical. I've been practicing medicine for almost twenty years, and I can hardly keep up with the changes."

"Twenty years? That's not possible. You don't look a day over thirty-five, and you're handsome, and if I weren't so in love with Fouad, I'd invite you to share my bed. Of course, I'm being outrageously silly, and having fun, and shouldn't even be flirting with you, but so what… it's true."

He laughed. "I've never had an offer quite like that. I think I'd better report you to Fouad."

"You wouldn't dare," she said, laughing.

"You're shameless, Sonia Rizk."

"So I've been told many times over."

* * *

A few days later, a nurse handed Sonia a letter that had just been delivered to the nursing station. She did not recognize the handwriting across the front of the envelope. Curious, she wondered why someone would take the time to write her a personal note and then drop it off anonymously when they could just as easily have delivered it in person.

She tried to open the sealed envelope but could not do it with one hand. Just as she was about to push the call button for the nurse, Dr. Salame returned to her room.

"Sorry, I left my stethoscope here."

"You've come just in time. I can't open this damn envelope." She held it up. "Would you please help me?"

"With pleasure." He took the envelope and slipped his finger under the seal at one end. He gently nudged it up, then slid his finger inside the ridge of the envelope, tearing it across the top until it opened.

"Voila."

"Masterfully done, thank you." When he tried to hand the envelope back to her, she said, "You've gone to all this trouble, why don't you read it to me."

He looked at her.

"Go ahead." She nodded, and he pulled the note out.

He lingered over the page before he finally lifted his eyes to meet hers.

"What? Is it some secret admirer with a message you're too embarrassed to read?"

"I… I don't want to be the one to tell you what it says, Sonia."

"What are you talking about?" She took the note from his hand and read it. It said: "I hope you die. Nadia."

CHAPTER NINETEEN

Nadia surprised not only Hassan but herself with her insatiable sexual appetite. After such a long absence, she liked having sex again and having a man lying beside her as naked as she was and whispering naughty things in his ear that aroused him. She had become a Sonia. *No surprise*, she thought. Sonia had been her sex instructor, explaining the different positions and the sorts of things she had men do to have sex be more exciting. Hassan was passionate and good at both receiving and drawing her out emotionally, something neither Elie nor Andrew had been able to do. And where was Andrew in all of this? A fond memory. *It was better that way*, she thought. By compromising herself, she had taken herself beyond anything Andrew would ever want to know about.

If Hassan was now Nadia's Sultan, she was still Scheherazade. She had been the one who had initiated sex with Hassan when he had least expected it. She had spent those long absences plotting how to take him on, how to tease and flatter him and ultimately gain his confidence. And, in anticipation of eventual sexual relations, she had the contraceptive pills she had asked Ani to get her so she would not get pregnant.

And as a reward for good behavior, she had gotten Ani back. And when she was not helping Nadia, she now walked around with a book under her arm. In fact, once she had broken her resistance with Hassan, the whole household had changed. Suddenly, she had become the mistress of the house. She allowed all the servants to use the library and pretty soon it was not just Ani but all members of the staff who were reading and teaching those who were illiterate to read. She became not only Hassan's shining light but the entire household's, and because of her sweetness and goodness, Hassan had changed too, revealing a side she had not known.

She never imagined him to be an excellent chef and yet, there they were, collecting fresh herbs and vegetables from his garden, then dismissing the kitchen staff and spending the day cooking together. He became her mentor in fine wines, and pretty soon she was the one tasting and choosing from his extensive wine cellar a particular wine they would drink with their evening meal. Whether in the kitchen or strolling through the grounds, or over afternoon tea, he spoke about his childhood. It was his mother who had sent him to Damascus to get an education, the one who had instilled in him his social etiquette skills and insisted he learn English and French along with Arabic. When he graduated from Damascus University, he earned a Masters at L'Ecole Polytechnique in Paris before joining the CIA.

And then one night, Hassan confided in Nadia that he had recently had an unpleasant encounter with a former acquaintance, an American named Robert Jenkins.

"Did you know him at Langley?"

Hassan turned and stared at her. Was he trying to decide how much to divulge?

She ran her hand down his chest. "You can tell me, Hassan. I couldn't possibly share what you say with anyone."

He laughed. "Yes, we met at Langley. He was a son of a bitch even then, but I couldn't say that to his face. I was just a lowly Syrian there to be taught a thing or two about Intelligence operations."

"What's he doing in Syria?"

"He's here to make trouble, and he wants me to help him."

"What did you tell him?"

"I told him to go to hell. What else would I tell a man who wants me to help him destroy my country?"

"How did he take that?"

"He laughed and said he'd ask again, and that next time I'd better have a different attitude or else I'd be crushed along with Assad and his clique."

"Oh, Hassan, does this mean all-out war for Syria?"

"I'm afraid so. The US is intent on weakening both Iran and Hezbollah, but to do that they need to destroy Syria, the linchpin between the two. That's why I made arrangements to get my family out of here. Years ago, as an investment, I bought a few apartments in Istanbul. Little did I know they'd provide sanctuary for my family. Do you know the city?"

"I was maybe twelve when I visited it with my parents. I remember it being very beautiful and green with gardens and delightful promenades."

"It still is, and if we have to leave, my darling, I know you'll like it there. Maybe we should just do it now before all hell breaks loose. Would I be able to trust you to come with me and not try to escape?"

"I'm yours completely, Hassan."

What was he thinking, she wondered? *She had no travel papers. How did he plan to get her out of the country?*

CHAPTER TWENTY

Fouad, a Maronite Christian, was deputy director of state security services. Had the traditional order of succession been maintained, the position of director would have gone to him. Lebanon's National Pact, though not a written constitutional text, implied that the president of the republic should be a Maronite, the prime minister a Sunni, and the Speaker of the parliament a Shiite.

This power-sharing pledge also reserved highly important jobs for certain religious communities. Maronite Christians were given the lion's share in vital sectors of state—commander of the army, the governor of the central bank, the heads of military Intelligence and the state security services. This unchallenged franchise ceased in 1989 when Taif, a Saudi agreement that ended the civil war, reapportioned many of those prestigious positions to the Sunnis. It was former Prime Minister Rafik Hariri's assassination in 2005 that dealt the final, fatal blow to this delicate power structure. The Sunni leadership, which blamed Syria for Hariri's death, insisted that Syria's oversight of Lebanon's governance structure, which was an integral part of the Taif Agreement, should end. As a result, some thirty thousand Syrian troops were forced to leave Lebanon. This created a near-cataclysmic earthquake in the Sunni-Shia balancing act that, until then, Syrian and Christian leadership had successfully maintained.

The 2006 war further undermined Lebanon's sectarian equation. Hezbollah's victory over Israel not only strengthened the Shiites politically, it seriously challenged Sunni dominance and diminished any remaining Maronite Christian power.

The current general director, Abdel Raki, was Fouad's boss. A former major general and hawkish Sunni, he had the full support of the Western-backed March 14th movement, the anti-Syrian political coalition colluding with the US to facilitate the entry of radical Sunni groups with ties to al-Qaeda into the country as a counter-balance to rising Shiite-Hezbollah influence. He also enjoyed a privileged relationship with both Saudi Arabia and the prime minister, the same prime minister who had not only kissed US Secretary of State Condolezza Rice on both cheeks when she visited his office shortly after the 2006 war, but had openly gloated when she announced, after Israel had destroyed scores of Shiite villages in south Lebanon, that the world had just witnessed the birth pangs of a new Middle East.

Fouad recognized this as a perilous time for Lebanon. The US was intent on provoking sectarian strife in Syria to undermine Assad's government. And even though he understood the Sunni's fear of a rising Shiite power, particularly since they had remained unchallenged and all-powerful until recently, he could not excuse their willingness, and in particular that of his country's prime minister, to choose religious affiliation over Lebanon's national security interests.

Fouad's office on the top floor of the state security headquarters, at the opposite end of the director's, overlooked the intersection of Damascus Street and Corniche Mazra near the National Museum. The exterior of state security's French-mandate five-story building with its Swiss-cheese-like pockmarks bore witness to the battles that had taken place during the civil war along Damascus Street. Inside, things also remained pretty much the same—the walls still painted the same dull grey, the outmoded fluorescent lights that flickered intermittently, transmitting a persistent low hum that drove most to distraction, along with the usual dose of nepotism, political and sectarian favoritism and corruption that was endemic throughout all state agencies.

Fouad's office had been recently equipped with air conditioning and a Wi-Fi connection as well as a newly minted plaque on his door that read "Deputy Director, General Security Services." Few outside the agency knew his official title; even fewer knew his name. In many ways, he embodied a persona similar to Hassan Jaafar's, without, thankfully, the same number of killings to his credit. Fouad was an affable, albeit slightly overweight, according to Sonia, relatively well-dressed, suave, but ruthless-when-necessary, individual who introduced himself in Lebanon's social circles as a successful IT executive.

On one wall in his spacious wood-paneled office hung the obligatory portrait of Lebanon's eleventh president, Michel Suleiman. Other furnishings included a leather couch, two matching chairs and an oriental carpet, in relatively decent condition, covering most of the chipped and badly stained marble floor. His desk showcased the standard government-issued memorabilia—a cedar tree carved out of oak, a coffee pot with four demitasse white cups, each embossed with the requisite Cedar of Lebanon, resting on a round bronze tray along with several pairs of worry beads—all vying for a limited space alongside a pile of classified documents, one of which he was perusing when a call came in on his secure line.

"*Naam?*" he asked abruptly.

"This is Hassan Jaafar," said the voice on the other end.

While Fouad liked and respected Hassan, they were often on opposite sides politically. Like many a spy master, Hassan Jaafar presented two conflicting personas… the cold-blooded killer responsible for thousands of disappeared men either killed outright, imprisoned in one of Syria's notorious hell-holes, or thrown into mass graves around Beirut and the debonair, well-educated, silver-tongued political figure courted by Lebanon's powerful figures, both Christian and Muslim. The two had been friends at Langley and had worked closely together on security issues when Jaafar was Syria's Intelligence czar.

"How the hell are you, Hassan? It's been too long."

"Yes, it has, and I have an apology to make. I never thanked you for your arrangement," Hassan said.

Fouad knew he was referring to the CIA agent who had gone missing from the American embassy in Beirut. He had kidnapped and tortured one of Hassan's best agents, then thrown his mutilated body along the side of Damascus Street not far from Fouad's office. A criminal investigation concluded that the American had been beaten to death by a jealous husband who had discovered him in bed with his wife. Fouad connected the dots and filled in the blanks, but he never denounced Hassan.

"I hated that bastard as much as you did," Fouad said. "I shed no tears when you took him out. He was arrogant and treated his Arab colleagues like they were trash. He deserved what he got. But Andrew Sullivan didn't deserve to lose Nadia. He wants her back, Hassan."

"I finally have the woman of my dreams, and I have her screaming from the rooftop every night. You can tell that son of a bitch that she loves it, and I'll never give her up. She rejected me once and then went and married that fool Elie. Why do you think I had him kidnapped? I knew eventually I'd get her to come to me, and she did, in Chtaura, when she found out Elie was still alive, and that's when I set the trap."

"You're a selfish bastard," Fouad said, "screwing two peoples' lives so you can enjoy a bit of sex."

"Come on Fouad, are you getting soft in the head? Why would I care about an American and his feelings when they're screwing up the entire Middle East? Now let's discuss the business I called you about."

"I didn't really think this call was about Nadia. How can I help you?"

"Robert Jenkins is here stirring up trouble... but I'm sure you already know that. Last week he summoned me to the US embassy and suggested I work with him to overthrow the Assad government. When I told him to go to hell, he recommended I adopt a more flexible attitude. There were ways of persuasion at his disposal, he said, that included rendition to some hell-hole as pay-back for a certain CIA agent tortured and killed."

"Jenkins is a bastard and a puppet of Washington's neocons," Fouad said. "He's here to do their dirty work."

"And it's always the same fucking agenda, isn't it? Topple the regimes of Israel's adversaries by whatever means necessary—managed proxy wars, pre-emptive strikes... whatever it takes to get the job done. Regardless of my differences with Assad and his inner circle, I'd never agree to help the Americans destroy my country. Did you know that Jenkins is already importing and training jihadists? And when the time comes, he'll use agitators to start the rioting and the killing and then blame it all on Assad. Jenkins has to be stopped, but I can't do it alone. I need your help."

"I have my own *merde* to deal with, Hassan. I've got a dozen dossiers of hardcore jihadists sitting on my desk right now, let into the country by our quisling Sunni leaders who would do just about anything to stop the Hezbollah-Iran strategic alliance. In the meantime, these jihadi lowlifes, most of whom are from Saudi Arabia, literally closed Saida a few days ago, holding the entire city hostage, and when the army tried to arrest their leaders and restore calm, they killed ten good soldiers. This means they're also armed and dangerous. So, as much as I'd like to help, only because it would mean a lot less trouble spilling over our border, I don't know what I can do for you."

"Jenkins is going to be named the new US ambassador to Syria."

"How do you know that?" Fouad asked.

"A tip-off from Syrian Intelligence."

"So that's why Jenkins contacted you. That confused me for a minute, but now it makes sense. You have access to Assad and his inner circle."

"Not anymore," said Jaafar. "I've retired."

"If that were true, Intelligence wouldn't have told you about Jenkins' new post. Look, if we're going to be working together, we have to be honest with each other, no secrets. Is that understood?"

"Understood."

"This must mean then that Jenkins doesn't have anyone on the inside, an informant or a double agent, and needs your help. Agree to work with him. Arrange it with your former Intelligence officers. Feed him information, make it sound reasonable, and he'll bite. Arrogance blinds men like him to most truths."

"That's a hell of a gamble I'd be making on my life."

"I'm not so sure. These men assume they're always right. They may actually believe they're doing the right thing. They're power freaks. They love to play Byzantine games, but audacity gets in their way, clouds their thinking. Go ahead and hatch an escape plan and be ready to implement it if needed."

"I'm way ahead of you," Hassan said. "I've made all the necessary arrangements."

You cannot do that, thought Fouad. *I have just made you my bait to ensnare and destroy Jenkins, so I do not want you going anywhere.*

"I'm willing to come to Damascus," Fouad said, "or anywhere of your choosing."

"All right, let's meet in Lattakia. How soon can you come?"

"I don't know yet. I have some urgent matters to attend to before I can leave the city. I'll be in touch soon."

* * *

When he hung up from Hassan, Fouad called his friend Roger in forensics who routinely worked with Syrian Intelligence. If Fouad hoped to stop Jenkins, such a collaboration was vitally important.

"Roger, I need to see you. It's urgent."

"I'm free this afternoon," he replied. "Where do you want to meet?"

"My office at three."

"I'll be there."

Fouad then called Joe who worked on counterterrorism issues when he was not providing security for Sonia and training Andrew. If Fouad were to decide to use Andrew to ensnare Jenkins or Jaafar, or both, he wanted Joe in on the planning.

Out of habit, Fouad called both Roger and Joe by their anglicized names. Like many of Fouad's agents, they used variants as a way of separating their Intelligence work from their personal lives. Roger, for example, was pronounced with a French accent, an inflection at the end on the "e." Joe wasn't really Joe but Joseph, pronounced with a strong "f" ending, or Yousef when saying his name in Arabic. Fouad's name, by contrast, was a common Christian name that did not have a stage name. And just as names changed according to needs, so did Lebanon's spoken languages. French and Arabic each enjoyed their own melodic pitch changes—French evoked a lighter, livelier, more lyrical sound, while Arabic conveyed harsher, more combative tone colors.

What interesting language and gene pools the Lebanese had, he thought. At the very least, they were a mix of Phoenicians and Greeks, Assyrians, Babylonians, Romans, Armenians and Turks. So, who were they really? And if others were to get interested in Lebanon's affairs, and decide to settle in, there was no telling what the DNA of future generations of Lebanese would look like.

He glanced at his watch. He had three hours until he met his new team, enough time to pay Sonia a visit. He grabbed his jacket, locked his door and rode the elevator to the ground floor. He exited the building on Damascus Street, crossed the tree-lined boulevard and walked two blocks along Corniche Mazra to Hotel Dieu Hospital. Along the way, he stopped to buy Sonia a bouquet of flowers. He knew she was not going to like what he had to say but hoped, if he handled the situation diplomatically, that she could, at least, be pacified into agreeing, at least short-term, to his change of plans. Before her accident, he had agreed to move in with her even though his small penthouse apartment on Badaro Street, with its spectacular view of the city, was just two blocks from his office. Sonia's was deep inside Achrafieh near the Sioufi gardens, a densely populated neighborhood that contended with day-long traffic jams. He had not considered this inconvenience when he had agreed to the new living arrangements.

Sonia had been recovering nicely, but she had let herself fall into a state of despondency over Nadia's note. She had lost her appetite. She refused physical therapy and complained of a sudden onset of acute pain necessitating renewed doses of morphine. In her fog of opioids, she slept poorly, and when she did finally nod off she suffered recurring nightmares.

She appeared to be sleeping when Fouad entered her room. He put the flowers on her side table and dragged the nearby chair closer to her bed. He inspected her facial wounds and was pleased to see that the swelling had subsided, and the cuts and bruises were healing. When he peered closer, he noticed Sonia's eyelids flicker and realized she was faking sleep. His first inclination, given his pressing state of affairs, was some surly remark he knew he would come to regret. Instead, he gently stroked her cheek to tease her out of her sullenness.

She opened her eyes and looked at him. "I'm so ashamed, Fouad. I can't bear myself."

"If you're feeling that badly, you could call Jaafar's bluff. He obviously had a malevolent reason for telling Nadia the truth about her kidnapping. Turn the tables. Talk to Nadia directly, ask her forgiveness, and explain the circumstances. You're good with words. You'd find the right thing to say."

"I have no way of contacting Nadia."

"Go public. We know she's being well treated, and presumably she watches television."

"I'd only make things worse for her."

"What could be worse than keeping Jaafar company?"

"Sooner or later, I'll have to do this, won't I?"

"Yes, but maybe it would be best if you waited until you were fully recovered."

"Yes, of course. What could I have been thinking. I'm not up to doing anything public right now. I look dreadful."

"Okay, then it's settled. Now, here's what I have planned. You're going home. A physical therapist will come every day, and you'll do as you're told. I've hired a cook who will prepare you nutritious meals, and I'll be there to make sure you do everything you're supposed to do."

"I love you, Fouad. I don't deserve you."

"Nonsense, warts and all, we're the definitive flawed pair. We deserve each other." *Oh, do we ever*, he thought. *We are such manipulative shits we would probably end up destroying one another.*

"And when I'm home, and you've moved in, I can make you an office in one of the spare bedrooms as long as you don't mind sharing it with my shoes and purses."

"I won't mind sharing anything with you, darling, but I have to hold off on the move for now."

"That's a blow, Fouad. We agreed."

"Yes, we did. You rather pushed me into it, but right now, I don't have the time to think about a move when my apartment is right next to my office, and I have a major crisis on my hands and can be there in minutes if I'm needed. I regret it very much, but I have to put urgent state matters ahead of us."

"Are you prepared to say what that urgent business is?"

"Yes, but you'd probably fall asleep in the middle of it."

"Are you sure you're not doing this because I'm so beaten up?"

"Don't be silly. Your shine is already coming back, and if I didn't have to attend a meeting I'd climb in bed with you right now. Scars and all, I love you."

He saw her wipe her eyes and wondered if she was emotional because of her fragile state or because he had said he loved her.

"You've been so marvelous. How lucky I am."

When Fouad bent down to kiss her goodbye, he found her already fast asleep.

CHAPTER TWENTY-ONE

Fouad knew one thing going into his conversation with Roger and Joe. Given their personalities, the two men probably would not like one another. This did not bother Fouad. They were the best at what they did, and he needed their expertise. They had already been briefed and were on board, and they would put aside any ideological differences or personal dislikes and get the job done. He had known Roger almost his entire life and had never given a thought to how he came across to others. Hands down, he was simply Fouad's best friend, but stacked up against a more cosmopolitan Joe, the two men could not have been more different. Roger, a six foot one, bushy white-haired, ruggedly handsome, often blunt, sun-baked outdoorsy-faced forty-three-year-old, usually wore a rumpled, outmoded *demi-season* light wool jacket, dress shirt, tie and scuffed desert boots. Joe, the affable sophisticate with a hint of proper Russian breeding, except for his occasional foul language, had blue eyes, arched eyebrows and a smile that lit fires in women's hearts. He usually wore blue jeans, a baby-blue linen shirt, sleeves rolled up to his elbows, a cotton sweater casually tossed over his shoulder and sockless Gucci loafers.

The two men arrived on the hour and Fouad, standing in front of his desk, made the introductions.

"*Merci d'être venus,*" said Fouad, having decided to conduct the meeting in French since many of his senior colleagues were more fluent in Arabic and English.

"Roger, I don't think you've ever met Joe. He's one of my best counter-terrorism experts and works undercover most of the time. He returned to Beirut several years ago after working at the CIA for some twenty-five years."

"If Fouad thinks so highly of you, that's good enough for me. *Vous etê le bienvenue,*" Roger said, shaking Joe's hand.

"Merci, Roger, it's a pleasure to meet you. I understand you and Fouad go back a long way."

"We played together as kids… chess champs, too, and I beat him every tournament. And boy, did he hate losing. And then we discovered spy thrillers, and by the time we were eighteen, we decided we wanted to do this kind of work. Somehow, we survived Langley, and here we are back in our old neighborhood trying to save Lebanon from itself." Roger turned to Fouad. "Does this make us sound like boring old men?"

Fouad smiled and shook his head. "Spies don't lead dull, boring lives."

"And they're not always lucky enough to have life-long friends," said Joe. "Not something that comes naturally with this kind of work. I'm envious."

"Twenty-five years at Langley… that's hard to believe," Roger said. "Why did you finally decide to leave?"

"I did a few tours in Iraq, saw Abu Ghraib and Camp Bucco, then spent some time at Guantanamo… the torture, the prisoner abuse, it got so I wasn't sleeping."

"I don't think we'll see anything that dramatic here," said Fouad, "but we are about to commit a quiet rebellion. Our boss's loyalties—"

"Are not to the state," said Roger. "They're to the fucking jihadists because they're Sunnis, and that's a treasonous act in my book. I'm proud to be doing something to stop him."

"How about you, Joe?" he asked. "Does any of this bother you?"

"I'm a Christian, and I have one loyalty and that's to Lebanon. I'll fight to the death, if need be, to save it."

"Thanks, guys," said Fouad. "We're solid and we're a team, and I'm grateful. Now, let's get started. We have a lot to cover."

Fouad suggested they bring their chairs closer to his so they would not have to speak loudly.

"You've both been briefed on Jaafar's call. And Joe, I've also filled Roger in on his kidnapping of Nadia Khoury and your relationship with Andrew because, going forward, we may decide to use one or both as decoys. At the moment, Jaafar's our concern. He's on the fence, not sure he wants to work with Jenkins, but I'm confident he'll come around."

"How can you be so sure?" Joe asked. "If it were me, I'd pack up and leave the country."

"He won't leave without Nadia," said Fouad. "A few phone calls to the right people would prevent him from taking a kidnap victim across any international border. If need be, when we meet in Lattakia and he isn't on board yet, I will remind him of that."

"So, we essentially blackmail Jaafar into working with Jenkins. Where does that get us?" asked Roger.

"Jenkins is the kingpin," said Fouad. "At the very least, we keep track of his moves, try to stay one step ahead of him, and with luck, trip him up so he fails in his mission."

"Okay, Jaafar's on board, we monitor Jenkins, then what?" Roger asked.

"You'll work with Jaafar and Syrian Intelligence to feed Jenkins info he thinks is important," said Fouad. "Jenkins considers Jaafar, even in retirement, to still be an insider. You have a working relationship with Syrian Intel, you figure out the logistics. For a start, interrogate the jihadists we already have in custody. If they won't talk, make them. We want to know who funnels them weapons and who recruits them at a hundred dollars a month to kill Alawites, Christians and Shiite infidels."

"How do we know any of this will stop an uprising that's already been set in motion?" Roger asked.

"We don't," said Fouad. "But we have to try."

"The uprising is a smoke screen for something bigger," Joe said. "In October, Qatar and Turkey agreed to form a working group to develop a gas pipeline that would transport gas from Qatar to Europe via Syria. Assad rejected the idea, and that's when the US started actively training and funding the jihadists."

"The training and the funding might be recent, but the idea of regime change began with Bush around 2003," Fouad said. "Obama's just continuing Bush's plan, and the Qatar pipeline is an added incentive to act."

"The uprising begins, Assad is forced out and a puppet who'll go along with the pipeline's corridor is installed," Roger said. "The bastards don't even bother writing a new script anymore, do they? They just dust off the old play book and hire new actors."

"Actually, it's still the same subset of actors, just a newer generation," Joe said.

"And they fail every time," said Roger.

"When you have your head up your ass, you don't see your mistakes," Joe said. "It's called hubris. It's what drives US foreign policy. Hegemony in this oil-rich region is of vital strategic importance to the West."

Fouad was pleased. This was exactly the kind of conversation he had hoped to have, and he liked the way Joe and Roger exchanged ideas.

"But the story could get even more complicated," Joe said. "My sources tell me that Assad is going to endorse a Russian approved pipeline that will run from Iran's side of the gas fields through Syria to our ports here. If this happens, it will make Shiite Iran, and not Sunni Qatar, the principal supplier to the European energy market and increase Iran's influence."

"And infuriate the Sunni powerhouses," said Fouad. "That's why they're on board with mega dollars to get rid of Assad. Plus, it's a double win for the US. By supporting their Sunni allies, they protect their military posture in the region."

"Don't be surprised if Russia eventually joins the party," said Joe. "They have strategic interests here too."

"Putin supports Syria at the UN. So do Iran and China for that matter, but he's given no indication that he'd intervene in an actual war," said Fouad.

"The Russians have a military alliance with Syria," Roger said. "They'll have to intervene."

"Roger is right. We'll see a lot of shit go down in Syria," said Joe, "but it'll be the Russians, not the Americans, who'll play the decisive role, and Jenkins and his ilk will suffer a decisive defeat."

"You talk as if the Russians have already decided to intervene," Roger said.

"You aren't working for them, are you, Joe?" asked Fouad.

"Roger," said Joe, ignoring Fouad's question, "my father was in Russian Intelligence. He defected to the UK when I was a teen. I'm not sure Fouad filled you in on that part of my background."

"Briefly."

"He was involved with a woman," Joe said. "Apparently she was a double agent... at least that's what my father's friends thought at the time. This was confirmed by one of his colleagues who reached out to me after my father died in a car accident... brakes apparently failed, and he skidded off a mountain road. The kind of death defectors get, I guess, for not playing by the rules."

"I'm sorry," said Roger.

"No need, except it destroyed my mother and frankly skewed my opinion of women in general. Guess that's why I've never married."

"Joe," insisted Fouad, "you didn't answer my question. Are you or aren't you working for the Russians?"

"When I was CIA, I was strictly CIA. I'm working for Lebanon now. And yes, I still maintain contact with my father's Russian friends. Does that make me a Russian spy? I work counter-terrorism. I'm supposed to work with all sides."

"Do you speak Russian?" Roger asked.

"Fluently. I also read and write it."

You are an even more valuable asset than I had imagined, thought Fouad.

"Now tell me what to do with Jaafar," Fouad said. "I need a plan."

"You've already suggested a viable one," Joe said. "Otherwise, offer him protection inside Lebanon. And if he brings Nadia back across the border, make no attempt to rescue her, and reassure him of that. I assume he's quite content with Nadia. Why wouldn't he be? I've heard she's gorgeous. A happy Jaafar will be more useful to us."

"Roger?"

"Screw Jaafar! We have more important things to worry about. The uprising's been set in motion whether Jaafar works with Jenkins or not. Once it starts, we'll have our hands full making sure it doesn't spill over our border."

"We still haven't decided on a plan so let's keep an open mind when we meet with Jaafar."

Fouad noticed both men looking at him. "Yes, I'd like both of you to accompany me to Lattakia when I meet with Jaafar."

"I'm in," Roger said.

"Me too," Joe said, standing up. "Sorry, but I need to get back to Broumana," he said as he extended a hand to Roger. "Pleased to meet you, and I look forward to working with you."

When he left, Roger turned to Fouad and asked, "Who is this Joe? Is he working for the Russians?"

"Just because his father was Russian doesn't make him a Russian spy, Roger. That kind of accusation is akin to the Americans blaming all Muslims for nine-eleven. Personally, I hope the Russians do intervene in Syria. Assad doesn't have a friend in the world, and if the Americans have their way, his country will be torn to shreds."

"So, are we looking at a new Great Game being played out?" Roger asked.

"Very possibly, only this time it will be the US and Russia and potentially far more dangerous."

CHAPTER TWENTY-TWO

Fouad was walking across the Damascus Street-Corniche Mazra intersection on his way to the office when his mobile rang.

"Robert Jenkins is back in the country," said Joe on the other end of the line.

"I want him kept under surveillance."

"It's already taken care of, boss," Joe said. "He's staying at the Phoenicia... pretty high-end for someone on a US government salary. I doubt he's paying the bill... probably one of his rich Gulf allies."

"Good work, Joe. Stay in touch. I'm on my way to the office now."

* * *

Fouad remembered Robert Jenkins well. He was fifteen years old when his father, an American diplomat, was posted to Lebanon. Quite by chance, he and Fouad had attended Louise Wegmann Academy, a French primary and secondary school near the National Museum. Two years older, Fouad was a senior when Robert began his sophomore year, and it was only at Langley, during a get-acquainted session, that they discovered their mutual past. They had become instant friends and spent many a night bar-hopping along M Street in Georgetown, an upscale neighborhood in Washington, DC. One evening as they walked back to their car, they were assaulted by two men at knife point. Fouad managed to disarm his assailant who fled the scene. Robert dragged his opponent into an adjacent dark alley and beat him to death. When Fouad saw the lifeless body, he helped Robert to his feet and together they took flight. The next day Fouad read in the Washington Post that an unidentified man had been found dead in an alley in Georgetown. Neither he nor Robert spoke of the incident, but a short time later Robert traded in his Intelligence credentials and entered the state department's foreign service, no doubt at his father's urging, with the goal of becoming part of its diplomatic corps. Instead of following his father's prestigious career in statecraft, Robert squandered his career in skullduggery and subversion. Through his Intelligence channels, Fouad knew that Robert was not only one of the key architects of regime change efforts in Syria but was also actively recruiting and training death squads in Saudi Arabia, Qatar and Turkey to be used in Syria.

Joe called Fouad again. One of his men had just finished recording a conversation between Jenkins and Jeff Fetter, former US ambassador to Lebanon, presumably in Beirut to meet Jenkins. They had met in the hotel coffee shop.

"Fetter has been busy since he left Beirut," Bob said. "He's now UN undersecretary-general for political affairs."

"Impressive title! What the hell does it mean?" Fouad asked.

"I didn't know either, but a quick Google check said his position consisted of setting the UN agenda on behalf of Washington on issues pertaining to conflict resolution in various political hotspots."

"Let me guess, the countries in need of conflict resolution are the ones targeted by US covert operations."

"You're spot on, boss."

"So, what did Fetter and Jenkins discuss?"

"Fetter had just arrived from Riyadh where he'd met with members of Saudi Intelligence. He instructed Jenkins to travel to Hama in Syria to meet with the opposition groups there and then report back to the Saudis. Fetter stressed that their goal was to create factional divisions that would lead to mass murder and extra-judicial killings... the end game being the destruction of Syria as a nation state."

"Filthy bastards. Where's Jenkins now?"

"He's in an elevator on his way to Eau de Vie, the restaurant on the top floor of the Phoenicia."

"I know it," said Fouad, remembering the first time he had met Sonia, dining there with Andrew, only hours after he had arrived in Beirut. "Is he alone?"

"No, his bodyguard is with him. As soon as they reach the eleventh floor, he'll probably wander in alone and take a table by himself, while Jenkins will sit somewhere else. He's hardly impressive, the bodyguard, must be a new recruit. He didn't know what to do with himself while Fetter and Jenkins chatted."

"Where did Fetter go?"

"Airport… waiting for his flight to Paris, then on to Dulles, DC."

"Good fucking riddance."

"Boss, one more thing Fetter said. Obama's new CIA chief will be playing a key role in organizing covert support to Syria's rebel forces, including infiltrating Syrian Intelligence."

"That's not good news."

"No, it's not. It'll be up to Jaafar and Roger to find the traitor and dispose of him."

"Good work, Joe. Where are you now?"

"I'm in the lobby of the Phoenicia. Come to the men's room when you arrive so I can wire you with a recording device before you meet with Jenkins."

"I'll try to keep the conversation interesting."

"I count on it. And stay a few extra minutes in the men's room after I leave. I'll need time to get in position before you arrive at the restaurant. You may need a bodyguard too."

"Be careful, Joe. Jenkins knows who you are."

"Not to worry, I haven't forgotten."

A short while later Fouad exited the elevator on the eleventh floor. As he walked through the cocktail lounge at Eau de Vie, he spotted Joe off to his right, seated at the dimly lit bar, talking to a beautiful blonde in a low cut mini dress. *Don't get too distracted, Joe, I might need you.* He entered the restaurant and waited for the maître'd to seat him. Fouad spotted Robert Jenkins at the far end of the restaurant. His table, next to a floor-to-ceiling window overlooked the Corniche. Fouad also noticed his bodyguard seated a few tables away. Joe was right. He was an easy spot.

Fouad followed the maître'd to his table. Without looking around, he sat. He was perusing the menu when he heard Robert's voice.

"Fouad Nasr, is that you?"

When he turned, Robert was already on his feet and coming toward him. He stood and smiled. "Damned if it isn't Robert Jenkins." He opened his arms and gave him a hug. "You come to my city and you don't look up an old friend?"

"Apologies, Fouad. I've only just arrived."

"I've missed not staying in touch," Fouad said. "I've always considered you a friend."

"I never picked that up from you. I thought you always considered me a snob."

"You were a snob." Fouad laughed. "But I liked you anyway, and after what happened in DC, I felt sorry for you, but then you left the CIA, and I haven't seen you since."

"I was lucky enough to be taken into the diplomatic corps, and that's kept me hopping around the globe."

"Yes, I've tried to stay abreast of your accomplishments, Bob. You've succeeded brilliantly."

"What do you say we have lunch together?" Robert asked. "I was waiting for someone else to arrive, but apparently he isn't coming."

"I'd like nothing better." And Fouad joined Robert at his table.

"I love this view," Fouad said, as he pulled his chair into the table and looked out over the Corniche and the sea. "From this height, the city still looks pristine, doesn't it? Too bad it's become such a cesspool, but that's *my* problem. Tell me about your career. You've held some pretty significant foreign policy positions. Maybe I should have followed your lead instead of staying in the Intelligence business."

"Don't kid yourself. It isn't all glory and praise. The world of foreign service isn't all it's made out to be."

"But that's part and parcel of what governments are about these days. It's hardball all the way," Fouad said.

"And a lot of shit happens along that rocky road," said Robert, "...a lot of shit."

"Let's order," Fouad said. "I'm starving, and what do you say to a bottle of Musar with lunch?"

"I never say no to Lebanese wine. It's still one of the best."

"I agree. Making good wine is the one thing we still do very well in this country."

When the waiter had taken their order, they continued talking.

"As to shit going on, I assume you're referring to Syria," said Fouad.

"What makes you think that?"

"I run an Intelligence unit in this country. It's my job to keep track of our illustrious foreign visitors, and I know you've been meeting with some unscrupulous characters, even by Lebanese standards. A lot of what's happening in Syria has US fingerprints all over it, so I put two and two together."

"You lay it all out there, don't you? I like that... no bullshit."

"You'd have seen right through me if I hadn't."

Fouad untied his napkin and placed it on his lap before speaking again.

"I know you're already working with some of our Sunni leaders, but I'm offering you my services too, and it comes with an entire department."

"Fair enough, old friend. You know I'm making contact with opposition groups, and you know how the game's played and how dirty it can get. You can assume we're laying the groundwork for an insurgency in Syria."

"I didn't need you to tell me that. It's been on the nightly news. Tell me something I don't already know."

The waiter returned with lunch, and when he'd opened and poured the wine Fouad lifted his glass and offered up a toast.

"Here's to you, Robert, and to your successful career."

"Thank you, and since this is a special occasion, I'll share something with an old friend that no one else in the field knows yet. I've just been named US ambassador to Syria. It's a recess appointment and will have to go through congressional hearings, but once it becomes official I'll be able to direct the insurgency from our embassy in Damascus."

"Congratulations, Bob, well done. So, Mr. Ambassador, can I ask you some questions?"

"Fire away."

"Generally, there's something that triggers an uprising. Here it was the Hariri assassination. People demonstrated and demanded the expulsion of Syrian troops. How will you start the one in Syria?"

"For our luck, we really won't have to do too much. Nature's done most of the work for us. Syria's experiencing its worst drought in nine hundred years."

"Jesus, I hadn't realized it was that serious."

"Without doing any recruiting locally, we already have about one and a half million angry, unemployed men, many of them farmers, who are ready to blame Assad for their misfortune. One little push from us, and they'll trigger the revolution."

"So, the goal is regime change with Assad completely out of the picture?"

"Our objective is to undermine Assad's ability to govern the country without physically removing him from office."

"Why not just remove him?"

"The Syrian people support him. And it isn't just the Alawites. He also protects the interests of Christians and Druze. His army supports him, too, and a large percentage of those troops are Sunni. So, the goal is to render him irrelevant. We deploy jihadists to capture and hold large sections of the country and make it impossible for the central government to control the state."

"That's a tall order."

"Not really Our plan breaks the country into disconnected enclaves, each ruled by an al-Qaeda affiliate."

"And you expect this to be done by a bunch of head-chopping jihadists?"

"They're the fodder who will lead the charge. We'll send in our Special Forces to do the heavy work and then initiate a country-wide no-fly zone."

"That's still a tall order, especially if the army still supports Assad. And I don't suppose Iran will sit idly by, or Hezbollah or the Russians for that matter."

"It'll be a hell of a mess, but sometimes you need to do ugly things to make the right things happen."

"But why turn Syria into another Iraq? Iraq had a highly educated successful middle class with good jobs, and now it's a destroyed country."

"I guess it depends on what kind of world you want to have," Bob said. "The US wants to see a world where terrorists and their backers are defeated. We're just trying to contribute to the greater good of the region."

Fouad agreed about the peaceful world part but not the way Jenkins wanted to go about it.

"But why go after Assad? He's just a doctor and probably not even in charge of anything. I feel sorry for him."

"Have you ever met him?" Bob asked.

"No, but I don't think he's the monster you make him out to be."

"You're an Intelligence officer, and you still believe that kind of rubbish? You're living here without a clue about what's really going on, my friend. That's why it's so important that we come in and fix things."

"Is destroying a country fixing things or making it worse?"

"Have you forgotten the suicide bombing at the Marine compound here in '83 when Iran sent in one of their so-called martyrs and killed several hundred Marines?"

"Of course I haven't forgotten that mess. Intelligence should have had a better handle on what was happening, and it failed."

"Exactly, and since you can't sort out this kind of behavior from a rogue state like Iran, hell, you can't even control Hezbollah right in your own back yard, that's why we have to do it. This isn't the Switzerland of the Middle East you think it is, Fouad, but maybe we can help make it what you want it to be."

"*Inchallah*," Fouad said, as the dishes were being cleared. "A bit more wine?"

"Yes, with pleasure. Wouldn't want those last drops to go to waste." And as Fouad was pouring the wine he heard a voice he recognized call out Bob's name.

"Sorry I'm so late, Bob. The prime minister asked to see me just as I was leaving to join you."

Fouad looked up to see his boss, Ahmad Raki.

CHAPTER TWENTY-THREE

Sonia was still in the doldrums over Nadia's note and a bit miffed at Fouad for reneging on their living arrangements, but when she saw the effort he'd put into her homecoming she forgot about feeling miserable.

Her apartment sparkled. The afternoon sun shown in on her apricot walls and dark burgundy and orange Persian carpets, casting an orangey blush over the living and dining rooms, and nothing could have been more inviting. The glass doors giving onto the balcony were open, and the scent of her Damascene roses filled the air. From the kitchen, the smell of meat and spice-scented kibbeh pies filled her nostrils, and she realized for the first time in a long while that she was hungry. She smiled. She was happy to be home.

"Your friends Camille and Leila called. They'd like to stop by tomorrow to pay you a visit," said Fouad over lunch. "I said yes. I hope you don't mind."

"Of course I don't."

"And I also invited Andrew and Paul, and Joe who might bring his lady friend Aziza, whom you've not yet met. Joe and Andrew have become good buddies. They've even found an apartment to share. It'll be a welcome home party to cheer you up, my darling."

"No need to apologize, and I'm glad you included Camille and Leila. She offered to help Andrew with his Arabic."

"From what I hear, Andrew's Arabic is actually quite good. He's understood, and his patients love him. He even says he's happy, although I don't see how that's possible. Working in a hellhole like Shatilla can't be easy."

* * *

Andrew was the first to arrive with a bouquet of flowers.
"For the lady of the hour," he said, bowing. "And how wonderful to see you home and doing so well. And you look very stylish with your eye patch."

"Thank you, darling, and for all your visits and good cheer."

Sonia was pleasantly surprised by how much Andrew changed every time she saw him. No, it was not so much a change, she thought, as a sense of self-confidence he had assumed about himself and his place in the world. He had put on another pound or two and even with the streaks of grey beginning to show in his thick crop of dark hair, he was still the most handsome and seductive man she knew. He made no mention of Nadia, for which she was grateful, and he joked with Paul as if he had known him for years. And she was delighted to see Joe again, his part alley cat part sage she had found so suave and drop-dead gorgeous when she had met him at the retreat. Aziza was captivating too, and apparently a star at Shatilla. Sonia was not sure how Joe knew her, but they appeared to know each other very well. Shortly after his arrival, Fouad grabbed Joe and led him to the balcony where they carried on a lengthy conversation, seemingly oblivious to everyone around them. *What could possibly be so important*, she wondered?

When Camille arrived and walked into the living room on his new prostheses, everyone cheered. And there was the beautiful Leila alongside her uncle, wearing a pretty dress that showed off her long, tanned arms with no makeup and smelling of jasmine, and Sonia was suddenly horribly jealous because here was a woman who did not need to do anything to make herself attractive. She had been tortured in Khiam prison, yet she had managed to put that behind her. And here *she* was, Sonia thought of herself, the woman who, at one time, could have seduced any man and now was nothing more than a broken, ugly wreck that no one wanted.

And when she broke out of her reverie, she saw Andrew and Leila in a corner talking, and she was reminded of the first time he had seen Nadia in her Georgetown house. She hated Leila for being so like Nadia, and even hated Andrew for choosing Nadia, and now possibly Leila, instead of her. In a brief moment of reflection, she reminded herself that she had agreed to change her vengeful ways. The hell with that idea, she thought. It was more fun hating the people she loved.

She did decide, on the spot, to lose weight and exercise, and turn herself back into the *femme fatale* she had once been.

Finally, Fouad and Joe rejoined the gathering and bottles of prosecco were opened and hors d'oeuvres were served. When the party began, she decided it was more fun, after all, to love the people she hated.

CHAPTER TWENTY-FOUR

Early morning was Andrew's favorite time to sit on his balcony. It was still relatively cool, especially since it was supposed to reach the high nineties later in the day. The sea was at its loveliest too, glittering as it did like specks of diamonds, its waves gently hugging the shoreline, careful not to awaken a city still dormant. In what would be his only quiet moment of the day, and cognizant of how lonely he was, he fell into a meditative state. While he tried to hold onto the memory of Nadia, Leila had walked into his life when he had least expected it, and he found himself, in spite of some guilt, quite smitten. There was a freshness about her that he rather liked and an intoxicating scent that lingered with him for hours. He decided to ask her to help him at Shatilla. She had volunteered there in the '80s. Not only did he need help, he rather liked the idea of having her by his side. Glancing at his watch, he realized he was running late. He sipped the rest of his Arabic coffee and finished his *zaatar manoushe.*

He hopped on his bike, pedaling up the steep, long hill from his apartment, past several blocks of expensive high rises to the newly renovated Kuwaiti embassy. The policeman at the intersection, a regular on his route and dressed in his dark grey uniform, matching cap and mid-calf black leather boots, smiled and waved. As a tribute to Andrew, who was a local celebrity, he brought the traffic in the roundabout to a halt, allowing him to pedal safely to the other side, adjacent to the *Stade de Cheila,* a large sports stadium where the local soccer teams played their matches. With a wave of thanks, Andrew continued down the road, weaving through the traffic-clogged neighborhood with cars, as usual, stopped helter-skelter, until he reached Rue Sabra, the main entrance into Shatilla where street vendors, their carts a colorful array of zucchini, eggplant, tomatoes and okra alongside watermelon, apricots, loquats and cherries, waited for the morning shoppers, mostly women who enjoyed the sport of price haggling.

Word had gotten around that he was the only American in the clinic system and a bit of a hero for some of the things he had done. Those who knew him along his route waved and shouted *"Marhaba, Hakeme,"* good morning, doctor, as he pedaled past. A passerby said hello, and he responded with a *Marhabtain*. He loved how *Marhaba* could be repeated to mean *good morning* twice in a language he was growing to love. And as he got better and more fluent, he realized how much it had altered not only his personality but the very things he used in his daily life. They took on a different feel, a different taste, a new smell. It was the first time he had become fluent in a foreign language, and with that came a wonderful sense of belonging. He was living in a foreign country and had been adopted and loved as one of its own, and he had never experienced anything like that before.

Since beginning his work at Shatilla, he was proud to see Rue Sabra, remembered as the place of mass slaughter, finally begin to distinguish itself and play host to local art exhibits and Arabic music festivals with musicians from Lebanon's Conservatory of Music participating. For the first time, the camp had also invited Palestinian Girl and Boy Scouts from all twelve refugee camps, each troop participating in an award ceremony and then parading up and down Rue Sabra, the girls in their green vests, white shirts and khaki skirts, the boys in their tan shirts, olive green trousers and red ties.

To his dismay, the situation in the camp began to dramatically deteriorate a few weeks later. Regular garbage collection suddenly stopped. Rubbish began to pile up along Rue Sabra until it became a mountain so high it reached the second floor level of an apartment building, leaving only a two-foot wide passageway, obliging anyone entering or leaving the camp to walk alongside it via a densely packed path. The stench, a smell akin to hydrogen sulfate mixed with methane gas, with a tinge of sickening sweetness like that from a carcass left to rot in the hot sun, might have been less offensive to the olfactory senses in a colder month, but it was thirty-six degrees Celsius. To keep from retching, Andrew took to covering his nose and mouth with his handkerchief every time he had to cross while a dozen young boys, bandanas tied around their nose and mouth, scavenged for things worth having. The first time he saw them doing this, he stopped his bike and shouted to them to leave because it was a health risk, but they ignored his warning and went about their business.

It was this very morning, as he had tried to navigate the pathway, that he was thrown into the garbage. He had to get off and push his bike through the passage since a rotund young woman with a couple of children waddled ahead of him. The children all began retching at the smell, and the woman suddenly fainted and fell sideways into the morass of garbage. Andrew set his bike on its stand and tried to pull the woman out. She came to, panicked, and dragged him in with her. Filthy and embarrassed, but not without words of gratitude, the mother and her children hurried off while Andrew, dripping with slime, hopped on his bike and hurried off to Aziza's office located in the former Palestinian Authority compound at the far end of Rue Sabra. He locked his bike beside the door and ran in to see if she was in her office where he hoped to clean himself up.

"Help me," he said, when he appeared at her office door.

"Oh my God, what happened?"

She jumped up from her chair behind her desk and came toward him but backed off when she smelled the stink.

"I fell in the garbage."

"What were you doing?" she asked.

"I lost my footing and fell."

Why bother her with all the wretched details? he thought.

She closed her office door, then turned and said, "Take off your clothes while I find you clean ones."

He looked at her with surprise.

"What? You plan to go to your clinic smelling like shit?" She left, closing the door behind her.

Andrew peeled off all his clothes and there he stood naked and embarrassed, especially since he had been standing in front of the woman responsible for sparking his libido. He felt a bit guilty about being attracted to Aziza when she was already attached to Joe and concluded it must be the Caucasian-Arab mix of thick black hair and deep dark eyes that so intrigued him. Maybe that was one of the reasons he stayed there. He liked the women, especially the strong, courageous ones who were descended from centuries of warriors, some of whom claimed to be Phoenician.

To avoid smelling the stench, Andrew opened the only window in the room, thankful it looked onto a deserted alley and not the main thoroughfare where everyone could have seen him. Being an American, he longed for the simplicity of jumping into a shower, hot water available at the flick of a knob. Here he was, instead, sweating and trying to swish off slime that had already caked onto his skin, and he wondered out loud what the fuck he was doing there.

Aziza returned with clothes, a towel, a bar of soap and a man Andrew knew from the camp who carried a tub of water. He laughed when he saw Andrew.

"What's Walid laughing about?" Andrew asked.

"He's just pleased and a bit embarrassed because he's been asked to help. Everyone in the camp is talking about what you did for that young mother. Now, let's get you washed up." She directed him to kneel over the water.

"I can do it myself," he said, still embarrassed.

"*Walou,* for once let someone help you, Andrew."

He said nothing and let her wash his hair, back and upper arms before handing him the soap and a towel.

"I'll let you do the rest while I get rid of these foul-smelling clothes."

"Check the pockets first," he said. "My billfold and ID should be in the right back pocket of my slacks." *And my photo of Nadia,* he thought. "My Nokia is in the other pocket. It's got all my telephone numbers, so I'd hate to lose it." He kept thinking Nadia might call.

"They're still there," she reassured him, removing them and wiping them off.

Aziza returned as he was trying to put on a pair of tennis shoes that were a bit too small.

"I was convinced that God had abandoned us," she said, "but then He sent us you."

"Please Aziza..."

"No, let me finish. Your dedication has infected everyone in this camp. You make us feel less forgotten. And we don't tell you often enough how much we appreciate you."

"Let's talk about something more serious. Fifteen thousand people use Rue Sabra every day. Why isn't anyone talking about the garbage crisis?"

"Do you think we haven't been discussing it? Well," she said, hesitating, "to be honest, I talk and talk and everyone here seems to be asleep. Maybe it's because it's summer and hot and people are depressed. I get that. I'm depressed too. I ask for help, and no one shows any interest in volunteering."

"So, I'll continue seeing patients with respiratory infections and skin lesions in my clinic? If this keeps up, Aziza, we'll have a cholera epidemic on our hands. That isn't just speculation. It's a real probability if we don't do something. Should I go to the Palestinian Authority and address the issue? They must have an office somewhere in Beirut."

"Of course they do, but as you've noticed, it isn't inside the camp. God forbid that those worthless, corrupt bastards would live with their own people."

"Okay, I guess that's a no. So should I go to the Lebanese authorities?"

"They hate us."

"Why can't we organize a garbage disposal system so we aren't dependent on anyone?"

"That's a great idea, but who will do it?"

"Maybe after my twelve-hour shift I can help in my spare time."

"What spare time?" she replied.

She missed my irony, he thought. *Maybe I should not be boasting about my Arabic language skills if I am not properly understood.*

"I'll try to find some volunteers, Aziza. I know you can't do everything yourself."

Annoyed by his own sense of powerlessness, he thanked her and walked out of her office and down a corridor past three other rooms that reeked of cigarette smoke. On the way in, he had not noticed either the portrait of Yasser Arafat with his trademark stubble and keffayah, or the posters of young martyrs who had recently been killed in Palestine plastered on the walls.

Once outside, he called Leila, thankful she had given him her cell phone number.

"Any chance you could start helping me at Shatilla?" he asked. "I'm a bit overwhelmed and—"

"No need to apologize. Uncle and I are in Beirut these days, and I'd be happy to help. When do you need me?"

"Now. I'm already having a lousy day, and it's only just begun."

"I can probably be there in about half an hour."

"Thanks. I'll have someone wait for you at the camp entrance."

"That won't be necessary... I know the camp well. I'll find you."

Back on Rue Sabra, he walked some twenty paces before entering a dimly lit alleyway. Taking a quick left, he then walked up the two wide cement steps to the next level, then right at the corner between a barber shop, already bustling with clients, and a video arcade full of unemployed men with nothing better to do. In certain places along his route, the passage was so narrow he could stretch out his arms and touch the damp walls, while overhead, dangling wet clothes from the upper floors of buildings, some scarcely penetrated by natural light, intersected with impossible tangles of black, snake-like wires hooked to loud generators, their motors pumping out power to the surrounding apartment buildings.

Andrew continued another half block, along a wider path that saw a bit more sun, and past a drycleaner and a hair salon squeezed in between dilapidated, cinder-block three and four-story buildings that looked to be on the point of collapse, until he reached his clinic. Once just another old house in ruin, it had been entirely refurbished with large welcoming windows on either side of a wide front door and painted steel gray. A bright red banner with the words "Doctors Without Borders" hung across the front of the clinic.

It was home to a staff of six doctors who each worked twelve-hour shifts, five days a week and every sixth weekend. The clinic employed a secretary and four full-time nurses. The staff wore white—the physicians, cotton jackets with the Doctors Without Borders logo on the breast pocket; the others, aprons with the same logo.

Wooden benches, hardly adequate for the number of patients who streamed through the door each day, lined either side of the clean, spacious, white-walled waiting room. The six examining rooms were sparsely equipped with a desk, two chairs and an examining table. Although Doctors Without Borders operated and funded thirteen medical facilities throughout the country, primarily in the Palestinian camps, Andrew realized that number was wholly inadequate for the number of patients in dire need of their services. And in contrast to the modern, well-equipped Hotel Dieu Hospital where Sonia had been treated, Shatilla's clinic had a basic x-ray machine and a lab that could only do a simple CBC, blood sugar and urine analysis.

Andrew and his colleagues treated everything from diabetes, hypertension and asthma to pregnancies, malnutrition, diarrhea and minor illnesses and could, when necessary, stabilize seriously ill patients before transferring them to a nearby hospital where they had referral privileges. Shatilla used to have its own hospital, the ten-story Gaza Hospital, run by the Palestine Red Crescent Society, but lack of funding had forced its closure years prior. The building now housed Syrian refugees.

That same day, after Aziza had cleaned him up, she turned up at his office with her sister Myriam. They brought him a bag full of falafel for lunch.

"I hate to bother you, Andrew, but we have a crisis," she said and handed him a wrinkled piece of colored cellophane.

"What's this?" Andrew asked, turning the paper over in his hand.

"It's a chewing gum wrapper. The gum was laced with heroin."

"We'd better talk inside," he said, and invited the two women to sit in white plastic chairs that he pulled in from one of the examining rooms.

"Okay, Aziza, what's this all about?" he asked.

"Since this concerns my twelve-year-old daughter," said Myriam, "I think I should tell the story."

"Go ahead," Andrew said, looking at the pretty woman with large dark eyes who did not look old enough to have a twelve-year-old child. Unlike Aziza, who dressed in jeans, tennis shoes and a loose blouse, Myriam wore a hijab, long robe and open-toed plastic slippers.

"My daughter is both a drug addict and a pusher. She's been selling drugs to other students," Myriam said, tears streaming down her cheeks. "Aziza, tell Dr. Andrew the rest, please. I'm not able…"

"My niece attends Ramallah School," Aziza continued where her sister left off. "It's one of the UN run schools."

"I thought their schools were better monitored. How long has this been going on?"

"Not long," said Aziza. "As soon as the staff discovered what she was doing, they suspended her. I only just found out because I happened to drop by to visit my sister this morning after you left my office and found her sobbing. As soon as she told me the story, I went to see the headmaster who assured me that since this came to light they'd become much more vigilant. I then visited the UN authorities to make sure they were aware of the problem."

"How did she pay for the drugs?" asked Andrew.

"So long as she sold the drugs to other students her handlers supplied her with her own personal stash," Aziza said.

"How is this possible? She's only twelve years old."

"Easy," Aziza said. "The dealers sell the drugs outside the primary and secondary school. They give someone like my niece free drug-injected candy. Once she's hooked, she'll do anything for her daily dose, and so agrees to sell to her fellow students."

"What kind of drugs are we talking about?"

Aziza held a paper up and said, "It includes everything from hashish, cocaine powder and crack to captagon and tramadol. What the drug dealers can't inject into candy and chewing gum, they rub on. And a chewing gum costs 250 Lebanese pounds, twenty-five cents, a minimal amount of money. The more expensive drugs like Tramadol cost five dollars for thirty pills, Zanax, seven dollars for eight pills."

"What's being done to address this problem?" Andrew asked. Was it his place to continually question the authorities? *Yes,* he thought, *if I am working here and trying to make things better, I have the right to speak up.*

"The camp's political and social committee is having a meeting tonight at seven. I've added this to the agenda so we can discuss it. Please come. We need you to help us."

"I'll be there, and thanks for bringing me lunch."

Aziza smiled. "After this morning's crisis, I thought you could do with a special treat."

After Aziza and her sister left, Andrew closed his office door, sat in his chair, tipped it back, put his feet on his desk and one by one popped a few of the falafel into his mouth. He was about to ask his secretary to bring him a coffee when someone knocked on his door.

He promptly brought his feet to the ground before responding. "Come in." The door opened and Leila walked in.

"Sorry I couldn't get here sooner. The traffic was impossible."

"No worries, I'm just relieved to see you," he said, standing and greeting her with a kiss on each cheek. "Just when I thought my horrid day couldn't get any worse, it just did. Apparently, we have a major drug crisis in the camp."

"Tell me what to do, and I'll do it." Leila smiled up into his eyes, she about six inches shorter than Andrew who was six foot two.

"Just stay close, and do whatever I tell you."

Later that afternoon, he asked one of his colleagues, Dr. Jahn Sewell, to join Leila and him in his office for a coffee break.

"Jahn, I'd like you to meet my friend Leila. She's going to be volunteering here."

"We should do this more often, especially if I get to meet a beautiful woman. Welcome Leila."

Jahn dropped into a chair and let out a sigh. A Norwegian, probably in his late fifties, he was tall, blonde, fair-skinned, well-built and fit except for a bit of bulge around his waist. "I'm so tired by the time I leave here that I can barely see to drive home."

"I know what you mean, except in my case, it's more dangerous. I ride a bike."

They all laughed and Jahn pulled a cigarette out of his breast pocket. "Mind if I light up?"

"Not at all," Andrew said, realizing how relaxed he had become about people smoking around him.

"Leila, any objections?"

"I'm Lebanese. Everyone smokes here."

As Andrew watched Jahn take a few drags, he told him about the drug crisis in the camp and the meeting that evening and why it was being called.

"Leila, I'll fill you in later on what happened here today, and I hope you'll be able to stay for the meeting."

"Of course."

"Jahn, did you know we had a drug problem in the camp?"

He shook his head. "But I'm not surprised. The youth in this camp are the target of the worst kind of scum. I've been here for five years."

"I hadn't realized you'd been here that long."

"I don't know how I've stuck it out for so long, frankly. I have a love-hate relationship with this place. And since we're talking about addiction, maybe this camp is my addiction and why I can't walk away from it. Over the years, I've watched things inside the camp get harder and harder for people—parents who are unemployed, marital abuse, disgruntled, bored teens—yet they somehow manage to pull themselves up and carry on. I love these people, Andrew. They've taught me what it means to be human in the face of extreme deprivation."

"That's one of the things that struck me the most when I visited the camp the first time," Andrew said. "You have the dead buried here and the living alongside them and somehow they manage this symbiotic relationship with great dignity even in the midst of despair."

"Aziza's parents are buried here. Did you know that?"

Andrew turned to Leila. "You met Aziza at Sonia's. She's Joe's friend."

"Yes, she's a remarkable woman for what she does here."

"Her father was the camp surgeon," Jahn said. "He ran Gaza Hospital during the Israeli invasion of '82. He was a real hero. The Israelis were carpet bombing the city, and there he was performing surgery under the most deplorable conditions."

"I remember him," Leila said. "I worked briefly in that hospital."

"Aziza is a lot like her father, isn't she?" Andrew asked.

"Indeed, and may the good Lord protect her," Jahn said. "Under the most impossible of odds, she never seems to lose faith."

Andrew opened the bag of falafel and offered some to Leila and Jahn.

"Thanks," Jahn said, taking one. "I was hungry. This will help until I get home."

Leila put up her hand. "I ate before I came."

"How did things get so bad for these people?" Andrew asked.

"Simple. Because no one cares," Jahn said. "They're the all-purpose scapegoats for all of Lebanon's problems. Unfortunately, to some degree, there's a reason for this."

"Why is that?"

"When Yasser Arafat was expelled from Jordan in '70, he came to Beirut and went about setting up a state within a state inside the camp, thinking himself impervious to Lebanese laws. To make matters worse, during the Israeli invasion when they were carpet bombing Beirut, he boasted that the road to Palestine led through Beirut. The Lebanese have long memories. They haven't forgotten his arrogance, and I'm not sure I blame them. Unfortunately, they lump all Palestinians in their hatred for Arafat. The drug problem is no different. Instead of addressing it as a Lebanese societal problem, they take the easy way out and blame it on the Palestinians, and nothing gets done to solve the problem."

"Leila knows a lot about that sordid period of history," Andrew said. "She was captured and tortured by the Israelis and thrown into Khiam prison for nine years."

"You're a rare Lebanese hero," Jahn said. "It's an honor to know you."

Leila bowed her head to acknowledge his comment.

"Sadly, it's the children who are paying the price for events that occurred before they were born," Leila said.

"Many of these problems could have been avoided if Lebanon had adhered to the 1951 Refugee Convention that granted Palestinians in Lebanon the same rights as refugees worldwide," she said. "That includes the right to work and the right to own a home."

"You're right, Leila," Jahn said. "We have 70 percent unemployment in this camp alone. It's no wonder the youth are turning to drugs. They see no future, no hope of anything ever getting better."

"Why hasn't Lebanon been called out on the international stage for its abuses?" Andrew asked.

"No one cares a damn about the Palestinians, not even their own diaspora," Jahn said, standing. "I could talk about this for hours, but it's time I got back to work. Thanks for lunch and for introducing me to Leila. About the meeting tonight, don't worry about your patients, just leave when you need to. I'll look after them."

"Thanks, Jahn."

"And Andrew," he said, as he was about to close the door, "I know I speak for all my colleagues when I say we're awfully glad you're here."

Before he resumed seeing patients, Andrew contacted Paul. He explained what was going on in the camp and asked if he would attend the meeting.

"Of course, and here is the perfect excuse for you to invite Leila," he said.

"What do you mean?" he said, looking at her and smiling.

"I know you're sweet on her, so go ahead and give her a call."

Andrew laughed. "I'm way ahead of you, friend. Leila is already here working with me, and Paul, if Joe's free, ask him to come too."

When he closed with Paul he looked at Leila. "He wanted me to invite you to the meeting."

She laughed. "I'm glad I have so many allies among your friends."

"So am I, and you are welcome to stay with Joe and me tonight so you won't have to drive home. It could be very late when we finish the meeting. We have a guest bedroom."

* * *

Andrew and Leila arrived at the hall just as the meeting was being called to order. Aziza, as camp leader, and two other women he didn't know sat on an improvised dais in a crowded room full of teachers, UN personnel and parents angry over the brazen drug selling targeting their kids.

Above the shouts and angry voices, Aziza attempted to call the meeting to order. Finally, someone in the audience whistled and got everyone's attention. After she read the committee reports, she explained in detail why she had added the additional item to the agenda.

"In light of a drug crisis that has come to our attention, our social committee has put together a list of resolutions we'd like your permission to pass," she said. "We plan to close down the illegal drug shops and the so-called pharmacies that sell these drugs."

"How do you propose doing that?" someone asked.

"We'll increase camp policing and establish a hotline to anonymously report drug transactions."

An elderly man stood up and asked to speak.

"*Sitt*, explain how more policing will help. Two days ago, three drug dealers were arrested inside our camp. They were held by camp security pending transfer the following morning to the Lebanese authorities. During the night, the dealers offered the camp guard a two thousand dollar bribe. The man earns two hundred a month so, of course, he took the bribe. I ask you, who among us can blame him?"

"We should all blame him," said one of the camp elders. "Where is the son of a bitch? He agreed to be part of our security team. He had a responsibility to act morally, and he didn't. He should be punished."

A woman standing and holding a small child said, "I agree. I have three school-aged children, and I'm scared for them. I have no way to protect them from drug dealers."

Aziza stood up. "We all need to help one another, and we need to adopt these resolutions so we can begin implementing them immediately. No more excuses, no more turning a blind eye to illicit crimes. If we all pledge to say no to petty corruption, we'll refuse to be corrupted over the bigger issues that confront us and our children."

A young man raised his hand and asked to speak.

"I sell drugs inside the camp." And before he could say another word, people began cursing him and demanding he be thrown out of the camp.

"Let me speak. I have something important to say," he said. "There's a reason I turned to crime, and I hold the camp leaders responsible. Our water is salty—"

"That's not our leader's fault," shouted a man in the back of the room. "Blame the Lebanese government."

The drug dealer continued. "We have little electricity. Two children on my street were electrocuted last month from bad wiring. Our air is polluted."

"All of Lebanon's air is unsafe to breathe, not just ours," mumbled someone, and everyone agreed.

"We have no regular garbage collection," he said. "Sewage runs down our streets when it rains. Our children don't have a playground, and our parents can't get work outside the camp."

"What he says is true," shouted someone in the audience.

"Even if it's true," said another, "that doesn't give him the right to become a drug dealer and sell drugs to our children."

"In Lebanon, there are basically only two jobs open to young Palestinian men like me," he said. "We can accept a gun and join one of the militias run by Lebanese politicians, or we can sell drugs, also supplied by the same politicians."

A middle-aged man stood up. "I condemn what he does, but his grievances are valid."

A respected older Palestinian man who ran an NGO inside the camp raised his hand and stood.

"Even if the Lebanese authorities do take camp drug dealers into custody, one of three things are likely to occur. The drug dealer pays a bribe and is let go, he is freed as the result of political protection by someone he works for, or after a few days, he will be released by the Lebanese police after agreeing to become a camp spy, a valued service for those monitoring camp affairs."

"These are just a few of the reasons we have so little confidence in our camp leadership's ability to make changes," another voice shouted out.

"We need outside help," another said.

"Yeah, but where is that going to come from? We're feared and despised by the Lebanese."

"That's precisely why we called this meeting tonight," shouted Aziza above the dissenting voices. "We need to take matters into our own hands. I acknowledge that we haven't lived up to your expectations, and some ugly things have happened, but I pledge to all of you that we will implement change, and it will begin immediately. We will clean out the camp from drug dealers and illicit pharmacies. If we don't, our children will continue to suffer, and that's why we need everyone to help. So, let's all agree to the proposed resolutions and that we're in this together for the long haul, and that we'll find a way to resolve our crises."

Aziza asked for a vote. Her resolutions were unanimously passed.

"Before I close this meeting, I have one more very important item we need to discuss. I've invited Dr. Andrew here tonight. He has something to say, and I respectfully ask that all of you listen very carefully."

"Thank you, Aziza," Andrew said, jumping onto the dais. "From a medical standpoint, I believe we have a perfect storm brewing in our camp. It's caused by two things… drugs and garbage. If we can't curtail the drug use and we continue to allow our garbage to pile up, we're going to have a cholera outbreak in the camp."

He found himself looking at a sea of shocked faces. He continued.

"Our children are the most vulnerable at the moment. They're the ones being targeted. Drug use weakens the immune system and makes them susceptible to all kinds of diseases. That in of itself is bad enough, but the situation is aggravated by the garbage problem."

"Doctor, what we need is an anti-drug intifada," yelled a young man.

"You take care of organizing your intifada, and I'll try to ward off a cholera epidemic. Now pay careful attention to the symptoms— diarrhea, nausea and vomiting, severe dehydration, rapid heart rate, thirst and muscle cramps. If you start to exhibit any of these symptoms, we want to see you at our clinic. Treatment includes oral hydration kits. We have a limited supply on hand but will try to get more from the other camps as soon as possible. For severe cases, we can administer IV fluids, antibiotics and zinc supplements. I'll close by promising that we will try to do something about the garbage, but as Aziza just said, we can't do it alone. It has to be a group effort, and I expect, for the good of our camp, that everyone will do their part. If you have any questions or want to volunteer, please come see me in my office. Thank you."

The audience applauded, and the meeting was adjourned. Andrew found it very gratifying to have so many people come up and thank him. When most had left, the drug dealer approached him.

"I appreciate what you do here. I'm part of the problem, but I want things in the camp to change. I'd like to help if you think I can."

"What's your name?"

When he said his name, Andrew said, "Come see me tomorrow at the clinic, Malik, and we'll talk about some of the ways you can help."

And as he turned to leave, Andrew said, "What you did tonight took a lot of courage. Thank you."

The young man nodded before he turned and left the room.

He found Leila, Paul and Joe at the back of the hall waiting for him. Paul shook his head. "I had no idea things had gotten to this level. We need to talk and figure out what to do. Let's have dinner. Joe, why don't you ask Aziza to join us?"

"Great idea," he said, and he went off to find her.

"Leila, since you're going to be working here, why don't you move into the spare bedroom Joe and I have. I'm sure he'd agree that a beautiful lady would be a welcome addition to our humble abode. It would also be more convenient than fighting traffic every morning."

Was he sounding too enthusiastic? he wondered. Hell, what did he care. He was suddenly happier than he had been in a long time.

"It's a deal. Give me a day to go home and pack."

"You realize though, that I don't really have any free time to devote to some of these problems, that you may end up doing more than you ever bargained for. I'm already swamped and—"

"Don't worry. I'll be here for you. I can act as your secretary or nurse. I do have some medical training... anything that will help make a difference."

"Hey, don't leave me out in the cold," Paul said. "I'd like to help too, maybe on one of the camp committees. Just point me in their direction."

"Paul, you'd be a true God-send," said Andrew. "He's forsaken these people, so if you can step in and perform some miracles on His behalf, you'd be mighty welcome. We have a plethora of needs. You could get your own team together and help install good water supply facilities throughout the camp or create multiple sewage networks because none exist at the moment. Maybe you'd prefer to help devise a desperately needed garbage disposal system. You saw the mountain of rubbish. Take your pick. They're all urgent projects."

"While you're deciding, Paul, can we please get to the restaurant?" asked Leila. "I'm about to faint from hunger."

"I wouldn't want that to happen," Andrew said, taking her hand. "Let's go."

Over dinner, Andrew told them about his day.

"You're a hero," Leila said. "You saved that woman's life. She might have suffocated in that mountain of garbage if you hadn't pulled her out."

"Nonsense, you're making much ado about nothing if you ask me."

"Okay, hero," said Joe, "if that's all it is, you can buy us all dinner tonight."

"By the way, Joe, we have a guest sleeping over tonight."

"Whose bed?" He laughed.

"Let's not rush things," Andrew responded, squeezing Leila's hand. "She'll sleep in the guest room."

* * *

Over a glass of wine on the terrace before retiring, Andrew finally asked Leila about her captivity, in part to understand what Nadia might be going through at the hands of Jaafar.

During his time in Marjeyoun, Andrew had heard many stories about Leila—the Palestinian sympathizer who volunteered at the Gaza Hospital, the girl-warrior who joined the resistance movement after the Israeli invasion in 1982, the patriot who attempted to murder the Israeli who oversaw his country's brutal occupation of south Lebanon. The assassination attempt had failed, and Leila was caught. After an initial interrogation in Israel, she was transferred back to the Israeli-run Khiam prison near Marjeyoun where she endured nine years of solitary confinement, rape and torture by electric shock.

For her refusal to become an Israeli collaborator, she was kept in a three cubic square foot concrete box, in sweltering heat or bitter cold, for weeks at a time, her hands tied behind her back, knees to her chest, her feet pressed against the wall. Leila did not talk about what she had endured very often, and when called a hero she rejected the designation.

"Why don't you like to be called a hero?" he asked.

"To me, a hero is someone who displayed moral courage. I attempted to kill someone, a justifiable act against an enemy in time of war, but still a crime."

"How could you bring yourself to kill a man? I ask only because I'm not sure I could do it."

"It was easy. He was an enemy of my country."

"Were you afraid?"

"Yes, I was terrified. My hand shook so badly I could hardly hold the gun."

"How did the Israeli act? I would have imagined him jumping on you, tossing the gun from your hand."

"Odd that you'd ask that. I can still see his eyes, staring at me, incredulous."

"You actually saw his fear?"

"Yes, I saw it in his eyes. That's what gave me the courage to pull the trigger. I would have wanted his fear to last longer, but by then he would have regained his senses and come after me."

"Was it an Israeli who raped you?"

"No, it was my own people—the pigs from the south Lebanon Army. It's still difficult for me to discuss. I try very hard to block such ugliness from my mind. It's much healthier to concentrate on the good things in my life... like you, Andrew."

"You're obviously strong-willed, but how did you keep from going crazy?"

"All I did was survive by my wits."

"Explain, please."

"I did math puzzles in my head and wrote poetry on scraps of paper."

"What are you," Andrew laughed, "some kind of math genius?"

"My father and I used to play such games, an alternative to playing chess. He was a math teacher and knew how to engage a young mind. He saved my sanity."

"You knew the consequences if you didn't agree to collaborate with the Israelis. Were you ever tempted to just say okay, I'll cooperate?"

"No, I love my country. I was willing to do whatever I could to protect and preserve it. I still feel that way."

"That's the highest form of patriotism, Leila."

Andrew was only beginning to understand what nationalism meant and the extremes to which people were willing to go to protect home and country. Andrew also admired Leila for respecting his loyalty to a woman he had not seen or heard from in years. Little did she know this had given him the time, intentionally or not, to fall in love with her.

Andrew saw that her glass was empty. "Shall I pour you another?"

"No thanks. I'm in need of sleep, not wine. Can you show me my room?"

"Of course." She followed Andrew to the last room down the corridor. "Good night, I hope you sleep well." He kissed her on the check and watched her walk into the room and close the door, wishing he could wrap his arms around her and take her to his room.

CHAPTER TWENTY-FIVE

Andrew was in his clinic late one afternoon trying to see the last of his patient load before heading home when Aziza brought in a young woman, barely able to walk.

"It happened in the alley next to my house," she explained. "I saw them attacking her. She was beaten unconscious and left for dead. When the men left, I went to her, revived her and brought her here."

Andrew noticed her swollen eyes and the cruel knife lacerations across her cheeks, chest and forearms.

Andrew lifted the girl into his arms and placed her on the examining table.

"Who did this to you?"

She looked up at him, her eyes full of tears, then turned to Aziza.

"It was her brothers. I overheard the two of them shouting obscenities at her for being raped. It's always the same story here. The family finds out, and they do what they always do to a woman who has been sexually assaulted. They send their male members to kill her because she's brought shame on the family."

"Ignorant people," said Andrew.

"At least, this time, they didn't succeed."

"She's still been badly injured," said Andrew, his voice barely audible. As he looked at this beautiful young woman with long auburn hair, doe-shaped black eyes and long slim body, he thought of Nadia and almost cried out. *Had Jaafar raped her? If she knew she would eventually have to give in to Jaafar, I hope it was done on her terms, not his. I could not bear the thought of her being physically abused and disfigured. Maybe this woman, like other rape victims, saw the inevitability of her assault and understood the futility and risk of resisting, but was that any reason for her family to want her dead?* Whatever their backward thinking, Andrew was furious that the practice of honor killing still existed and insisted the men be found and brought to the clinic.

"They won't come," Aziza said.

"Have the camp police round them up then."

"You should know by now that women have few rights in our male-dominated culture," said Aziza.

Even though both Aziza and his nurse were present, the woman was embarrassed and pushed Andrew's hand away when he tried to examine her. Andrew understood her reluctance. After what she had been through, why would she want another male touching her body. He took great care to soothe her fears, speaking in a calm, reassuring voice, and she eventually relaxed and let him tend to her broken ribs, lacerated breasts and acute abdominal pain. He was claiming outrage at the men who tried to kill this woman, but what had he done to rescue Nadia? He had sworn to protect her from Jaafar, and he had failed at that too. He had trained with Joe and been prepared to carry out even the most extreme action to get her back, but then years had passed and here he was thinking about another woman. In his head, he tried to justify his moving on from a first bloom of love with Nadia that had lasted a brief six months to a woman who had endured nine years of torture and rape at the hands of her captors in the infamous Khiam prison.

When he had finished examining the woman, he offered a suggestion.

"Instead of sending her back home where she'll surely be subjected to more abuse, let's try to find her somewhere else to stay."

"I'll take her home with me," said Aziza. "No one will dare come for her there."

As he watched Aziza and his nurse walk the woman out of his examining room, and with his mind still full of Nadia, he wondered if Fouad had known all these years where she was. Did Joe, who had stepped into the role of protective older brother, know too? Was this deception their way of protecting him, or was this just the definition of a friend in a place like Beirut where most everything, including friendship, appeared as an illusion.

He sat at his desk, rested his head in his hands and closed his eyes. He jumped when he heard the clinic door open and someone shout.

"Andy?"

He recognized Paul's voice calling from the waiting room.

"I'm in my office," he shouted. "Come on back."

"What are you still doing here?" Paul asked.

"I could ask the same of you, my friend. How is the garbage recycling program going?"

"Very well, actually. We're making headway. I'm quite pleased, especially with the young men I have working with me. They are full of energy and have some great ideas."

"I'm glad someone I know is in high spirits."

"You're not?"

"I've found myself in a predicament that I'm not sure I know how to handle."

"This could only be about Leila."

"It has more to do with Nadia."

"Do you want to talk about it?"

"I try to convince myself that I'm waiting for her to return, but in the everyday crush of what I'm doing here, days, sometimes weeks pass, and she's completely absent from my mind. And then today, because of a rape victim I treated, thoughts of her came rushing back, stirring up emotions I thought I'd forgotten. And now something else has gone and happened to me, and it's not what I expected to happen and…"

"Now you're referring to Leila. I know you like her. I've seen you two together. It's so tender the way you interact."

"Yes, she's walked into my life and stolen my heart."

"It's okay to still care so deeply for one and yet love another. What a beautiful tribute to a woman you knew only six months. She must be quite remarkable, but it has been a long time, and she probably isn't coming back. People who fall into Syria's black hole usually don't resurface. So, enjoy Leila and love her. She's strong and vibrant and full of love for you. I'd say you're quite lucky."

"For some reason, it must be your Godly connection, Paul, it feels right that this advice should come from you."

"I'll always be here for you, Andrew, but I do worry about you. You're worn out. You never say no to anyone. You want to save mankind, but you're only one person."

Andrew nodded. "It's the hopeless, unwinnable battles I have to fight every day that wear me down. I love this place, but it's frightening."

"Lebanon has always been a complex country. It's because of this post-war decadence, where everything is permitted, that it's become an even darker place."

"And that's what's so confounding. On the surface, it's a seductive, sophisticated twenty-first century city you fall in love with and never want to leave, and then the veneer comes peeling off, and suddenly you see all its shit. And then there's me in all of this, a simple man trying to do a decent job."

"To these people, you're a miracle worker. I hear them talking in the camp. You're like a god to them."

A god? I am nothing of the kind, thought Andrew. *Here I am, ready to give up on a woman who spent thirteen years waiting for her husband and loving another who spent nine years in Khiam prison for her patriotism. They are the real heroes.*

Paul stood and pulled Andrew up from his chair. "I know the perfect cure for your ills. Go home and spend the evening with Leila. Tomorrow you'll feel like a new person. Come on, I'll walk you to your bike."

CHAPTER TWENTY-SIX

Nadia had a difficult time controlling her temper. Hassan wanted her to agree to marry him so they could travel to Istanbul. He had not actually proposed, at least not in the way she would have wanted. Instead, he had suggested an utterly outrageous idea, and for this she decided to play with his religious beliefs and did, until she figured out the real reason he was desperate to leave the country.

In all ways, she was already his wife, or whore, depending on who was asked, so what did an official paper mean to her other than a possible means of escape from a captor with whom she had a complicated love-hate relationship. *But why Istanbul?* she wondered. She was restless and in need of a change of scenery, but Paris would have been a far better option. Whatever they finally agreed to do, it would have to come with concessions.

Recently their conversations around the question of marriage had gone something like this:

"Why rush into marriage, Hassan, and why Istanbul?" she asked. "It's another terrible regime."

"Terrible or not, it's a place where I can keep you safe. No certainties, but I don't think the Turks will be part of the next war. They know the region is in a death spiral. The US wants regime change but doesn't know what it's doing. In the meantime, the Russians are waiting on the sidelines to see what the US will do.

"My immediate concern is Assad's approval of a pipeline running from Iran's side of the gas field to ports in Tarsus and Lebanon. It's going to upset the Sunnis."

"So, it's not just Iraq replayed for gas and oil reserves," Nadia said. "It's an ever-worsening Shiite-Sunni rift."

"The Saudis are already nervous. Their oil fields are in the Shiite-controlled part of their kingdom."

"Could the Saudis put down a Shiite uprising if it were to happen?"

"If the Iranians decided to intervene to protect the Shiites, probably not. But that's just the half of it. The US has plans to balkanize the country by allowing the jihadists to move across the Iraqi border from Mosul and Ramada into Deir Ezzor and Raqqa in eastern Syria to form a caliphate because—"

"Let me guess. That's the proposed route of the Qatari pipeline."

Hassan nodded. "Now you see why I want us to leave, Nadia. The Sunnis and the US see an urgent need to get rid of Assad, and if their jihadists are beheading Shiites in Iraq, what's to stop them from doing the same in Syria?"

"I wouldn't be any safer as a Christian. So, is this marriage proposal of yours a serious one?"

"It's the only way I can get you a passport."

"That's not what I asked."

"It is if you agree to become an Alawite." He didn't speak for a minute, probably hoping she would calmly consider his idea. And then out of that same silence came, "So, will you convert?"

The presumption that she would consider such a proposition threw Nadia into a rage.

"Why on earth would I convert? I don't practice my own religion, and for that matter, neither do you. In fact, I don't have to convert to any Muslim sect to marry you, but I'm sure you already know that, so how dare you try to trick me. Just in case you've forgotten, let me remind you. Any Muslim, whether he be a Sunni, Shiite or Alawite, can marry a non-Muslim woman if she be Christian or Jewish because they're both 'people of the book.' The Alawite religion is beautiful, and you're defaming it by making claims that aren't true."

"What do you know about my religion?" he asked, still trying to defend his request.

"I know that the Sunni-Shiite divide dates back to the years immediately following the death of the Prophet Mohammed in 632 and that he died without appointing an heir. The Sunnis thought it should have been his advisor, Abu Bakr. The Shiites insisted it should have been Mohammed's cousin and son-in-law, Ali."

During Hassan's long absences, Nadia had taken advantage of his library to study up on the Alawites—things particular to matters of marriage and other minutiae she had found interesting such as Alawites comprised about 12 percent of Syria's twenty-three million people. This meant that Bashar, an Alawite, ruled over a 74 percent majority Sunni population. Christians, including both Armenians and Assyrians, represented another 10 percent, and the Druze weighed in at only three.

Nadia continued. "The Alawites are a recent religion dating back to only the ninth and tenth centuries, and their beliefs include bits of both Judaism and Christianity. No wonder the Sunnis consider Alawites infidels, and the fact that they believe in Jesus and celebrate Christmas makes them worse than infidels.

"So, Hassan, if anyone needs to convert, it's you since you believe in as many Christian tenets as I do."

"*Touché*." He laughed, putting up his hands in mock surrender. "I apologize. I should have been more thoughtful."

"Thoughtful? No, you should have been honest. This marriage proposal is about what's best for you. You want me to consent so you can keep me prisoner and take me across the border into Turkey so you can escape the jihadists. In exchange, you're not willing to give me what I want."

"And what is that, Nadia?"

"Damn it, Hassan, I want the right to choose to become your wife without coercion or fear of being killed by crazed fanatics."

"Does this mean you'll consider my proposal?"

"It means there are concessions that need to be made, concessions that only you can agree to."

She sat quiet for a moment, waiting to see what he would say next.

"Nadia," he said, finally, taking her hand in his and kissing it. "I sincerely apologize. I love you with my whole being. I hope you know that I'd never intentionally insult you."

"Apology accepted, Hassan, but let's come to an understanding. I'll answer your question when you're prepared to respond to mine."

Nadia remained adamant but not without some trepidation. For the first time since her capture, she was in a position to extract an important concession, and then he had gone and spoiled it.

"I'll be away most of tomorrow, but I promise you an answer over dinner."

"What?" Nadia said. "You're going to make me wait until tomorrow? What could be more important than this discussion?"

"Stopping the Americans from destroying my country. I'm meeting a Lebanese colleague in Lattakia for lunch tomorrow to discuss the latest developments."

Nadia stared at Hassan. Suddenly she understood. "This isn't about the jihadists, is it Hassan? It's Robert Jenkins you're afraid of, and who you want to escape from."

When he looked at her, Nadia saw the fear in his eyes.

"Yes, he has the power to do anything he wants with me."

"What did he threaten you with?"

"Throwing me into some hell-hole where no one could find me and torturing me until I die."

"Why would he say such a hideous thing?"

"Years ago, I killed one of his agents in Beirut. It was pretty well covered up thanks to my colleague in Beirut, and the bastard deserved what he got, but somehow Jenkins found out, and he's using it as blackmail to force me to help him destroy my country."

"What are you going to do?"

"Fight him as much as I'm able. I've told him this although there's not much I can do to stop a conspiracy that's been planned for years. I'm a Syrian patriot, no different than any other man who loves his country. There's going to be a third world war here, Nadia, and I'll do whatever I can to prevent it."

Syria was hardly a democracy but then what country was, Nadia wondered. But it was the last highly educated, independent, secular Arab nationalist state in the Middle East. As important, it was religiously ecumenical and a staunch refuge for minorities, particularly Christians.

As Hassan had reminded her, Syria had opened its doors to at least half a million Chaldean Christians fleeing Iraq.

The claim that Syria was part of the "Axis of Evil," the US government's Syria Accountability Act of 2002 charging Syria with the crime of supporting terrorism and seeking chemical weapons, and most recently, new sanctions aimed at diminishing its oil revenues from oil exports—all of this, Hassan had explained, was an effort to break down the government and increase public opposition to the regime.

"Israel sees the destruction of Syria as a way to weaken its archrival, Iran," said Hassan. "Saudi Arabia has similar intentions but with religious overtones. Carving up Syria will satisfy everyone, and Jenkins is their principal front man. As the new US ambassador to Syria, he will be well positioned to make it happen."

CHAPTER TWENTY-SEVEN

After saying goodbye to Paul, Andrew climbed on his bike and made his way home. The effort he put into pedaling uphill to the roundabout was enough to get his heartbeat going and clear his head. As a reward for his effort, he soared effortlessly downhill, arriving at his seaside apartment full of energy. He parked and locked his bike, then called the elevator. When he exited on the sixth floor, he heard music, then smelled the chicken cooking and realized he was hungry. It was not until he closed the door that Leila heard him and stepped into the hallway.

She stood barefoot in a sleeveless, short, bright red dress. He loved the simple way she was dressed, modest yet unintentionally sexy, with her hair piled on top of her head, long, waving strands falling along the sides of her face. Blown away by her appearance, he went up to her and put his arms around her.

"Don't we have Joe here tonight?" he asked.

"No, he's gone to Syria with Fouad."

"Oh, so we're finally alone. I think we need to take advantage of such an opportune occasion." He lifted her chin and kissed her hard and then, taking her hand, led her to his bedroom.

He liked that she was both comfortable and sexy in her nakedness. Though she had lived in hell for nine years, her body badly beaten and tortured, she possessed a beauty that touched his heart and like his friend Paul, her righteous, moral core counter-balanced the ugliness in this corrupt, amoral place.

They lay silent for a while until she laughed and shouted, "Finally!"

"What?" he asked, propping himself up on his elbow.

"You, me, together. I love it."

"Well, I had a few things I needed to work out before it could happen."

"And are they finally worked out?"

He wrapped his arm around her and pulled her into his chest. "Yes, I'm quite sure they are."

Suddenly, she sat up and shouted, "My chicken!" and she ran naked out of the room, down the hall and into the kitchen.

Laughing, he put on his shorts and followed her into the kitchen.

"It isn't ready yet," she said.

"While we're waiting," he said, his arms wrapped around her body, "let's jump in the shower."

* * *

Slipping back into her red dress, Leila returned to the kitchen to finish dinner while Andrew went to the balcony. Nadia was on his mind, and he needed to be alone with his thoughts. If he had been with her all those years, he wondered, would he have been as attracted to a woman like Leila? Probably not, but then everything got distorted with her kidnapping, and such reasoning no longer held sway. While Nadia was the elegant, sophisticated diplomat, Leila was earthy and authentic and the perfect partner for the physician who had found his calling. With no regrets, he said his goodbye to Nadia and walked back inside to help Leila with dinner.

A full moon and a fresh breeze off the sea added a bit of magic to an already perfect evening as they ate by candlelight on the balcony. Lifting his glass of a Ksara white, Andrew offered a toast.

"To you, Leila. Thank you for bringing joy into my life."

"And to you, Andrew, for allowing me in," she said, touching her glass to his. "From the moment I met you in Marjeyoun, I admired the way you loved my uncle Camille. And then, when I started working in the camp and saw your compassion, I couldn't help but fall in love with you. I didn't dare say anything. I respected your love and loyalty to Nadia."

She stayed silent a moment and then added, "There was a time when I was in Khiam, particularly after I was raped, when I wasn't sure I could ever love anyone, so I thank you, Andrew, for opening up my heart."

She sipped the last of her wine and without waiting for Andrew to respond, she glanced at her watch. "Joe won't be back for hours."

"Good, then we can leave the dishes until morning." He took her hand and led her back into the bedroom.

CHAPTER TWENTY-EIGHT

Fouad invited Roger and Joe to accompany him to Lattakia where he had agreed to meet Jaafar. Their entourage included not only Fouad's armed driver in his comfortable Range Rover but a backup Rover with two men carrying firearms. He had not been to the north of Lebanon in a number of years, and mindful it would add an additional half hour to their already four-hour trip to Lattakia, he had asked his driver to leave the main highway and take instead the old, more picturesque route along the sea. Thankfully, war had not touched this pristine part of Lebanon where you could still find a rustic shoreline dotted with the occasional red-roofed Lebanese stone villa overlooking a calm, clear turquoise sea… a vista starkly at odds with the over-built, congested, traffic-snarled area between Beirut and Jounieh. Fouad remembered a quaint little café just outside Byblos where he had them stop for coffee. He wanted time to strategize about what they were going to discuss with Jaafar.

The café, little more than an open space with a few chairs, tables and a thatched roof, sat right along the water. Like a child enthralled by the sea's ebb and flow, Fouad stared over the edge and watched the gentle waves splash up against the concrete siding before receding. *If life could only be this simple and calm and predictable,* he thought. He had been troubled for some time by how he had deceived Andrew. It was not in his habit to manage a friendship in such a duplicitous manner, but if he had told Andrew where Nadia was, he might have gone off and done something stupid. And Fouad knew Andrew would have been no match for the goons who kept watch over Jaafar and his prisoner.

This must have been weighing heavily on Joe's mind too, because after they had ordered coffee and manoushe, he asked, "What are we going to say to Jaafar about Andrew?"

"Since I don't even know this guy," said Roger, "I'll let you work out the logistics while I take a stroll along the water. I rarely get to do this sort of thing."

"I'm Andrew's friend too," Joe said, after Roger left, taking the driver with him, "and I feel terrible keeping all of this from him. He'll be devastated and deeply hurt when he finds out."

"I know, but it's for his own good. And to answer your question, yes, Andrew will be a topic of discussion, and I'll nail Hassan for attempted murder. If he tries to call my bluff, I'll produce the photos of his goons beating up on Andrew."

"There may be one bright hope," Joe said. "Andrew seems very interested in Leila these days. Maybe we'll see a time when he won't care as much about Nadia."

"We'll see," Fouad said, looking at his watch. "While I pay, call Roger and the driver. We need to get back on the road."

They drove through Tripoli, the last large Lebanese metropolis before finally reaching Dabousie, the Lebanese-Syria border crossing. The three men and their driver paid their respects to the border patrol on the Lebanese side of the border before getting back into their Range Rover and driving the few meters to the Syrian side. Even at the height of the civil war, it was enough to have either a Lebanese or Syrian ID to cross the border hassle-free. After the Hariri assassination and the expulsion of Syrian troops, crossing became more bureaucratic and time consuming. This time, Fouad and his entourage were the invited guests of Hassan Jaafar and once their identity was verified they were whisked across the border. For a supposedly retired former Intelligence chief, Hassan apparently still had plenty of clout.

Once inside Syria, they passed alongside the port of Tarsus where Joe pointed out the fleet of Russian naval ships.

"Tarsus is now an official port of the Black Sea Fleet, and they're busy renovating and expanding it so they can bring in their major naval vessels."

"You were right about the Russians, Joe," Roger said. "This sends a pretty clear message to the US and Israel that they're here to stay."

Even with their coffee stop, they arrived at Spiro's Restaurant with a quarter hour to spare. They parked the car near the port and strolled along the waterfront until it was time to meet Hassan.

Fouad had not seen him in a number of years, but there he was— still the same imposing presence with the perfect manners, wearing his ubiquitous sunglasses, the well-tailored suit and silk tie, and the crisp dress shirt, still trim and tanned. And here *he* was, he thought, in an old suit and looking quite underdressed for the occasion.

"My dear debonair friend, you're looking fit and happy."

The two men embraced, their years of friendship outweighing their political differences. Fouad introduced Joe and Roger as trusted colleagues fully versed on the crisis about to befall Syria. And because the meeting was between two top Intelligence chiefs, Fouad surmised Jaafar had given orders ahead of time to have the private banquet room prepared and sealed off from the public. Once seated, Hassan's guests were offered either Bargylus, a new Syrian wine produced locally, or arak to accompany the dozens of traditional *mezze* dishes Hassan had no doubt ordered ahead of time, for the table was already set with copious amounts of food. Fouad knew to pace himself. Since Spiro's was renowned for its seafood, he anticipated platters of just-caught fish to come after the *mezze*, followed by Arabic sweets, seasonal fruits and, of course, a strong Arabic coffee with a dash of cardamom.

"Have you been in contact with Robert Jenkins since we spoke?" asked Fouad.

"If you mean since he threatened to send me to some hell-hole if I didn't cooperate, yes, indirectly. He sent a message saying he knows I have a UN diplomat and where I'm keeping her."

"Nadia! How the hell," Fouad said. "Jenkins must be either bribing or blackmailing someone in your household into cooperating."

"I don't see how that's possible. My people have been with me for years. I doubt any…" He appeared to be mentally checking off each of his staff.

"Do any of them routinely leave your compound?" Roger asked.

"Just my two drivers, Khalid and Moussa. If I don't need them, they run errands for the staff."

"Maybe it isn't someone on your staff, Hassan," Fouad said, even more troubled by that prospect since, aside from Sonia, he had only shared the particulars surrounding Nadia's capture with Roger and Joe.

"Thankfully, Nadia and I are leaving as soon as I take care of some final details."

"You can't take Nadia anywhere," Fouad said.

"I can if we marry. She isn't part of this mess, but Jenkins has made her his pawn. Whatever you think of me, Fouad, I love her and will do whatever I can to protect her. My options are limited at this point. With Jenkins' threat, we've moved beyond anything I can do to stop him. That will have to be done from your end."

"Does Nadia know any of this?"

"On the marriage issue, she's held off giving her consent until I agree to her demands. About the other wrinkle, why upset her?"

"It's more than a fucking wrinkle," Fouad retorted. "It's Nadia's life that might be in danger."

"What good is she to Jenkins?" Joe asked.

"He could use her to get information I have about him."

"Care to share what that might be?" asked Fouad.

"I have evidence that Jenkins personally ordered the assassination of the Shiite Grand Ayatollah. As you may recall, he survived, but the explosion killed eighty-five people. He also ordered the assassination of Hezbollah's operations mastermind. Both incidents were meant to incite a Shiite-Sunni war here."

"How does Jenkins know you have this evidence?" Joe asked.

"I made two copies of my findings. One I keep in my safe, the other I shared with the head of Internal Security. I was still Syria's Intelligence chief at the time, and as a courtesy, I…"

"Where do you keep the key to your safe?" asked Roger, cutting Hassan off.

"On a chain around my neck."

He put his hand inside his shirt to pull out the key, but it wasn't there. "What the…?" He thought a moment. "I put it on the bathroom counter while I showered. I was in a hurry to leave and must have forgotten it there."

"Your missing key isn't the problem," Fouad said. "It would appear the trouble is on my end… and something I'll need to take care of."

The four men continued to serve themselves from the numerous *mezze* dishes, grateful for the silence. More wine and arak were poured as the platters of fish arrived—spicy fish kibbeh balls, the tiny Sultan Brahim, fried and crispy and eaten in their entirety, bones and all, and a La Ouse, a local whole white fish, smothered in tahini sauce and topped with pine nuts and spices.

Fouad popped a fish kibbeh into his mouth. "Delicious," he said, wiping his mouth with his napkin before drinking more wine. "My compliments to the family who produced this wine, Hassan. It's excellent."

"Thank you. We're very proud of our wines, as you Lebanese are of yours. The owners are two brothers from the Saadi family here in Lattakia."

"Tell me, Hassan, does the proposed Qatari pipeline have anything to do with the trouble brewing here?" Roger asked.

"Not really. The West has always wanted our gas and oil reserves, and they're not particular about where they get it. There's a much bigger issue now," said Hassan. "The US has a vested interest in a permanent state of war in the region. Their Sunni allies control access to all key US military bases in the region, and the US military and Intelligence communities want to protect those existing arrangements. It's a fucking game they all play. You help us fight our wars. We'll let you keep your bases. We'll supply the funding and the jihadists. You supply the planes and the military hardware."

"We're talking about a proxy war that will pit the US and its regional allies against Iran," Fouad said. "It's pretty straightforward."

"What's Israel's role in all of this?" Joe asked.

"They back not only any escalation that'll topple Assad but a prolonged war that will grind down the Iranians and weaken and isolate Hezbollah so they can attack and destroy them."

"Hassan, you're an Alawite. Whose side are you on?" Roger asked.

"I'm on the side of the Syrian people. I don't want to see either Iran or Russia, or the US and Israel for that matter, deciding my country's fate. If Bashar Assad needs to be removed from power, it's the Syrian people who should decide that... no one else."

"I agree," said Joe, "and this time the US has badly miscalculated its regime change demands. The Russians won't sit back and watch them destroy Syria without intervening on Assad's behalf. There's a reason they're fortifying their naval base in Tarsus."

"There you go again, Joe, jumping way ahead of yourself," Roger said. "Syria isn't broken yet, and you're already suggesting the Russians will ride in to save Assad."

"I'm doing more than that, Roger. I'm predicting a twenty-first century Great War using regional proxies right on our border."

Fouad did not give either of them a chance to continue their riling.

"Hassan, you sent your goons to kill a very good friend of mine shortly after you kidnapped Nadia. Care to tell me why?"

"I don't know what you're talking about."

"Andrew Sullivan, Nadia's fiancé. Your men beat him almost to death."

"You have no proof."

"Not true, one of the guards who rescued Andrew took photos of your men as they fled. I can positively identify Khalid. He's about to be taken care of, so that leaves one more. His name is Moussa."

On cue, Joe stood and left the room. Hassan understood what was about to happen.

"Next time you order someone dead," Fouad said, "make sure he isn't one of my friends."

"I'll keep that in mind," Hassan said, his face expressionless and seemingly indifferent that his long-time butler and chauffeur was about to be killed.

Instead, with complete *sang-froid*, and while coffee was being served, he invited his guests to enjoy the dessert. "The knafeh is our local specialty. Be sure to try it. Fouad, since you've relieved me of my driver, I assume you've arranged to have someone else drive me home?"

"I'll call him," Roger said, standing. "I'm off to the men's room anyway. I'll have him pull his Land Rover around to the front of the restaurant."

Hassan stood, as did Fouad, and the two embraced. "Let's not wait years before our next reunion," Fouad said. "I've missed you."

"Thanks Fouad, that means a lot to me. We'll be in touch."

Fouad accompanied Hassan to the restaurant's lobby and watched him walk out. As Hassan waited by the parking lot for his new driver, a bomb exploded rocking the restaurant, splintering the wooden front door into pieces and shattering all the windows. When the smoke cleared, Fouad rushed to what was now a gaping hole and saw what was left of Hassan Jaafar. His remains, a piece of charred meat, lay in a pool of blood.

A second bomb exploded with whirlwind force and lifted Fouad off the ground, propelling him back into the restaurant, smacking his body against a stone wall.

CHAPTER TWENTY-NINE

Nadia was in the library reading when Ani came rushing into the room, sobbing.

"*Sitt* Nadia, there was an explosion. Mr. Jaafar is dead."

Ani grabbed the remote and turned on the television. They sat together on the couch, Ani holding Nadia's limp hand.

> "This afternoon just outside Spiro's Restaurant near Lattakia's seaport a bomb blast killed Syria's former head of Intelligence, Hassan Jaafar, as he was walking to his car. His chauffeur was also found dead at the scene. A member of Lebanon's Internal Security was critically wounded and transported by helicopter back to Beirut for treatment."

Nadia fell back into the sofa's soft cushions. Unable to speak, she stared at the screen before a flood of mixed emotions poured over her. She had lived intimately with the man who had just been killed. And even though she had been his prisoner, their relationship came with complicated emotional components. Had she come to love Hassan Jaafar? Yes, on some level she had, and now he was gone and she was no longer his prisoner. How strange to suddenly be able to say, *I'm now a free woman.*

Ani, still holding Nadia's hand, continued to cry. When she finally calmed down, Nadia said, "We need to leave here before the Mokhabarat show up. Can you find us a car? I can drive, if no one else can."

"*Sitt,* I'll ask Moussa, Mr. Jaafar's driver. He'll help us."

"Good, make the arrangements. We haven't much time."

CHAPTER THIRTY

As soon as Ani left the library, Nadia ran upstairs. She needed clothes, but more importantly, she needed cash to pay her way out of Syria. She searched the other rooms on the second floor to be sure she was alone before entering Hassan's bedroom. She closed the door, locked it, and then glanced around the room, not sure where to begin. She smelled his Givenchy Pour Hommes cologne and followed its scent into the bathroom. Like other memories centered around Hassan, that cologne was who he was, a man so frightfully powerful yet so physically attractive that she had willingly given herself and become his lover. Such reckless behavior had begun long before her capture. As a university student, she'd been smitten by the attention of such an important figure and, had it not been for her parents' horror, she would have, at the very least, let him take her to bed. Fifteen years later, when they'd met in Chtaura, that same sensual thrill was still there. And this morning, before leaving the house, he had awakened her and made love to her with the hunger and passion of a first encounter and, though his prisoner, she had, with the same erotic draw, let the man who had gradually won his way into her heart enter her, take her and own her as his partner for life. And now, she felt a profound loss she dared admit only to herself.

When she turned to leave the bathroom, she saw the key to his safe. After they had sex, Hassan had showered in a hurry. As he dressed, he had made a bit of a fuss about being late and had forgotten to put the key and its chain back around his neck. She took it, went to his armoire and opened the double doors. Again, his scent, his phantom presence, scrambled her emotions as she ran her fingers along the sleeves of his suits which were hung according to color. And then she saw the magnificent paintings, ones she would have admired had she seen them hanging in his house. And then it hit her. He had removed them to give her a free hand to hang paintings she loved. He truly wanted her to be mistress of his house. Through tears, she parted his clothes, as she had seen Hassan do to reveal the safe, and inserted the key. The lock clicked, and the door sprung open. Inside, on the top shelf, she found wads of cash—dozens of piles of hundred dollar bills, euros and Syrian pounds along with the staff's ID cards. She also took two gold bars, Hassan's Rolex watch and two pair of his gold cufflinks—useful bribes should she need them. She looked for something to put all of this in and found, next to his shoes, a soft leather travel bag. And then she saw the manila envelope. She pulled out the first few pages and quickly perused them. Hassan had confided in her that he had enough incriminating evidence to blackmail Robert Jenkins should it become necessary. A quick overview mentioned his involvement in the attempted murder of an important Shiite cleric and the assassination of a high-level Hezbollah operative in early 2004. She slid the pages back in, sealed the envelope and put it in the bag. This could be her ticket out of there, she thought. She put the key in the safe, closed the door and listened to it click shut.

Back in her own bedroom, she had just finished stuffing some clothes from her own closet into the bag when Ani appeared at her door.

"We should leave now, *Sitt*."

Nadia grabbed a few more items, zippered the bag closed and shut the bedroom door behind her. Ani was waiting for her at the bottom of the stairs.

"I found everyone's papers."

Ani followed her into the dining room and watched as she lay the identity cards out on the table.

"Look for yours, Ani, while I call the others."

And as the staff gathered around the table, each gratefully snatching back their papers, she pulled out some of the Syrian pounds, each fifty-pound bill equating to one US dollar, and put them on the table for them to take.

"There's plenty for everyone, so please share equally."

A man she had seen around the compound approached her and said, "We need to leave now. The Mokhabarat will be here soon."

Ani took her bag and escorted her out the front door. The car was just outside, motor running. She turned, said goodbye to the staff, and walked to the car. The same man was standing by the back door, holding it open. He helped her in, then closed the door.

Ani hopped into the passenger seat and waited for the man to climb in behind the wheel before turning around to address Nadia.

"*Sitt,* this is my friend Moussa. He will take us to my parents' house in Lattakia."

"Thank you for helping us, Moussa."

He looked at her through his rearview mirror and gave her a nod.

As they pulled away from the house and exited the gate, Nadia glanced one last time at the mansion that had been her prison. She had been brought there in the dark of night and had only noticed a brightly lit mansion on top of a hill meant to welcome her. Now, as she looked back, she saw not only Hassan's impenetrable fortress, not unlike Saladin's castle where Asmit had been kept, but a thick pine forest surrounding it, assuring neither easy access nor means of escape.

"Moussa, if there's a secondary road to the coast, take it. By now the Mokhabarat has probably set up roadblocks around Lattakia. I don't have my Lebanese papers and do not wish to get arrested."

"I understand, *Sitt.* I know this area well… don't worry."

"Ani told me you were one of Mr. Jaafar's drivers."

"Yes, *Sitt,* for many years."

"How fortunate it wasn't you who drove Mr. Hassan today. Khalid's death must have come as quite a shock."

"Yes, *Sitt,* but *Hamdelilah,* by the Grace of God."

As he turned onto a secondary road, a short distance from the house, Nadia glanced down into a lush green valley seemingly untouched by human life—no church steeples or mosque minarets towering over the tree tops, not even a meandering road snaking through the forest. Was it possible all this land belonged to Hassan? She noticed intermittent beams of light off to her left. It was a car advancing up the main road, its lights fading in and out as it careened around turns, shining into the darkening edges of twilight one minute then hiding behind a bend in the road the next. Relieved they had left in time, Nadia closed her eyes and gave a prayer of thanks.

Unaware of how much time had passed, she felt the car slow down abruptly. She opened her eyes and saw, on a road seemingly wide enough for only one car, another vehicle coming toward them and making no attempt to slow down. Moussa had no choice but to pull over to the scantest of shoulder and allow the car to pass.

"*Sharmoota,*" he yelled, cursing the driver. "He almost got us killed."

Nadia looked out her window as the car passed. She stared at the man with fading sandy hair, seated alone in the back seat. She knew who he was. Hassan had described him perfectly. From his reaction, he recognized her too. This unsettled her because she realized why he was making his way to Hassan's house and what he was after.

She turned and watched the car continue past them up the road. "Moussa," she shouted suddenly. "I see red lights. I think the driver might be turning around."

"I know, *Sitt,* I've been watching him too."

"You've got to get us off this road. Can't you go any faster?"

"*Sitt,* the road is bad and there's gravel. If I go too fast on a turn, we could slide off the road. Wouldn't want to end up in the valley."

"Neither would I. Just do your best."

Nadia glanced behind her again. "The car's coming back!" she shouted.

"We'll be on the main highway soon. I'll lose them there."

When Nadia looked again, she saw that the car was maintaining its distance, apparently in no hurry to overtake them. Why?

Nadia made what she hoped would be a wise decision. She removed the manila envelope from her bag and wrote her father's phone number across the top.

"Ani," she said, handing her the envelope, "I want you to take this and keep it somewhere safe."

"*Sitt,* I will help in any way I can but…"

Nadia did not wait for Ani to finish.

"You see the phone number on the top of the envelope?" she asked, pointing. "That's my father's number in Beirut. Please call him. Say 'I have news from Nadia,' so he will know to trust you. Tell him, too, that you have an envelope from Nadia that she wants him to have. Work out how you'll deliver it to him. He can come to Lattakia, if that's easier, and pick it up himself. Tell him that I promised you would be compensated for your help."

She nodded.

"And one more thing, Ani. Don't look inside the envelope. The information could get you killed."

Nadia ignored her wide-eyed expression and looked behind her again, checking on the car.

"Ani, give me your parents' phone number in case I need to contact you."

She watched as Ani searched in her purse for a piece of paper. She scribbled the number on the back of an envelope and handed it to Nadia.

"*Sitt, w*hat is this about?"

"The man in the car is after me."

"Why?" asked Ani.

"He knew Mr. Jaafar and wants to ask me some questions."

"What if he's from the Mokhabarat?"

"He isn't. Don't worry."

"How do you know…?"

Nadia was about to reply when Moussa cried out, "Look! Up ahead, a checkpoint."

When she saw the wooden barrier across the road and the flashing red light, her heart almost leaped out of her chest. She had been through this kind of high drama before at another Syrian checkpoint. That time, she had been with her then-husband Elie, whom she had just sprung from a Syrian prison, Andrew and Samir, her father's chauffeur. It was Hassan's doing then, trying to frighten her. Now, she thought, it will be either Syrian soldiers or the Mokhabarat hauling her off to their infamous underground Palmyra prison in the Syrian desert. Maybe they would throw her into a filthy, rat-infested prison cell instead, like the one Elie had occupied for thirteen years, and let her rot there until she died.

Moussa slowed down and inched the car forward before coming to a full stop. Two men approached the car, one on either side, and ordered everyone out. She watched Moussa open his door, then Ani, her hands trembling as she fumbled in her purse for her Syrian papers. Their identity verified, she and Moussa were ordered back into the car and told not to move.

One of the armed men came up to Nadia's side of the car. When he opened her door, she stopped breathing. "You need a special invitation? Out." Weak-kneed, Nadia climbed out. Her head spun, and her heart forgot to pump, leaving her dizzy. She leaned against the car so she would not fall.

The man shouted at her. "Your papers!"

Nadia shook her head. "I have none."

"What?"

"I was kidnapped by Hassan Jaafar and kept his prisoner, until today."

"We'll see about that," he said and spun her around, pulling her arms behind her back and handcuffing her. As Nadia was being marched to his car, she and Ani exchanged worried looks. The man who had been searching the car had just asked Ani to hand over the leather bag.

Hands were on Nadia's back, pushing her into the back seat of the car when she heard a second vehicle arrive. Was this more trouble? Would someone come from behind, slip a bag over her head, force her to the ground, then rape her and throw her body into a ditch?

The car door opened and closed. Someone walked toward them.

She turned her head and saw the American.

"*Shokran, shabab*," he said, thanking them. "I'll take over from here. Before you leave, remove the lady's handcuffs and hand over the bag."

Hands freed, Nadia swung around and said, "For some strange reason, you appear to be in charge here, so please tell these men to let my friends go. They've done nothing wrong. They were simply trying to help me."

He peered inside the car at Ani and Moussa, then looking into Nadia's eyes said, "*Shabab*, let them go."

When Nadia was sure they were far enough away and not being followed, she turned back to the American. "Thank you."

"You don't mind if I check your bag, do you?"

"Go right ahead."

He looked through the bag, lifting items out, then putting them back. "A lot of Jaafar's stuff."

"Yes, I thought I might need it."

"You *may* still need it," he said, and he closed the bag. "I'll carry it to the car for you."

When she reached the car, his driver had already opened the back door. He helped her climb in while the American hopped in on the other side, placing her bag on the floor between them.

Settled back into his seat, he addressed Nadia for the first time.

"It's a pleasure to finally meet you, Nadia Khoury."

This might be your most important Scheherazade role yet, Nadia. Play it well.

"And you are?"

"Bob Jenkins."

"How do you know who I am?"

"It was a well-known secret that Jaafar had kidnapped a beautiful woman. And now that I've seen you, 'beautiful' doesn't begin to describe how stunning you are."

She ignored his remark and asked, "If my kidnapping was such an open secret, why didn't some shining knight ever come to my rescue?"

"I can't answer that, but as the US ambassador-designate to Syria, I am completely at your service."

"I'm also a diplomat. I serve, or did, before being kidnapped, on the UN Commission on Human Rights, though I'm temporarily without official documents of any kind to prove it. Jaafar didn't worry about such things when he had me kidnapped and brought to Syria."

"And you've been kept at his mansion all this time?"

"Yes."

"Should we, I mean, should I assume that you found yourself in an abusive situation. If so, is there anything I can help with, any medical attention you might need?"

"Are you trying to ask me if I was raped?"

"Well, yes, I mean I'll understand if you don't want to tell me. You don't even know me so... don't feel obliged to answer."

"Well, it is a lot more complicated than just saying yes. I was kidnapped and held against my will, so isn't that the same thing as being raped? And the inevitability of eventually giving into my kidnapper, even if I made it my choice not to resist, is still rape, is it not?" She looked over at him and said, "Does that answer your question?"

"Completely... I mean, yes, and I didn't mean to pry. I just feel badly that you had to endure all those years in captivity."

"I appreciate your concern, Mr. Jenkins."

"Please call me Bob."

"You're very kind, Bob, and if I appear ungrateful, I'm not. It's just that after not seeing anyone other than Jaafar and his staff for so many years, well, I find it a bit awkward talking to a stranger." She turned and smiled. "Even if that stranger is the perfect gentleman, it's going to take me a while to get used to being free again and in the company of others."

"I'd be honored to keep you company anytime, Nadia."

That was probably true, she thought. She had been forced into a rarified situation that completely altered not only who she was but who she had become. She knew perfectly well what Jenkins was up to with his polite talk and concern for her well-being. Just because she had allowed herself to become Jaafar's whore, it did not mean she would become his.

"Thank you, Bob."

They sat silent for a while before he spoke again.

"Do you mind if I ask you a question?"

"Of course not."

"Did Jaafar ever talk to you about his work?"

"His work? It was an open book, Bob. He was head of Syrian Intelligence and a major player in Lebanese politics, as you probably already know. Even our presidential elections were subject to his approval. He killed some, disappeared others. That was his job as dictated by the Assad regime. On a personal level, he was debonair, well-educated and well-mannered. I had known him well years ago. We dated for a while, but when he asked me to marry him, I turned him down. He was part of the Syrian regime, and that frightened me. A short time later, I married my college professor. In revenge, Jaafar abducted him and held him in a Syrian prison for thirteen years. So, what more is there to know about Jaafar's work?"

"If you knew what he did, and hated it, why did you date him?"

"I was a wealthy, young, pampered woman who thought it her due to be courted by a powerful, older man, and I enjoyed it. Not a good reason, but an honest answer to your question."

"You don't act like a spoiled brat."

She laughed. "I grew up and got over such silliness. After my husband was disappeared, I left the country, concentrated on my studies and got my law degrees. All that hard work sobered me up."

"And then you met Andrew Sullivan."

"You know Andrew?"

"I met him a while back in Broumana. He was a guest in a rehab center."

"What was he doing there? Did something happen to him?"

"Jaafar tried to have him killed."

"Andrew?" she whispered, her eyes flooding at the mere mention of his name. She looked at Jenkins, puzzled.

"He was beaten almost to death by some thugs. He suffered massive injuries and spent close to a year recovering."

And then it hit her like a bullet to her heart. It must have happened right after Andrew's CNN interview. She saw the scene flash across her mind's eye. Jaafar had become irate when he discovered she had a fiancé. He had stormed out of the room and then, out of a completely silent house, she had heard him shouting to someone. He was giving orders to kill her darling Andrew.

"Tell me more about Andrew. Did he regain his health? What is he doing now?"

"It's been a few months since I saw him, but even then he was well into recovery mode. I joined him for a bit of sparring one morning, and he just about knocked me out." He laughed. "A bit of a surprise, I must say. I did some boxing in college, but I was no match for him. He's quite an incredible man, actually. He was studying Arabic so he could work in one of the Palestinian camps. He wanted to do something you'd be proud of."

"He actually said that?" *Yes*, she thought, *it was the kind of thing this altruistic man would say and do.*

Jenkins nodded as he pulled out a handkerchief from his pocket. He handed it to Nadia and gave her time to cry before he spoke again.

"How did you meet Andrew?"

"Through a mutual friend in Washington, DC. We were both invited to a party at her home." She laughed. "As soon as we were properly introduced, he told me he was going to marry me," and she cried again. "Such a kind, gentle, loving man."

"I must say, I was impressed when I met him. I even offered him a job."

"What did he say?" She was curious if Andrew liked Jenkins as much as Jenkins claimed to have liked him.

"He refused… said he'd found his calling as a physician. You must be eager to see him again."

Nadia burst into tears. "I don't know if I can ever face him again after what I've had to do to survive."

"This is a man who was ready to risk his life to rescue you, Nadia. He'll certainly forgive you."

"I'm not so sure." Surely, he remembered his old Nadia, not the woman she had become. "He was really going to come rescue me?"

"Yes, he was actively training to do just that."

Nadia was too heartbroken to respond. By her actions, she had lost a remarkable man.

"I'm curious, and again I apologize for asking so many questions. It's just that…"

"Go ahead, Bob, ask. If I don't want to answer, I won't."

"Were you upset when you heard Jaafar had been killed?"

"That's a callous question, Bob. He's only been dead a few hours, and I'm still feeling quite numb. No one should have to die such a horrific death. Once the shock has worn off, I'm quite certain I'll feel very sad. In his own misguided way, he deeply loved me. And how ironic, even his death hasn't freed me. With no travel documents, I can't even get back to Lebanon."

"I'll take care of arranging that, Nadia. With my diplomatic status, I'll get you home, but before I do, I'd be honored if you'd be my guest in Damascus for a few days so you can rest and recover."

"Thank you, Bob, but I've had enough of Syria and want to leave this place as soon as possible. So, if you could just get me to the Dabousie border crossing, I can take a taxi from there to my father's house."

"I wouldn't dream of leaving you at the border. It would be my honor to accompany you back home. Will you allow me to do that?"

"Yes," she said, smiling at him. "That's very kind of you."

Jenkins gave instructions to the driver and then turned his attention back to Nadia.

"Did Jaafar ever bring his work home?"

"I wouldn't know, Bob. In some respects, he was a very private man, particularly about his affairs."

* * *

When they reached the Dabousie border crossing, Bob insisted Nadia wait in the car while he took care of formalities. She agreed, relieved she did not have to face questioning from either the Syrian or Lebanese officials.

When he climbed back in the car, he smiled and said, "Nadia, you are free to enter Lebanon."

"I'm very appreciative of everything you've done. I'm not sure what I would have done without your help. Of course, my father would have come to meet me somewhere in Syria with my Lebanese papers, but you've made everything so much easier. I'm very grateful."

"Grateful enough to let me see you again once you've recovered?"

"We'll see," she said, smiling. "First, I need to become a free woman again."

"Wouldn't you like to call your father to tell him you're on your way home?" Bob said, handing her his mobile.

"Yes," she replied, trying to hold back her tears.

She was unable to see the numbers and instead dictated them to Bob. The phone rang four times before Victor answered.

"Papa," was all she could say.

"Oh, my Nadia, I can hardly believe... Where are you? Are you okay? Shall we come to get you?"

"No, Papa," she said, clearing her throat. "I've crossed the Dabousie border with the help of a very kind gentleman." As she said this, she looked over at Bob. "We should be there in about an hour and a half."

"*Hamdellah.* Your mother and I will be waiting, my darling."

She closed the mobile and handed it back to Bob.

"And now I'm totally at your mercy, Mr. Bob Jenkins."

"Good, and I plan to take full advantage once you've had time to settle back into your life."

"It's been a very emotional day, Bob, and as you can see I'm not doing a very good job controlling my feelings. Would you think unkindly of me if I just sat quietly for a while and looked out the window? It's been such a long time since I've seen the outside world."

"Not at all, and I'll make sure you're not disturbed."

And as she stared out the window at the day coming to an end she saw street vendors pushing their empty carts through Tripoli's congested neighborhoods back to its main market; fishermen preparing their nets before setting off in their lantern-equipped boats for night fishing; a shepherd on a distant hill leading his herd of sheep back home; a mother cradling her baby in her arms, her eyes darting right and left as she gingerly crossed a busy intersection; children, their faces weary after a long day, peering from their school bus windows—everyday occurrences that in the past she would have shrugged off as inconsequential now shone as wondrous acts of ordinariness.

* * *

She felt someone touch her hand and call her name. She had not realized she had drifted off.

"Nadia, we're almost in Beirut. Would you mind giving my driver directions to your father's house?"

"Yes, of course," and she indicated the best way to reach Hazmieh.

"I'd like you to meet my parents," she said, as they approached the house. "They'll want to thank you for all you've done."

"It would be my honor to meet them... thank you."

Her tears began again as soon as she saw the open gate, the archway of rosemary bushes and overgrown olive trees, and there they were, her parents, Victor and Carole, holding hands, waiting for their daughter's return.

"I thought I'd never see them again," she sobbed.

As soon as the car came to a halt, she opened the door.

"May I take my bag?" she asked.

"Yes, but let me carry it for you."

"No need." She jumped out, slinging it over her arm as she ran toward her parents and into their waiting arms, hugging and kissing them and letting flow tears of joy. She appreciated that Bob had waited for the appropriate moment to exit the car. And when he did, Victor broke away, rushed up to him and gave him a hug.

"We can't thank you enough for what you've done for our Nadia," she heard him say, as she left them and began walking arm in arm with her mother toward the house. At the front porch, she turned and caught Bob's eye as he glanced at her. She smiled. Knowing her father, he was peppering him with dozens of questions, most of which he would not be able to answer.

The men eventually joined Nadia and her mother in the living room, and Carole insisted Bob also invite his driver in for coffee.

"Won't you stay for dinner?" Carole asked.

"I wouldn't dream of intruding on this joyous reunion, but if Nadia allows me, I'll come back in a few days, once she's had time to relax."

"I'll walk you to your car, Bob," she said.

And once outside, he asked, "Does this mean I can see you again?"

"Yes," she said, smiling.

"You're even more beautiful when you smile, Nadia."

When they reached his car, he kissed her on the cheek.

"I'll be counting the minutes until I see you again."

When she saw the car exit the driveway, she turned and smiled as she made her way back to the house. She had played her Scheherazade role very well.

CHAPTER THIRTY-ONE

Sonia thought of her rooftop apartment on the heights of Achrafieh as her private Eden isolated from a city in perpetual turmoil. When it was not shrouded in layers of pollutants, she could see all the way to the turquoise waters of the Mediterranean. She was in the midst of the sophisticated City Center with its waterfront skyscrapers and luxury hotels and, standing alongside one another, the mosques and churches that had meant, at one time, to symbolically represent religious harmony in a country with seventeen different sects, but now, due to renewed suicide bombings, shed, instead, a glaring spotlight on the country's mounting sectarian frictions.

Still in her nightgown, her bare feet stroking the cool marble floor, Sonia took her breakfast of coffee, and lebneh with pita, tomatoes and olives on her garden balcony, perusing several local newspapers until the time her therapist arrived to work on her hand. She could now wiggle her fingers, hold a glass without fear of dropping it, and use her computer. Her doctors were pleased with her progress. *Quite a miraculous feat*, she thought, considering how mangled her forearm had been. Her left eye was another matter. While she could eventually look forward to a robotic eye, it could not happen soon enough.

Her greatest champion throughout this ordeal had been Fouad. He was the driving force behind her push to regain her health. More importantly, he had returned to her bed. Though not fully moved in as a permanent resident, claiming high security priorities, he came regularly enough to satisfy her sexual needs, and his.

Joe, her trainer, deserved major kudos too. She had converted one of her bedrooms into an exercise room, equipping it with a Pilates-reformer, a rowing machine, a stationary bike and various weights, and Joe came three days a week to give her a rigorous workout, helping to slim and tone her back into her former self. She had been annoyed that Joe had called earlier that morning to cancel their session. Fouad had apparently insisted he accompany him to an urgent out-of-town meeting.

"You know how important these sessions are to me, Joe. I simply hate missing even one."

"Don't fret, Sonia. I've arranged to have one of my assistants come at the usual time this afternoon, if that's all right with you."

"If he's as handsome as you, I won't mind."

"You're incorrigible, Sonia. Now I know why Fouad is so crazy about you. You keep us men on our toes."

"I hope so," she said with a laugh. "And tell Fouad that I missed him in bed last night."

"I will." And he hung up.

After breakfast, and before her therapist arrived, Sonia took time to catch up on what was happening in Syria. She knew from Fouad that trouble was brewing. There would be stories to tell, with accuracy and honesty, and that, she decided, would be her job going forward.

From her time in Marjeyoun with Camille and his friends, she knew that there had been a regime change in Syria on US foreign policy agenda since the early 2000s. The idea was to take out Syria to weaken Iran and Hezbollah in order to appease Israel, but given the Iraq fiasco, it made no sense, in her opinion, to destroy yet another Middle East country, and particularly Syria, the only remaining independent secular state in the Arab world. Its base, inherited from the dominant Baath party, had as its ideology a mix of nationalism, pan-Arabism and socialism. Founded by Michel Aflac, a Christian, the party integrated Muslims, Christians and Druze—all interested in a stable, thriving country. And yet, there they were—the US in cahoots with Israel and its Sunni allies—poised to destroy that country and set the region further aflame.

As a seasoned war correspondent, she knew how easily governments fabricated lies and disseminated misinformation to a gullible public. Iraq and its weapons of mass destruction had been a conspicuous example of such purposeful misdeeds. What crime would the West fabricate to make its case for war with Syria? Whatever it was, Sonia would expose their lies.

* * *

That afternoon, a dashing, young, well-built man named Naji rang her doorbell and introduced himself as Joe's assistant.

"You'll do nicely." She laughed, grabbed his hand and invited him in. "I assume Joe instructed you about my usual workout?"

"No worries, *Sitt* Sonia, he explained everything."

"I go by Sonia, so please drop the *Sitt.* When someone as young and as handsome as you uses that word, it makes me feel old."

With Naji, it was easy to remember how commonly she had flirted with men and gotten them into bed. In this instance, he was simply indulging a much older woman who had been beaten up.

After an hour and a half workout, Naji called the session to a close and complimented her. "Great job, Sonia. You're doing remarkably well. I wish all my clients were as dedicated as you."

As she bid Naji goodbye and closed the door, she heard the television blaring from the kitchen. She was about to tell Hasna to turn the volume down when she heard the news.

"This is a live update. This afternoon near Lattakia's port, former Syrian Intelligence Chief Hassan Jaafar was killed in a bomb blast. His chauffeur was also discovered dead at the scene. An officer from Lebanon's security apparatus was injured in the blast and transported back to Beirut for treatment."

Sonia leaned against the wall and slid to the floor. Nadia was now a free woman. Stunned and scared, she wrapped her arms around her knees, hugged them to her chest and cried.

She eventually climbed off the floor, grabbed her cell phone and punched in Paul's number. She did not ask where he was or what he was doing.

"Come, I need you."

"Give me fifteen minutes," he said, and hung up.

She showered and changed, and by the time she had dried her hair and put on a dress, Paul was waiting for her in the living room.

"Thank God you're here," she said, as he kissed her on the cheek.

"I've got a serious problem, Paul, and need your advice."

He sat down and watched her pace back and forth.

"I need a plan, and fast."

"I assume this is about Nadia."

"Of course, why else would I have called you so urgently? With Jaafar dead, she'll come right back here."

"I don't see a problem. She doesn't know you set her up to be kidnapped."

"She does know. Jaafar told her. She sent me a note while I was in the hospital. It read, 'I hope you die. Nadia.'"

Paul shook his head. "Sonia, come here." He patted the space next to him on the couch.

"Nadia's not your priority right now, Fouad is."

"What are you talking about?"

"He was the one wounded in the blast that killed Jaafar. He's..."

"Oh my God, I didn't make the connection when I heard the news. Is he going to...?"

"His condition isn't life threatening. That's all I know. Joe had him transported back to Hotel Dieu by helicopter. He's being worked up now."

"Paul, take me to him. I need to be there."

"There will be plenty of time for that. Besides, Joe gave strict orders that you weren't to come. He'll call as soon as he knows something."

Sonia called out to Hasna. "Please bring us a bottle of whiskey, two glasses, ice and some nibbles."

She sat back against the cushions. "Why was Fouad meeting with Jaafar? Was he trying to negotiate Nadia's release?"

"No, they were trying to find a way to stop the Americans from toppling Assad." Paul was silent for a minute. "And someone found out."

Hasna entered the room carrying a tray. She placed it on the coffee table.

"Thanks, Hasna, I'll call you if we need anything else."

Sonia poured two whiskeys, added a bit of water and one ice cube and gave one to Paul.

"Someone found out. Yes, just like Nadia found out. She hates me, Paul. She'll lash out and crush me, and that'll be her right. I destroyed her life."

"I have no advice to give, Sonia. This is your mess. You're going to have to figure out a way to deal with it. At the very least, you should have told Andrew. He won't take it well if he hears it from Nadia."

"I agree," Sonia said, throwing her head back. "And why wouldn't she tell him?"

CHAPTER THIRTY-TWO

Andrew awoke when he heard Joe come in. He climbed out of bed, put on some clothes and closed the door behind him. He found Joe sitting in the living room, his head back against the sofa cushion.

Joe's head jerked forward, and his eyes popped open when he heard Andrew.

"Looks like you had a bad night," Andrew said. "Where have you been, or shouldn't I ask?"

"I need coffee."

Leila heard this as she walked in to join them.

"I'll get it for you, and how about some breakfast too?"

"That would be perfect… thanks Leila."

"We'll have to eat in the kitchen. I left a bit of a mess on the balcony after last night's dinner."

"So, where were you all night, Joe?" Andrew asked.

"I was at Hotel Dieu. I've been there since late yesterday afternoon, with Fouad."

"Why? Did something happen to him?" asked Leila.

"He was in an accident."

"What? And you didn't let me know?" Andrew said.

"Joe," said Leila, "You're going every which way and not telling us much. What's going on?"

"You haven't seen or heard the news?" he asked.

"No, we didn't turn on the TV last night."

"A bomb blast killed Hassan Jaafar yesterday in Lattakia. Fouad was there with him. So was I. There was a secondary blast, and Fouad took it in his chest. I had him transported back here by helicopter and…"

"Why the hell didn't you call us? We would have come and kept you company at the hospital," said Andrew.

"After his initial work-up, he was transferred to ICU. You couldn't have done anything for him. You'll have plenty of time to visit him when he's discharged from ICU and in his own room."

It was hard for Andrew to stay calm after what he had heard. Finally, he blurted out, "What the fuck was Fouad doing meeting with Jaafar?"

Leila put her hand on his arm to calm him.

"Fouad's been horsing around with me all this time when he knew all along how to reach Jaafar, hasn't he?" Andrew waited before he spoke again. "Did he at least ask about Nadia?"

"As a matter of fact, he did. Apparently, she and Hassan had planned to marry and move away."

CHAPTER THIRTY-THREE

Though Joe had insisted there was no need for Sonia to go to the hospital, she decided otherwise. No one was going to tell *her* what she could or could not do if Fouad was seriously injured. As soon as Paul left her apartment, she grabbed her cell phone and called Dr. Richard Salame.

"Richard, this is Sonia Rizk."

"I've been expecting your call."

"How's Fouad? Is he…?" she asked, her voice trembling.

"I'm doing everything I can to make sure he pulls through this. So far, his vital signs are good. I'm cautiously optimistic that he'll make a full recovery."

She gave a nervous laugh. "You're not just saying that so I won't get hysterical?"

"I wouldn't do that to you, Sonia."

"How badly was he hurt?" she asked, reaching for her iPad so she could type everything he said.

"He sustained a primary blast lung injury as a result of his direct exposure to the secondary explosion."

"Didn't I have a similar injury?"

"Yes, but unlike you, Fouad was already in acute respiratory distress by the time the medical helicopter reached Lattakia. That complicated things a bit. He would have died en route to Beirut had the medics not administered high-flow oxygen. His injury also caused a pulmonary contusion…"

"What's that?"

"It's a bruising of the capillaries of the lung tissue. Because it can develop into something more serious, I admitted him to ICU and put him on a ventilator. He's heavily sedated, and I'll be monitoring him for possible acute respiratory distress syndrome."

"Hold on, you're going too fast."

"What?" he asked.

"I'm typing as you speak."

Sonia could hear him laughing.

"I forgot... journalists write everything down."

"What was that you said about a syndrome?"

"It's a complication oftentimes associated with pulmonary contusions, but since he's otherwise in good health, I expect him to respond."

"When will you know he's out of danger?"

"I can't say, but I'll keep him in ICU until he shows signs of recovering."

"Richard, I know I can't be in ICU with him, but I desperately need to be near him. As his friend and mine, could you arrange for Fouad to have a suite so I can stay with him when he's out of ICU?"

"It has already been handled. He has good insurance that will cover such incidentals. I even anticipated that you'd want to move in with him, so I've asked housekeeping to have an extra bed brought into his room. Does this meet with your approval?"

"Totally. Thank you, Richard."

"I'm glad my friend is so loved, Sonia. He's a lucky man."

"I'm the lucky one, Richard. I've needed a man like Fouad in my life for a long time."

She and Fouad made the perfect, imperfect pair. She knew she was blessed to be so loved and accepted with all her frailties.

She was practically giddy when she got off the phone with Richard. Fouad would make a full recovery. She tried a number of hair styles before deciding to wear it down, the fullness around her face drawing attention away from her eye patch. Dressed in a sleeveless silk dress with a flared skirt that fell just below her knees, she examined herself in the full-length mirror. Satisfied with her modest look, she pulled a small suitcase from her closet. Into it, she put a pair of slacks and matching sweater set, a two-piece suit appropriate for receiving visitors, underwear, nightgown and slippers, and a comfortable pair of heels along with her cosmetics and toiletries. She threw in a book and her computer and iPad before closing it and asking Hasna to carry it to the front door, and then called a taxi.

Ever since the attempt on her life, Sonia had been constantly on guard against another attack of some kind and only took cabs. Oftentimes, she wore a wig when she had to be out in public and removed her eye patch and concealed her eye with sunglasses. It was never talked about, but she knew Fouad worried that the Israelis would try again to take her out, the reason that Joe or one of his men were close by whenever she left her apartment.

Aside from an occasional walk around the hospital grounds and a quick meal in the cafeteria, Sonia divided the next two days between Fouad's suite, where she kept abreast of events as they unfolded in Syria, and standing outside the ICU, where she peered through a glass window and observed Fouad on his ventilator and hooked up to multiple IV lines with nurses monitoring his breathing and blood pressure on an overhead computer screen. Andrew and Leila came after work each day as did Paul, along with Joe and Roger, his security buddies. Grateful for these distractions, she received her visitors in what served as the living room of Fouad's two-room suite. It was comfortably furnished with a couch and two cushioned high back chairs, all done in a tasteful navy with gold trim, with a coffee table and two end tables. The inner room was Fouad's and otherwise sparsely furnished except for Sonia's bed.

On the morning of the third day, Fouad was finally transported to his suite. Sonia waited impatiently while the nurses hooked him back up to his IV drips and, as a final touch, attached a clip to his index finger that would record his vital signs, everything displayed on a wall-mounted monitor. Instead of a ventilator, he had graduated to small oxygen tubes inserted up his nostrils.

When the nurses finally left, Sonia tiptoed in to see him. His eyes were closed so she pulled a chair up to his bedside and sat quietly, content to finally be close enough to touch him, hear him breathe, and know he was mending. In the dimly lit room, silent except for the steady beep of the monitor, she also closed her eyes. She was startled out of a brief reverie when Fouad suddenly spoke.

"Hello, lady. The nurses told me that you were camped out here the last two days. Is that true?"

"Yes, my darling, didn't you feel my presence?" She laughed through her tears, relieved to hear his voice.

"Indeed, I did, thank you. I needed you here." He moved his head and looked around the room. "What an exquisite bouquet of flowers," he said when he spotted the vase next to his bed.

"From yours truly, with all my love," she said, stroking his cheek. "I'm so relieved you'll make a full recovery."

She leaned in and kissed his cheek, careful not to dislodge the oxygen tube.

Sonia noticed his eyes suddenly flood and his lips quiver. He tried to say something but could not get the words out. She patted his hand but otherwise let him be. He lay quiet for a while, staring at the ceiling, until he finally spoke.

"When I close my eyes, I see body parts and blood splattered everywhere. I see a strangely quiet place too."

"Everyone in such situations thinks they've seen God. It's quite normal. I wonder if I didn't see him, too, when I was injured. It felt very real, that momentary calmness, but we'll never know if it was real. It could have all been nonsense. If Paul were here, he'd advise you not to claim a conversion on the road to Damascus."

"Regardless of what it was, I'm not sure I'll ever recover from this."

"I am. I was where you are now. Don't you remember? You practically threatened to leave me if I didn't snap out of my depression, and since I didn't want to lose you, I worked hard to overcome a lot of obstacles."

He shook his head. "You're strong-willed. I'm not."

"Nonsense, I'll issue no threats, but I will suggest a palatable idea. We stop all this nonsense and retire. You give up trying to save the country, and I'll give up journalism, and we'll find some quiet, out-of-the-way place and live a peaceful life before the Israelis try again to kill me. We could go to Paris if you'd prefer somewhere livelier."

"You'll be just as safe here with me and my team watching over you."

She nodded. He was probably right.

"Don't get me wrong. I don't disagree with you about retiring, and I know I should stop what I'm doing and maybe someday we'll get out of here, but I betrayed a friend and that makes me feel very guilty, and I need to make right what I've done before I do anything else."

"Are you referring to Andrew?"

"Yes, I need to see him so I can explain why I met with Jaafar. Would you call him?"

"Surely that can wait until you're feeling better."

"On the contrary, I'll only feel better when I tell my friend what I did and why. Ask Paul to come too. He has a way of placating contentious situations."

"Okay, my darling, I'll call them if you think that will make you less agitated."

She left his bedside and was about to leave his room when she heard a bell ring outside. She went to the window and glanced out. A grade school abutted the hospital grounds. It was recess, and the children were rushing out the door to the playground, the girls to jump rope or play hop-scotch, the boys kicking soccer balls or playing tag. Such innocence—she had long forgotten what it meant to be so unspoiled and angelic. Hers had been a lifetime of lies and betrayal. She envied Fouad his integrity and honesty, his ability to confess a wrong. *I have no such virtues*, she thought, *and could never admit to Andrew that I arranged Nadia's kidnapping and destroyed their lives.*

She turned away from the window when she heard Fouad toss a bit in his bed.

"You're still here?" he asked. "I thought you were going to call Andrew and Paul."

"Right away, darling. In the meantime, get some rest."

She left his room and closed the door behind her.

* * *

onia waited for Andrew by the nursing station. He had promised to be there by eleven. When the elevator door opened on the sixth floor, she was surprised to see both Paul and him exit. She had not seen Andrew in about six weeks and was pleased to see him so happy and relaxed, in sharp contrast to the way she and Fouad felt.

"We walked into the lobby at the same time," said Paul, kissing her on the cheek. "How's Fouad today?"

"Ever so much better, thank God, but he's out of sorts… depressed, in fact. It's not like him to let anything get him down."

"This isn't just any old thing, Sonia," said Andrew, taking his turn to give her a kiss on her cheek. "He saw a man blown to bits. That would unsettle anyone."

"Do you know why he wants to see us?" asked Paul.

I will let Fouad tell them, she thought, and she shook her head.

"I just know he's anxious to see you both."

They followed her to his suite, tucked away at the end of the corridor.

"I hope Fouad was duly impressed by his luxury surroundings," said Andrew.

"I don't think he realizes where he is yet," she said.

"How did you rate such a suite?"

"Connections, my dear man, and good insurance." She laughed as she opened the door to Fouad's room and waved them in.

"Darling, look who I found wandering the corridors."

Fouad lifted his hand and beckoned to Andrew and Paul to come closer. Paul went and shook his hand while Andrew stood at the foot of his bed.

"Hello, friend. You're out of ICU which means you're doing much better. Congratulations."

"I'll feel even better when I've confessed a few things. I've asked both of you here for that very reason. Andrew, bring up a chair and sit here," he said, patting the right side of his bed. "Paul, you sit on the other side next to Sonia.

"Knowing Sonia, she's already warned you that I'm a bit out of sorts. There's a reason. I've wronged you, Andrew, by meeting with Jaafar behind your back, and I want to put things right. It's a complicated story, so bear with me."

"Are you sure you're up to this?" asked Sonia, as she plumped up his pillows so he could see everyone without straining his neck.

He turned to Paul and said, "*C'est ma seule confession, alors fait tres attention.*"

Paul laughed and responded, "I'll be listening to your every word."

Sonia knew this was going to be a serious discussion and even though diplomacy had only one official language—French—it was not Andrew's, and she knew they would conduct their conversation in English.

"Fair enough," said Fouad, and he began.

"Andrew, I'm not sure I ever told you that I've known Hassan Jaafar for a very long time."

Andrew shook his head. "No, but it stands to reason since you're both in Intelligence."

Sonia brought a bottle of 7Up with a straw to Fouad's mouth and let him take a sip.

"We trained together at Langley. Unlike me, who began in a rather low-level position in Internal Security and had to work my way up to the top, Jaafar rose in the ranks in Syrian Intelligence very quickly. Not only was he well introduced into the Assad clan, he married into a wealthy and influential family who opened doors for the dashing, young Intelligence officer. He served as Syria's Military Intelligence Chief in Lebanon from 1982 to 2002 and, through diplomacy and bribery, and quite a bit of brute force, became the most feared man in Lebanon with the power to order the arrest and oftentimes the murder of anyone he deemed an enemy."

"Why did the Lebanese allow him such free reign?" Andrew asked.

"They had no choice. At the time, Syria was under the reign of Hafez al-Assad, Bashar's father. A shrewd politician, he had aligned himself with Bush senior during the first Gulf War. His reward was *carte blanche* to maintain control of Lebanon, including keeping thirty-five thousand of his troops here until George W. ordered them out after blaming Bashar Assad for the Hariri assassination in 2005."

"It makes no sense that one country could essentially own another."

"The blurring of strategic and self-interest is not easily understood, even for a seasoned expat," said Paul, "but inexplicable things do happen. Surely you've figured that out by now."

"Yes, I have—the hard way."

"It was during this time that Jaafar met Nadia and fell in love with her. I assume she filled you in on the details of their brief affair and how she had refused to marry him. He kidnapped her husband and threw him in a Syrian prison for thirteen years."

"And then she was kidnapped, and I was almost killed. Tell me something I don't already know, Fouad," Andrew said testily. "Otherwise, I see no need to flush out such painful memories."

"Okay, how's this for raw truth. I knew all along where Jaafar was keeping Nadia but chose not to rescue her."

Andrew stood abruptly and gave Fouad a piercing look. "You son of a bitch!" he shouted. "How could you...?" He paced the room and at one point raised his fist about to hit the wall.

Sonia played with her empty coffee cup, squeezing it, while in her mind she kept repeating "This is all my fault, all my fault." She started to get up and go to him, but Paul put out his hand and stopped her.

"Leave him. He needs to burn off his anger."

She ignored Paul's remark.

"Andrew, I know you're angry, but this is important, so sit down and listen."

"Fine," he said, returning to Fouad's bedside. "So, let me get this straight. You allowed Nadia to be kept a prisoner all that time when you could have rescued her. What a goddamn idiot I've been... and here I thought you were my friend. What the fuck were you doing playing with her life like that? Who gave you that right? If you weren't already beaten up in your bed, I'd tear your fucking head off."

"I know, my friend," said Fouad, "and all I can do is apologize. And I deserve a good box in the head."

Sonia knew he was trying to disarm Andrew. He was being earnest, not trying to justify his actions, but Andrew wasn't willing to let him get away with any of it.

"I can't accept any excuses for your betrayal. That's bullshit," said Andrew.

"What would have been the right thing to do, Andrew? Isn't it better to sacrifice one individual for the sake of a whole country?"

"For a whole country, yes, okay, but what is the decent thing to do? Isn't it to work harder to try and change the system that allows us to continue to always do the wrong things? Maybe this is naïve thinking, but it's the kind of world I'd rather live in. Look at what we have now."

Andrew got up and paced again, stopping this time in front of the window and staring out. Paul went to him and put his arm on his shoulder. "Are you all right, my man?"

"No, I'm not," Andrew replied, as he turned to Paul. "I suspected something was going on between Fouad and Joe, but I never dreamed I was the fool in their scheme."

He turned and looked at Fouad. "And you knew nothing of her condition? Or did you? Were you in contact with Jaafar all along? Did he tell you he was having a frolicking good time with her and not to worry? Is that how it played out?"

"Come back and sit down, Andrew," Fouad said. "I have a lot more to say."

"Why should I give a rat's ass what else you have to say? I've heard enough."

"Please, Andrew," implored Sonia. "At least let him finish."

"Oh, so now you're the righteous voice of reason? Were you up to your neck in this 'keep Andrew in the dark' scheme too?"

"No, she wasn't, Andrew. Sonia knows nothing about what I'm about to say, so please let me explain what I did and why, and then you can judge me."

All Sonia could think about was how much trouble Fouad's confession was going to cause. He was essentially telling Andrew a lie, and there would be huge consequences as a result. She tried to get Fouad's attention to signal he should stop, but he paid her no attention.

Andrew turned and stared again out the window while the three others sat in silence, waiting to see what he decided to do. He eventually turned, came back to his chair and sat.

"Thank you," Fouad said, as he was about to take another sip of his 7Up.

"After Rafic Hariri's assassination in March 2005 and the expulsion of Syrian forces from Lebanon, we experienced an internal war within our Intelligence units, essentially pitting the newly formed Information Branch, which enjoyed the backing of the opposition Sunni coalition, against the traditional Christian armed forces and the Shiite-led General Security offices. As it turned out, Adnan Kassab, the man who led the Information Branch, had many loyalties."

"You're wasting my time, Fouad. What does this Kassab guy have to do with Nadia?"

"A lot, so shut up and let me continue."

When he coughed and winced in pain, Sonia said, "Maybe we should postpone this until you're feeling better."

"No," he insisted, "I'm fine, but I'll take some more 7Up, please." He took a sip.

"It turns out that Kassab was working closely with Saudi Intelligence to facilitate the transfer of arms and money to the jihadists training to overthrow Bashar Assad. An old acquaintance of mine, Robert Jenkins, was also working with Kassab."

"He's the American I met when I was in rehab," said Andrew.

"The very same," replied Fouad. "Jenkins was with Jaafar and me at Langley. He was one of those privileged bastards who literally got away with murder. Well, when I found out Kassab and Jenkins were collaborating in Assad's overthrow, I contacted Jaafar and told him what they were up to. At first, he backed off, said he was happily retired and wanted nothing more to do with Intelligence work. I played on his love of country until finally he wanted to know what he'd get out of it. I asked him what he wanted."

"I want Nadia Khoury," he said. "I love her and want to marry her."

Sonia was listening to this interchange and was shocked when she heard Jaafar's demand.

"I knew he'd always been mad about her, ever since he'd served in Lebanon, so I couldn't refuse," said Fouad. "It was a way to save my country. It seemed reasonable to me, and so I assured him I could do that as long as he got rid of Kassab."

Sonia watched Andrew to see how he would respond. She found Fouad a bit too brutally honest.

"You gave her away just like that?" Andrew said. "People mean nothing to you, do they?"

"That's not true," Fouad said. "Yes, I placed loyalty to Lebanon above Nadia. In exchange for Jaafar's help, I willingly sacrificed her so I could in some small way stop the flow of arms to the jihadists. It was probably a useless act on my part because it was going to happen sooner or later no matter what I did to try and stop them." He paused. "Believe me when I say I knew she wasn't being harmed in any way."

Andrew stood up, put his hands on his head, and turned to Fouad.

"How can you say such an outrageous thing, Fouad? She *was* being harmed. She was a prisoner. That's a form of abuse, in case you didn't know. Did Jaafar say she had agreed to marry him?"

"No, he didn't, only that he hoped she'd eventually agree. As his wife, she'd have travel documents, and they could leave Syria."

"So even if she had agreed, it would have been to ultimately obtain her freedom. Is that what you're saying?"

"Yes, in all probability, but I stand by my decision, however painful it is to have you hear. Most Lebanese don't want to see regime change in Syria, nor do we want an Islamic state in Lebanon. For the most part, we're minorities and hate the idea of a bunch of Sunni lunatics running things. Democracy has its flaws, but right now it's the only thing we have."

"What was Jaafar's role in all of this?" Andrew asked. "What did he have to give up? Who was he asked to betray?"

"Jaafar made good on his promise. Kassab was caught red-handed smuggling arms into Syria, and Jaafar took him out. The incident was quietly hushed up because no one in Kassab's coalition, let alone his Sunni handlers, wanted anyone to know what he had been doing on the Turkish border. He was buried in a shallow, dusty grave there.

"On my end, my unit drove a car to a quiet neighborhood in Achrafieh. They placed sixty kilos of C4 explosives inside the car. Then, they took an unidentified body from the city morgue, put it in the car and blew it up. I regret to say that two innocent bystanders died when the car exploded. The story that was released to the press was that Kassab kept a small apartment near the site of the explosion and unbeknownst to his office had returned from a trip abroad ahead of time and spent the night there. The next morning, when he started his car, it blew up. All that remained of the body were pieces of burned flesh. His death was announced, and he was given a state funeral with all the pomp and circumstance befitting a man of his stature."

"Wasn't C4 the explosive used in my assassination attempt?" asked Sonia.

"Yes, but in Kassab's case, we used a larger amount of explosives to make sure the body would be unidentifiable."

"And no one ever suspected what really happened?" asked Paul.

"The leak came from the Lebanese side that it was Jaafar who'd killed Kassab. It was from Internal Security, one of my Damascus Street colleagues, in fact, who leaked the information. They all hated Jaafar.

"Robert Jenkins must have figured it out too, but he wasn't going to come forward and implicate himself. And that's why I'm awfully sure he's the one who arranged Jaafar's assassination. The Saudis probably knew too, especially since Kassab was one of their most loyal lieutenants. Jaafar knew, sooner or later, that they'd put all the pieces together, and that's why he was eager to leave the country as soon as possible."

"How can you play with the lives of other people and still live with yourself?" asked Andrew. "Okay, you got rid of Kassab, but you killed two innocent people to do it."

"Those kinds of choices come with the job, Andrew. I pledged loyalty to my country when I began working in Intelligence. Oftentimes, in order to save a country, and in particular Lebanon, which has already suffered fifteen years of civil war, you make hard choices, and neither the decision I made to take out Kassab at the cost of two innocent lives nor the decision I made to let Jaafar keep Nadia were, in my opinion, too steep a price to pay to help save the country from further instability. If regime change does take place in Syria, we will inevitably have trouble on our border with the jihadists trying to infiltrate, particularly in the Bekaa, and I'll continue to do whatever it takes to, if not completely stop them, at least curtail their impact on this country that I love and have sworn to protect."

Andrew got up and walked around the room again, his emotions winding down enough to allow him to think rationally again. "What a complicated mess. Do all countries function this way?"

"Pretty much," replied Fouad, "when they need to."

"What are you going to do about Robert Jenkins?"

"At the moment, nothing... he's just been appointed the new US ambassador to Syria. I'll know where to find him when it comes time for revenge."

Before Andrew could say anything else, his cell phone rang. Sonia watched him pull out his Nokia. He flipped it open and answered. He wore the face of a beat-up, defeated person. She had seen him wear that face once before—the day Nadia was kidnapped.

It took her a few minutes to realize that he was talking to Nadia. She tried to listen in, but Andrew moved to the window and lowered his voice. He stared out, oblivious to her and the others in the room, all silent, all staring at him, trying to figure out what he was saying.

She heard Andrew say where he was, and she knew they were arranging a rendezvous.

"I'll be there," he said, and he snapped the phone shut before turning around.

Sonia did not want it to be blatantly obvious that she had been listening. Should she go up to him? Instead, she found herself saying, "Still got that old phone?"

When he turned around and glared at her, Paul came up to him. "Are you going to be okay?"

"I have to leave, Paul." He shook his hand, opened the door and left without looking back.

CHAPTER THIRTY-FOUR

Nadia awoke to someone knocking on her door. "Ani, where are you? Why aren't you answering?"

"Nadia, it's me, your mother."

Nadia opened her eyes and studied her surroundings.

"Sorry, Mama, I hadn't remembered I was home."

"Ani just called."

"Please come in, Mama."

"I didn't want to disturb you," Carole said, opening the door and peering in, "but…"

"Good morning, Mama, how nice to see you."

"And you, darling. Ani wanted directions to the house. She's already crossed the border, and if there's no traffic, she hopes to be here in about an hour and a half. I thought you might want to be up in time to receive her."

"Is she coming alone?"

"No, a man named Moussa is driving her."

Nadia was pleased that Ani had acted so promptly. It had reaffirmed her loyalty. After explaining the details surrounding her escape the previous evening, Victor had wondered about possible compensation for the two. That was when Nadia had said they were both unemployed and probably looking for work. She was curious to see what would happen once Ani and Moussa arrived. Thinking ahead to the trap she intended to set for Bob Jenkins, she concluded it would be useful to have them both here under her control should she need trustworthy accomplices to help carry out her plan.

"I'll shower and dress and be down shortly, Mama."

Reluctant to get up just yet, Nadia lingered a while longer in bed. She had slept poorly. The last time she had been in this room she had snuck Andrew in after her parents had retired for the evening. Like eager young lovers, they had torn off each other's clothes and made love. Such joyously happy and carefree days—before her dreams had been stolen and her life destroyed. Even as a prisoner, with no foreseeable means of escape, she had clung to the notion, however implausible, that she would see Andrew again. It was shortly after Sonia had almost lost her life, and she had initiated sex with Hassan, that she knew she would never be able to go back to Andrew. She dreaded their reunion because he would know as soon as he saw her that she was not the Nadia he had known and loved.

Perhaps none of us are the people we thought we once were, she reasoned. She knew that on one level there was an emotionally pure Nadia who still loved Andrew, but at the moment she *could* not, or *did* not, want to reveal that woman because only the Nadia of lost innocence would be able to avenge Hassan's death through actions the virtuous Nadia would never be able to carry out.

She glanced at the clock and, realizing the hour, threw off her sheet and climbed out of bed. She opened her bedroom door, walked to the top of the stairs and called down, "Mama, please make me a coffee."

"Of course, darling."

Already she missed her quiet morning ritual when Ani had brought a coffee to her in bed. After so much time together, and without her ever having asked, Ani had taken care of her every need.

"Will you be wanting breakfast too, or shall I clear the table?" Carole asked.

"Leave breakfast. I'll put the things away when I'm finished."

Nadia's challenge would not only be adjusting to her newly-gained freedom. She also needed a dose of patience to deal with her parents who had their own habits and sensitivities. To their credit, they had been discreet in front of Bob Jenkins, when he had delivered her home, not to bombard her with questions, confident, apparently, that with time she would tell all. That would not happen. She had changed in ways they would never understand. It was enough that they would discover how bossy and argumentative she had become, a consequence, no doubt, of running Hassan's household. She might also have to explain the subtle changes in her diction and expanded vocabulary, an unexpected reward for reading so many books during her captivity. And if they did ask, she would lovingly describe for them the room that smelled of fine leather and cigars, where the sun streamed in through the high windows, warming her shoulders and neck as she sat on the couch and read. Now that Hassan was gone, she wondered what would happen to his estate and all his books.

Despite these challenges, Nadia resolved to try to be the daughter her parents remembered, the formally designated *Madame la Commisssaire,* a title that came with her appointment to the UN High Commission on Human Rights, the daughter who loved to cuddle up on the love seat and have her father prepare her coffee the way she liked it. All those things she would attempt to be again.

When she recalled the previous evening, she realized that with practically no effort there had been minimal friction. When Bob Jenkins finally departed, Carole had invited Nadia to join them for a late dinner.

"Merci, Mama, I'm actually famished. I can't remember when I ate last. And Papa, I'd like a whisky, if you don't mind, two shots over ice."

He had looked at her surprised. "You never used to like whiskey."

"I didn't, you're right, but my tastes have changed, and now I do. You'll discover a lot of new habits, Papa. I hope none of them will offend you."

"Indeed not, we're just thankful to have you back," said Carole, choking on her words. "And to be honest, you'll find us older and more set in our ways."

"Never mind that, Mama. I acquired some pretty bad habits myself when dealing with Hassan's staff. So, I ask your indulgence while I adjust to living in the real world again."

"It's strange to hear you refer to Jaafar by his first name," Victor said.

"Papa, I lived with the man a long time. Regardless of what you may think, we did establish a code of civility."

"I didn't mean to meddle in whatever transpired between the two of you."

"I know, Papa. I realize how hard it is to even imagine such a thing."

An awkward silence passed before Victor spoke again.

"I can't get over how amazingly fit you look for someone who's been held captive for so long."

"I swam and worked out in Hassan's gym... never missed a day. It was one of the smartest things I did during my captivity since I was alone for long stretches when he was away on business. Now that I'm home, I'll miss my routine. By chance, do we have an old treadmill somewhere in the house?"

"I'm afraid not," Victor said. "As you may recall, our daily exercise included laps in the pool. We never felt the need to invest in any equipment."

"If it's all right with you, I'd like to look into buying a few machines. I could set up a small gym in the basement."

"Heavens, why the basement?" Carole asked. "It's dark and musty. You can transform the guest bedroom upstairs into your gym, if you'd like. It's sunny with a delightful view of my rose gardens."

"That's a great idea, Mama. Merci."

"As to my other activities, Papa, I listened to music and read hundreds of books. Bad things can be said about the monster Jaafar, all of them no doubt true, but he was extremely cultured and had a library that would have been the envy of most. When he put me in charge of his household staff, I gave them permission to borrow books from his library. It had been the first time any of them had been given such an opportunity, and the most amazing thing happened. When they'd finished their work, they'd search out a quiet corner, pull out their book and read. It was rewarding to see them stimulated and curious and learning new things. So, there you have it, a brief overview of my time in captivity."

"Thankfully, this is all behind you, Nadia, and you can pick up the life you were forced to abandon. I'm referring to Andrew, of course," Carole said. "Would you like to see him? Shall I—?"

"No, Mama, not yet. I'm not ready."

She did not dare tell her parents that she was in mourning. She had just lost the man who had gently etched his way into her heart, the same man they had feared and despised all those years ago. Though melancholy, Nadia also recognized the irony in Hassan's death. He had given her back her freedom.

She saw them exchange glances but chose to remain silent. This was her private business, not theirs.

* * *

Nadia answered the door when Ani and Moussa arrived and invited them in. She hugged Ani, shook hands with Moussa and introduced them to her parents who had joined her in the foyer. Ani handed her the envelope, then asked how she had gotten home. After a brief overview of the journey, her parents invited them into the living room. Nadia stood behind her mother's chair and leaning over its high back, listened to the four of them chatting about the situation in Syria, where their families lived, and whether or not they were looking for work. After the requisite polite small talk, her mother invited Ani to come with her to the kitchen while Victor took Moussa to the garage to show him around. Left alone, Nadia retrieved the leather travel bag from her room, retreated to her father's study, shut the door and sat in his swivel leather chair behind his desk and emptied out the contents of the bag on the desk. She opened the envelope and began reading. It described Bob Jenkins as a gifted diplomat who spoke not only Arabic but Turkish, German and French. He had served as US ambassador to Algeria prior to the so-called Arab uprising, had ordered the assassination of some powerful clerics, and, until recently, had been his government's number two man in Iraq, in charge of recruiting and training terrorist brigade units in Turkey, Jordan, Qatar, Saudi Arabia and Libya—a man more powerful and more terrifying than Hassan but with one major weakness—beautiful women. He loved them and bedded them. Was she bothered by that? On the contrary, it just meant it would be easier to trap him. Did that mean she would agree to see him again? Yes, in due time. She planned to expose and destroy him, but first she needed to say goodbye to Andrew and send him away. She did not want him involved in any way in what she was planning to do. He was the good American. She collected all the pages and returned them to their envelope just as her father popped his head inside the door.

"Nadia, can we see you?"

"Yes, Papa." She exited the study to see Ani and Moussa, along with her mother, standing in the foyer.

"We have some good news to announce," Victor said. "Your mother has decided to hire Ani to help in the kitchen, and I've agreed to take on Moussa as my chauffeur. He has proven that he knows the city streets well enough and has a clean driving record, and since Samir's old room is vacant—my chauffeur just took another job in the north—I've agreed to let Moussa live there."

"Ani, do you think you'll be happy here?" Nadia asked.

"Yes, *Sitt,* and I'm very appreciative, as I know Moussa is. We both help our parents financially, so this opportunity means a great deal to both of us."

"Well then, it's settled," Nadia said. "Welcome to the Khoury household. I trust everyone will be happy."

Carole took Ani and left the room.

"Moussa, I have an errand to run, and I'll need a driver."

"I'll be in the garage, *Sitt.* Whenever you're ready, just let me know."

After he left the room, Nadia asked her father to join her in his study.

He followed her across the foyer and closed the door behind him. He stood for a moment and looked around the room.

"When you were a child, you'd bring me in here when I got home and quiz me on the cases I'd presented that day in court. Such fond memories—you the inquisitive child lawyer long before you became one. Best of all, it was our special private time."

"How could I forget, Papa, some of my fondest childhood memories. Do you ever wish you could go back to those innocent times?"

"No, because they'd probably be a disappointment."

She nodded. "I agree." After all she had been through, yet another reason she could not go back to Andrew.

"I took some important documents from Hassan's safe, along with a wad of cash and other valuables." She showed him the bag. "I need a secure place to keep everything, Papa. I'd rather not divulge the contents just yet, or why I took them. It's safer this way... trust me."

He nodded. "You can use the safe in this room."

"But I need to keep you out of this."

"If you want to do that, you'll need to get a safety deposit box at the bank. If you're looking for convenience and easy accessibility, use my safe. But then, I'd automatically be involved. Your choice." He took a key from his pocket and opened the safe. "Put your stuff inside until you decide what you want to do."

Before she put the envelope and leather bag in the safe, she removed some cash.

"Merci, Papa."

"If there's any legal work you need done," he said, as he locked the safe and returned the key to his pocket, "I'll be happy to take care of it."

"I'll keep that in mind."

"Do you want me to prepare a press release about your return?"

"Yes, why don't you do that while I contact my mission at the United Nations. They'll also want to issue a statement."

"I'll write up something tonight. Better that it come from us as soon as possible, and not from someone like Sonia."

"That bitch! She's the one who arranged my kidnapping and destroyed my life."

"What? That's outrageous!" Victor remained quiet for a moment and then asked, "You're sure about this?"

"Yes, Hassan confirmed it. He gave her information about the Hariri assassination in exchange for me."

"We must expose her."

"I intend to, but I'd like to tell Andrew before I go public. He was just as affected as I was."

"I can't imagine how he'll take it."

"He'll be as crushed and as angry as I am. Friends don't do that to friends."

"And get away with it," Victor said.

* * *

A s she left the library, she saw her mother coming out of the kitchen.
"I was just about to come looking for you, Mama."

"What do you need?" Carole asked.

"Clothes. My tastes have changed, and I don't like anything in my closet. It feels like so long since I've shopped here, and I've no idea where to go."

"But you have beautiful things, Nadia."

"I'll share a secret, Mama. When I got to Jaafar's mansion, I discovered that he'd gone ahead and stocked a closet full of expensive designer wear for me. This is all I wore—the best cashmeres, silks, linens and wools. I've been spoiled and don't want to go back to wearing ordinary clothes, and since money is no object, why not buy and wear what pleases me. So, dear Mama, that's why I'm going shopping."

"In that case, you'd best go downtown. I'd be happy to go with you if you'd like, and I can show you all the recent changes."

"I'd love to have you come along. I don't have a current credit card. Even my passport needs to be renewed, but I do have wads of cash, and you and I can buy whatever we want."

"I don't need a thing, Nadia."

"Nonsense, Mama, it's not about needing. It's about spending money and having fun and being free to walk around and do as I please. Shall we have Moussa drive us?"

"Of course," Carole said. "It's impossible to park anywhere in town."

"Then it's settled. Let's go get dressed."

Nadia put a great deal of care into getting herself ready. Lebanese women did not leave home unless they were well put together. It was a matter of pride and social etiquette to look one's best anytime, anywhere. How would they be waited on in a high-end shop if they did not look like they belonged there? Nadia chose a sleeveless white silk blouse, a string of pearls, a short black skirt and high heels—the basic chic outfit that showed off her well-toned arms and long, lean legs. She brushed her hair to a shiny luster and left it down to fall in layers around her face, then applied eye liner, soft brown shadow and mascara, rouge for her cheeks and a glossy fire-engine red to her lips. She inspected herself in the mirror. Satisfied, she left her room and descended the stairs to the foyer. Her mother was already there, dressed in a similar outfit. Nadia laughed.

"No one will ever guess we're mother and daughter."

Chuckling, Carole grabbed her daughter's arm and led her out the front door.

Moussa dropped them off on Rue Clemenceau. At Chanel's, Nadia bought several silk blouses, skirts and two summer dresses. Carole may have thought they were too tight or too short, but Nadia appreciated that her mother spared her any adverse comments. She had been cooped up for years, and she was having a marvelous time walking about, looking gorgeous and having men stare at her.

After four hours, Nadia was ready to keep going, but her mother protested.

"You're going to have to get me a wheelchair if we don't stop right now."

"Okay, how about a compromise. While we have a light lunch, I'll call Moussa and have him collect our bags. Will that do?"

Carole laughed. "Very nicely, my dear. I might even be persuaded to show you the new souks. They just opened last year."

* * *

As a child, Nadia had walked through the ancient souks with her father and then remembered them being reduced to rubble during the fifteen year long civil war. The new Beirut souks which had only opened in 2009, with their meandering alleyways and vaulted ceiling, inundated the senses with their two hundred shops, twenty-five restaurants and fourteen cinemas. She might have been impressed by the billions of dollars spent to restore Beirut's downtown, but as it was Saudi Arabia's money, that was a problem. As Lebanon's major investor, the Saudis could hold the country hostage anytime they wanted, particularly if things did not go their way in the current Sunni-Shiite battle for influence across the region.

From a wealthy Greek Orthodox family, Nadia had been born into a privileged world where education, a successful career and the right socially-connected marriage were all that mattered, but that was before the civil war had gone and shattered that utopian dream. It also used to matter to her that her five-thousand-year-old city, where Phoenicians had traded their precious purple dyes to Persians and Babylonians, and where Cleopatra was thought to have strolled in 48 BCE, could vanish in a war and then be rebuilt into something spectacular only to be destroyed again in the next inevitable conflict. Feeling empty and soulless, she no longer cared about any of these things.

* * *

By her third morning home, Nadia was missing Hassan, wanting him beside her. During the last few months he had come to her bed every night. It was almost as if he knew something was going to happen. He was all over her and driving her crazy because he wanted her to marry him. And now he was gone, and she missed him. And she realized, yet again, that this was another reason she could not go back to Andrew. She could play the Sonia card and prey on Andrew's emotions, but she was not Sonia, and she would never do that to Andrew.

She spent the morning mulling over how she would deal with him. Finally, she pulled up his number and dialed his cell phone.

After some awkward moments, she said, "How about a stroll along the Corniche. I feel the need for open spaces and fresh air. I'll come with the chauffeur to pick you up. Where are you now?"

"I'm at Hotel Dieu."

"Meet me on the corner of the Damascus Street-Mazra intersection in half an hour."

"I'll be there."

When she hung up, she asked Moussa to have the car ready.

* * *

She was not sure Andrew would recognize her father's Mercedes, but from across the intersection, he was already waving. As soon as Moussa pulled the car up to the curb, Andrew opened the back door and climbed in.

At the sight of him, her emotions overwhelmed her and, arms extended, she embraced him. She had not intended to let this happen, but it had, and now she had to find a way to bring her feelings back under control.

She pulled away from him and examined his face, all the while trying to adjust her short skirt and cover her thighs.

"Oh Andrew…" She took hold of his hand and patted it before leaning back in her seat.

She watched him staring at her. "Have I changed that much?"

"Of course you've changed, and so have I, and I stare because I'm in shock."

"You never were a good liar, Andrew Sullivan. Out with it."

"It's the first time I've seen you wearing makeup. You never used to."

"I'd forgotten that." She had gotten used to lying to Jaafar, and so it seemed only natural to lie to Andrew. When you become a modern-day Scheherazade, you lie all the time.

"I remember everything about you, Nadia. You never used to dress like that either."

"There are a lot of things I do now that I never did before," she said, sighing. "You've gone and grown up on me, Andrew. You didn't used to be so assertive."

"I never felt the need. I always thought you were pretty damned-near perfect."

She laughed and said, "Well, shame on me for changing."

She was surprised by how much it bothered Andrew. Of course, she had also taken notice of how much she had changed. She was simply pretending not to. It had started with small changes—a little makeup on the eyes and lips, shorter and tighter skirts, a bit more cleavage—and then, because it pleased Hassan, a bit more of everything.

"You made it easy to fall in love with you, Andrew. You were innocent and trusting. We were only together six months. Sometimes I think those were the best months of my life, but what did we really know about each other?"

When she compared their relationship to her marriage with Elie, she realized she had not known her husband all that well, either, and, in the end, had found she hated him.

"Were we so blindly in love that our relationship never got beyond the bed sheets?"

As soon as she said that, she knew it was unduly cruel.

"That's not how I'd have described our affair."

He looked at Moussa, and Nadia said, "It's okay, he doesn't speak English.

"Never mind all of that, darling," she resumed. "We're two people with very fond memories, and I'm glad we got to share them. Now, let's get to the Corniche so we can have a walk."

Pointing to the driver, she said, "Andrew, I'd like you to meet Moussa, our new chauffeur. Moussa, this is my friend Andrew."

"Technically, I'm still your fiancé."

"Yes, so you are," she said, laughing. "Moussa and his friend Ani helped me escape after Jaafar was killed. Since they both needed a job, Papa hired him as his chauffeur and Ani as part of the kitchen staff."

Nadia noticed Andrew give her driver a curious look and wondered why.

Moussa gave a nod and tipped his cap. She was annoyed he had not turned around when introduced. She intended to reprimand him for his bad manners when they got home.

Andrew spoke to Moussa in Arabic. "Thank you for what you did for *Sitt* Nadia."

"*Kirmalek*," he replied, as he pulled away from the curb, merging onto Mazra Boulevard. Heading due west, and with little traffic, they reached the Corniche in minutes.

Nadia asked Moussa to drop them off at the beginning of the promenade across from the Crazy Horse Cafe. When he stopped the car, Andrew got out first, then lent Nadia his hand and helped her out. She, in turn, slipped her arm through his, and they began a slow stroll along the sea.

They had not gotten very far when Andrew stopped abruptly. He turned and pointed to the Phoenicia Hotel behind them.

"Your parents put me up there the day I arrived."

"I'd forgotten that, but then I was off meeting Jaafar, wasn't I, trying to find out if Elie was still alive. Those were such god-awful times, Andrew."

"There were some good times too. Surely you haven't forgotten I'd come to celebrate our engagement party."

She leaned into his chest and said, "Of course I haven't." But she had.

"I remember waking up early the next morning. I was anxious about meeting your parents and knew a good jog would settle my nerves, so I came down here. It was a cool morning, running along the Corniche under the palm trees with waves crashing up along the sea wall. By the time I'd run the three miles to the lighthouse and back, I was ready to take on the world."

She stared at him as he rattled on. He was nervous. That was why he could not stop talking. But damn if he did not look even more handsome, and *he* was dressed differently too. He used to wear the usual physician attire—the long-sleeve dress shirt, pleated trousers and fancy shoes—and now he sported a polo shirt, khakis and sockless loafers, like a man at ease with himself.

"I know I'm babbling like an idiot," Andrew said, "and you've got a curious look on your face like you don't recognize me."

"I don't... I mean I'd forgotten how goofy you get when you're nervous."

"Yes, I guess I do still get that way."

"Have I changed, Andrew?"

"Yes, but in ways I hadn't expected. You're fit and trim, not exactly the image of the kidnap victim I'd envisioned. Sorry, I don't know what I'm saying. I stayed in Lebanon so I'd be here when you came home, and I started working in Shatilla to make you proud, and I expected our first meeting to be joyous, and here we are talking at each other like perfect strangers instead of lovers."

Part of her wanted to be her former self and tell Andrew she still loved him, but she could not say what he wanted to hear.

"It's normal to feel that way after such a long absence, Andrew."

"Is it?"

They stopped and leaned across the railing. To their east, they could see the coastline all the way to Jounieh and Mount Lebanon with its snow-capped summit. The St. George Hotel was nearby as were a half-dozen other luxury hotels. Farther up the Corniche, past multi-million-dollar apartment buildings, stood the American University of Beirut, better known as AUB, with its sprawling sixty-acre campus.

Nadia took a deep breath and turned to Andrew. "I'm not the same person you knew before, and I'll tell you a bit more, but right now I want to hear about you and your work. Papa told me about some of the extraordinary things you're doing in Shatilla. And I can't believe you went and learned Arabic. You're amazing. Say something for me in Arabic."

"Another time. Between us, I prefer English. It's our language."

"Yes, you're right."

"After you were abducted, I needed distractions. Otherwise, I would have gone mad. So yes, I studied Arabic and well, aside from the obvious accent, which I'll probably never manage to lose, I actually do quite well, thank you very much."

"Well done, Andrew, and you look in top form too."

"After my accident…"

"It wasn't an accident. Don't trivialize something so serious. It was an assault with intent to kill, and I know it took you a full year to recover."

"Anyway, during rehab, I started working out with a trainer named Joe. We became friends, and now we share an apartment. I'll get around to telling you more, but now I want to know how you survived your captivity."

"It's complicated. I did what I had to do to survive. It's best we leave it at that. I will only say that I was not abused."

"Are you kidding me?" he said, wide-eyed. "Kidnapping is a form of abuse. Everything you had to do with that man was abuse of some sort."

"Yes, in theory, you're right, but that's not how it was."

He let out a nervous laugh. "Joe was training me for the day I would come and save you. That was my incentive to go to the gym and work out." He sighed. "That was a silly idea, wasn't it?"

"My knight in shining armor. How very noble you are, but fortunately I didn't need rescuing."

"No, I guess you didn't."

He just made a fool of himself, and you poked fun at him, Nadia, and he is only now realizing it, so say something nice.

"What I meant was that you'd have gotten yourself killed if you'd ever tried coming anywhere near Jaafar's compound."

"How did you finally escape?"

"My maid Ani and her friend Moussa, our new driver, got me out of the house as soon as we learned that Jaafar had been killed. Along the way, our car was stopped by a man named Robert Jenkins. Apparently, he was on his way to Jaafar's house when he spotted our car and pulled us over. He insisted on escorting me back to Beirut."

"He's a dangerous man, Nadia. I ran into him while I was in rehab. He comes across as a nice person, but he actually runs death squads in Iraq and plans to do the same in Syria."

"Yes, I know. Jaafar called him the ultimate predator."

"There's something else I need to tell you. I've started a relationship with Leila."

Nadia hoped he had not noticed the sense of relief that had just shown up on her face.

"No apologies needed, Andrew, I've done worse."

"This isn't a competition."

"No, I didn't mean it that way."

"I want you to know it wasn't intentional."

"Andrew, stop, please. I understand."

"If we could go back to the time before…"

She stood before him and took his hands in hers. "We can't go back, Andrew. We had something beautiful, and it was stolen from us. Our lives were thrown into chaos, and now we're different people. You understand that, don't you? And now you need to discover if your relationship with Leila will make you happy. And I hope it does, and that she'll bring you great joy."

"Do you mean that, Nadia?"

"Yes, Andrew, I do, with all my heart."

Not only had Andrew announced a new romance, he had also managed to maintain his inner goodness while she had lost hers. Hassan had seen to that when he had turned her into his whore.

Neither spoke for a while, preferring, instead, to stop and lean on the railing to watch the action around them—the dozen or so fishermen each sitting on a colorful, short plastic stool along the rocky edges below the Corniche, a group of young boys daring one another to jump into the cold water, and two young lovers sitting arm in arm, their heads together, looking aimlessly out to sea.

Nadia nudged him. "Do you remember our visit to the Beaufort Castle with Camille?"

"How could I forget? It was there that you finally told me you'd divorce Elie and be mine forever."

"This is how I'll always remember you, Andrew, noble and honorable."

He looked at Nadia and smiled. "We had something special, didn't we?"

"Until Sonia went and spoiled it."

"What are you saying?"

"She's the one who arranged my kidnapping. She made a deal with Jaafar—me in exchange for information about the Hariri assassination."

"Sonia did this for a fucking story? I had no idea... I can't believe it," he said, dumbfounded. "What are we going to do about it?"

"I'm going to have that bitch's tongue torn out."

"Bitch that she is, of course, she deserves to have something happen to her, but she already has. She's blinded in one eye and without a fully-functioning arm, so maybe karma has already punished her."

"Screw karma. That woman deserves to die."

Nadia knew she was probably going to have to compromise and share the material she had on Jenkins with Sonia, and this would be getting two birds with one stone because that information would get her killed.

"I want her punished too, but..."

"She should be tortured and bled to death," Nadia interrupted.

He shook his head. "My Nadia would never have gone to that extreme."

"Don't you understand yet, Andrew? That Nadia is gone. I am the new Nadia, the one you don't want back, and I will not put up with people like Sonia ever again."

She shook her head and stamped her foot. "You're so goddamned righteous, Andrew. Yet another reason I fell in love with you." She threw up her hands in mock surrender. "Okay, maybe it's enough that she knows I know."

"How is that?"

"Let's just say she knows and leave it at that." Nadia tightened her grip on his arm and said, "Come on, let's walk to the end of the Corniche before I call Moussa."

When they eventually reached the waiting car, she asked, "Can we drop you somewhere?"

"If you don't mind, I'd appreciate a lift to somewhere near Damascus Street."

Sad, yet relieved to have gotten through their encounter with enough dignity to save face, she neither turned nor waved when he said goodbye and climbed out of the car.

As soon as she got home, she retreated to her bedroom and cried. She knew that she had lost the better part of herself and now was ready to move on as a Sonia. Did this mean she would now turn her attention to Robert Jenkins? Why not. He thought of her as an exotic harem queen. That could be both exciting and useful, perhaps even a green card should she need it once her diplomatic status ended. Ultimately, however she decided to carry out her plan... the goal was the same. Jenkins represented, on a macrocosmic level, the ultimate rapist who ruined countries, the people and their culture. Bastards like him deserved to be wiped off the planet. The closer she got to the man who killed Hassan, the easier it would be to destroy him, and she had the evidence to do just that.

In a world of extreme uncertainty, with al-Qaeda and its ilk claiming a foothold, not just in Syria but also in Lebanon, she was grateful to Hassan for having overseen her transition. He had understood the threats and helped mold her into the emotionally stronger, more assertive person he knew she would need to be to survive in the treacherous, fanatic world where the Robert Jenkinses were intent on unleashing a proxy war on her homeland.

She dug her cell phone out of her purse and punched in Jenkins' number.

CHAPTER THIRTY-FIVE

Andrew leaned against a stone wall along Damascus Street and thought about everything that had just happened. It was all he could do to hold it together and not cry like a child. Caught in a traffic jam after leaving the Corniche, he had asked Nadia and Moussa to drop him off at the beginning of Damascus Street about two miles from where he wanted to meet Leila. As their car pulled away from the curb, Andrew waved, but Nadia did not bother to turn to watch him walk away. This had been the final crushing blow from the woman who had just betrayed him.

He walked a few blocks before he could bring himself to call Leila.

"How did it go?"

"I'm free." Even as he said those words, he knew he was lying. Nadia would never be completely out of his head. "Let's meet at the Armenian restaurant on the corner of Badaro and Damascus Streets. We can talk there."

"Good choice. I like their food."

When he hung up, everything hit him—Fouad, who had known all along where Jaafar was holding Nadia, and Joe, who had pushed him to train for that soon-to-happen-rescue-mission that he knew would never materialize, all the while in cahoots with Fouad. Fuck you, Joe. Both men had offered false friendships. Both were as flawed as the country they served. He fantasized about beating the shit out of Joe but thought it best if he and Leila simply moved out of the apartment. But even that relationship was now in jeopardy. He had just lied to Leila, and she would soon discover his cowardliness. The duplicitous Sonia, singularly responsible for destroying his life in exchange for ill-gotten fame, should have died in the explosion. And Nadia… the bitterest of disappointments. Where was his former beloved, the woman he would have gone back to even though he had already begun an affair with Leila?

It had taken him a long time to fall in love with Leila, and even in his present state of confusion that represented something special. She had shown the utmost respect for his loyalty to Nadia and had been happy when she was finally freed. She worried how she would ever stand up to the beautiful Nadia, the UN special envoy, the woman who had done the impossible and freed her husband from a Syrian prison.

Respectful of Leila's concerns, Andrew had let her know he was meeting Nadia.

"It's something I need to do," he had explained.

"Just remember, I can't keep competing against the memory you have of her, so you will need to make a decision."

"Yes, I know."

He had envisioned Leila's furrowed brow as she delivered that ultimatum and knew such boldness disguised her underlying fear of losing him. She had wanted an affirmation of his love, but he could not give it, and now he would have to explain how Nadia had humiliated him and beg for empathy. She had been through her own tragedies and found the strength to heal, but on such a delicate issue of the heart, would she sympathize with his dilemma, or would she find him ambivalent and gutless and walk away?

* * *

He had been as nervous as an adolescent on his first date at the thought of seeing Nadia again. Yet, when he climbed into her car and took her in his arms, he had marveled at how natural it felt, two lovers still engaged to be married, hearts throbbing, finally united. Nadia had been the first to pull apart and attempt to regain her composure. Andrew was relieved. He had not been the only one feeling awkward after such an emotional greeting, one he could not have predicted.

She had sat across from him, her body pressed against the door, smiling, her hands in her lap, legs crossed. And even with the sun shining through the open window, highlighting her stunning beauty and silky skin, Andrew saw that she was not the same woman in the photo he had kept in his wallet all those years. The scent of Damascene roses, which, in his mind, he had associated with her long, auburn hair, was gone. The amount of makeup she wore and the way she dressed—a sleeveless white silk blouse cut low enough to expose the tops of her breasts, short, tight skirt and high heels—reminded him more of Sonia. This was surely Jaafar's doing. Damn his soul for cheapening her.

When he had gently scolded her for wearing makeup she did not need, she accused him of making a fuss about nothing. And while she admitted the six months they had spent together were probably the most joyous of her life, she insisted they knew very little about each other since, according to her, their relationship had never gotten beyond the bed sheets. Had Andrew thought that, he would not have spent all that time waiting for her to return or felt so guilt-stricken when he had fallen in love with Leila. Even Victor had questioned the durability of a brief six-month affair, followed by such a long absence. Andrew should have listened to his admonition.

* * *

When Andrew arrived at the restaurant he was relieved to see that Leila had gotten there early enough to secure an outdoor table. She had already ordered a bottle of Ksara red along with meat pies, spicy sausage, basturma and pickled veggies, all Armenian specialties.

He saw her studying him as he made his way to her table. No doubt his haggard face, rigid jaw, red eyes and slumped shoulders told her everything she needed to know about his emotional state.

"Here," she said, pouring him a glass of wine and handing it to him. "You look like you've been chewed up pretty badly. Was it that terrible?"

He nodded. "I didn't expect it to be, but it was."

"At the risk of making you even more upset, I need to know something before we begin discussing this. Would you have set me aside to keep your original promise to Nadia?"

He had not anticipated her question and hesitated before responding. "If it had been the old Nadia who'd come back, yes."

He saw the hurt in her eyes and knew he had said the wrong thing. Was it naïve on his part to tell the truth to save his own virtue, or would it have been better to lie to protect the feelings of the woman he loved? Eventually, she would have detected his lie and never trusted him again, and that was not how he wanted to build on their new relationship.

He reached over and took her hand. "I'll never lie to you, Leila. I love and respect you too much to ever do that."

"Part of me wishes you had," she said, her voice choking on her tears. "You can't have Nadia, so you'll settle for me. Second best isn't something I want to be."

"I don't see it that way. We've just begun our relationship, and going forward we now have a clean slate to build on."

"With Nadia's shadow looming over us."

"No, it's the hurt that's there, not her. I didn't wait all that time to be so cold-heartedly dismissed. I'll get over it and ask for your patience. I don't want to lose you."

She took a long sip of wine and stared into the void. If he could have rescinded his words and eased her pain, he would have.

"She's become someone I don't know. It was all rather sad the way it unfolded, but I'm relieved it's over if that makes you feel any better."

"Andrew, I'm beginning to think I know you better than you know yourself. You started by telling the truth. It upset me, yet I appreciated that you didn't lie, but don't start trying to pick your words and saying you're relieved it's over when you aren't."

"I'm not trying to do that, Leila. I admit I'm more emotional than I should be, and brooding when I shouldn't, and for that I beg your indulgence, but let me tell you everything that happened, and then you be the judge. Where would you like me to begin?"

"Is she still as beautiful?"

"She's a cheapened version of the Nadia I knew, too much like Sonia for my taste."

"What did you talk about?"

"Basically, shared memories. She mentioned our visit to the Beaufort Castle, and that triggered the memory of other things we'd done together like getting her husband out of his Syrian prison and back across the Lebanese border, a terrifying ordeal I'll never forget. While at your uncle's house, she asked Elie for a divorce, as you may recall, and then I remembered our stressful UN convoy out of Marjeyoun and all the friends we lost. None of this is news to you. You were there with us. You were even at Victor's house when Nadia was kidnapped."

"A god-awful night," Leila said. "Sonia had sent Nadia to the car to get her computer and when she didn't come back, you dashed out, certain that something had happened."

"Yes, and with all that history, she goes and dismisses me in the most cavalier and offhanded way. She didn't even refer to me as her fiancé when she introduced me to her father's new chauffeur, Moussa, who helped her escape Jaafar's compound. I'm not sure why, but I took an instant dislike to the man. He was unfriendly and tried to hide his face, as if he didn't want me to see him."

"Maybe he had something to hide."

Suddenly, Andrew sat bolt upright, choking on a piece of sausage he had just popped into his mouth.

"Are you all right?"

Andrew shook his head, and with a raspy voice, said, "No."

"Here," she said, handing him his wine. "Take a sip."

He gasped. "Moussa... he was one of the bastards who tried to kill me."

"What! You're sure?"

Andrew, still trying to clear his throat, nodded. "Certain. He was the one who bound my hands before blindfolding me. And later, when I fell on the beach, he pulled me up and beat me until I passed out."

"Do you think Nadia knows this?"

He shook his head. "No. I'll go straight to Victor with this and keep her out of it."

He sat, lost in thought. Finally, shaking his head, he said, "There were so many things that disturbed me about my meeting with Nadia.

She insisted she hadn't been abused. Can you believe that? She actually got defensive when I suggested kidnapping was a form of abuse."

"Would it have been better if she'd sulked and felt sorry for herself while a prisoner?" asked Leila. "No, she decided to make the best of a worse-case scenario. That was a smart move on her part. What else could she have done?"

"In theory, you're right, but he was a vicious animal."

"Yes, he was, but he loved her."

"Then, I made the mistake of telling her I had started training so I could rescue her. She laughed and called me her knight in shining armor."

"Were you offended?"

"Yes, of course. At the time, I thought I was about to do something noble. She did finally apologize when she saw how upset I was. I don't think she imagines how much I've been through for her."

"Or, maybe she no longer cares."

"That's when I realized it was useless to wish she'd come back unchanged."

Andrew did not mention their conversation about Robert Jenkins, the man who promoted himself as the brave warrior out to save the world from the bad guys when he was really one of them. Leila had yet to learn of his plans for Syria. Nadia confirmed that Jaafar hated him for what he planned to do to his country and also suspected he'd have no qualms about feeding Syria's Christians to the lions like the Americans had done in Iraq. It was a story as old as time.

Andrew served Leila the few remaining slices of basturma and pickled veggies then tensely leaned forward.

"It was Sonia who set up Nadia's kidnapping."

Leila's mouth dropped. "Sonia? But she's such a nice person."

"She made a deal with Jaafar—Nadia in exchange for information about the Hariri assassination."

"I can't believe she'd do something so treacherous."

"My head's still in a spin over it," he said. "That she'd do such a thing for a fucking story."

"Oh my God," she said, bolting upright in her chair and staring at him wide-eyed. "Now I'm remembering. We were at Carole's table having dinner. Nadia had been outside a long time. Suddenly, you jumped up from the table to go find her. Sonia physically tried to stop you. At the time, I found that quite odd. Now, it's as clear as day why she didn't want you to go outside. What are you going to do about her?"

"Nadia wants to have her tongue torn out, and I suggested she'd already been busted up pretty badly and that karma had punished her, but she'd have none of it."

"I'm with Nadia on this," Leila said. "You don't forgive someone who has committed such a monstrous and self-serving crime."

"No, you don't, but there's more," he said. "Fouad and Joe knew all along where Jaafar was keeping Nadia. They've been toying with me all this time. I'm particularly irate about Joe's behavior. He's been not only my fucking roommate the last two years, but my trainer, supposedly getting me ready to rescue Nadia. These were people I thought were my friends. You don't forgive that kind of betrayal either."

"No, you don't," Leila said, gravely. "Joe's deception is particularly hard to swallow. You've every right to feel bitter."

She waited before asking, "What did you finally decide to do about Sonia?"

"Reluctantly, Nadia agreed it was enough that Sonia knew she knew."

"How does she figure that?"

"I'm not sure. She just said Sonia knows."

"I told Nadia about us, Leila. I thought it was the right thing to do."

"What did she say? Was she upset?"

"She said there was no need for explanations or apologies, that she'd done worse."

That was when Nadia had put on her sunglasses and looked up at the sun. He saw how gorgeous she still was—her long auburn hair, her throat, and as she thrust her head in the air, her breasts raised as much as Sonia's would have in the right bra—but he also saw how vulgar she had become. Leila was not as glamourous or as beautiful as Nadia, but she was the woman he wanted as his life partner.

"She wished us the best, Leila, and hoped we'd be happy."

Her eyes flooded. "Can we get past all of this, Andrew?"

"I say we can. We've both been wronged in different ways by others. We're also two people who stand on principle, which is why I needed to tell you everything. There aren't many like us who respect truth and live by it in this corrupt country and yet, here we are, boldly determined to make it a better place. I love you, Leila, and I want to move on with you, if you'll have me."

She smiled sadly into his eyes, then stood. "I need to visit the bathroom."

Andrew knew he had deeply wounded her. Going forward, he hoped he would be forgiven. Elie, Nadia's former husband, had been the albatross that had hung over their relationship, almost tearing it apart, while it was Nadia's shadow that had loomed heavily over his budding love story with Leila. How ironic it was, in the end, that it had been Jaafar who had transformed his Nadia into someone he did not want back.

Andrew sat back and wondered if Leila would return. When lovers enter into that world of duality, it can be both painful and risky. Though it had ripped open her heart, he thought she had appreciated his truthfulness, but what if it had also destroyed everything between them?

He looked at the people seated around him chatting, eating, enjoying each other's company, willfully oblivious to what was really going on around them. Maybe that is what Leila would have preferred. Why did none of this matter, or had the Lebanese simply adopted amnesia as a way of surviving in a city so prone to periodically self-destruct? In a place that called itself a country but was, in fact, nothing more than a mosaic of religions and tribes, each with its own clan leaders and loyal followers, the detachment was even more obvious. Those former clan leaders, turned warlords, who now served in Parliament did not care enough about Lebanon's survival to separate their religious differences from politics even when their animus played into the hands of its neighbors, ever eager to exploit the schism.

Feeling rather glum, Andrew thought he might just leave and go back to his apartment. Leila had been gone a long time. Maybe she had already fled out the back door. Mixed in with his dark mood and his bitterness at having been so deceived, he heard himself say he could always go back to the US, but he immediately realized that was impossible. He had changed too much. Just then, he looked up and, with a sigh of relief, saw Leila threading her way through the tables. She had been crying. It disheartened him to think that he had fucked up so badly that he had caused the woman he loved so much pain. He had yet to learn that a strategic lie was sometimes better than the truth. Occasionally, it also preserved love when it hung in the balance. Seeing how sad she looked, he assumed she had decided to end their relationship.

Andrew stood and pulled out her chair. When they were both seated, she looked across the table, gazed into his anxious eyes, and said, "Okay, Andrew, let's try to make a go of it."

His eyes teared as he took her hands and kissed them. "There's no one I'd rather spend the rest of my life with than you, Leila."

And they began to stitch together their wounds, hoping the stitches would hold.

ACKNOWLEDGEMENTS

To my editor, Ian Graham Leask, who steadfastly supports my effort to dispel common myths about an ancient land that are systematically and oftentimes falsely perpetuated by government and mainstream media. To my daughter Nayla, who recommended vital changes to the manuscript, and to my readers Michel Farid, Sheila Perelman, Michel Saade and Joe Golibart for their invaluable input. And finally, to Michel, my husband of fifty-two years, for his support and encouragement.

ABOUT THE AUTHOR

Cathy Sultan is an award-winning author of three nonfiction books: *A Beirut Heart: One Woman's War*; *Israeli & Palestinian Voices: A Dialogue with Both Sides*; and *Tragedy in South Lebanon*. *A Beirut Heart* was translated into Chinese in 2013. *The Syrian*, a political thriller, was her first work of fiction. Sultan is also a peace activist who recently stepped down from six years on the Board of Directors of the Interfaith Peace Builders (IFPB), an NGO based in Washington, D.C. She took her first trip to Israel/Palestine in March 2002 and subsequently co-lead five delegations there on behalf of IFPB, including one to Gaza in 2012.

Sultan won USA's Best Book Award and Best Autobiography of 2006 for *A Beirut Heart*; USA's Best Book of the Year in the category of History/Politics for *Israeli and Palestinian Voices: A Dialogue with both Sides*; 2006 Midwest Book Awards-Honorable Mention in the Category of Political Science for *Israeli and Palestinian Voices*. *Tragedy in South Lebanon* was nominated for Best Book of the Year in the Category of Political Science for 2008.

Made in the USA
Columbia, SC
05 August 2018